Chinnery's

Jaysinh Birjépatil

BODIAM BOOKS LIMITED

Published in the UK by
Bodiam Books Ltd
East Sussex TN32 5RH
info@bodiambooks.co.uk

Revised Edition January 2005

First published in Great Britain 2004 by Whydown Books Limited
Sedlescombe, East Sussex TN33 ORN www.whydownbooks.com
http://www.whydownbooks.com

Cover by Tim Segar in association with PABPS, London.

Typeset by PABPS, London.

ISBN 0-9549539-0-8

To the memory of my sister
KUMUD

ACKNOWLEDGEMENTS

Help arrived from several directions and in many forms during the making of **Chinnery's Hotel.**

First I should like to thank Shanta Acharya for finding it a good home...

For useful comments and insights I am grateful to Tony Connor, Rani Dharker, John Drew, Judi and David Ray, Christy McCormick of Royal Highlanders (Canada, Retd), Joëlle Delbourgo and Mary Martinez.

I am also indebted to John Hayes, Dean of Marlboro College, Vermont, for financial support. This made it possible for me to travel to different parts of England to interview retired army officers and to visit museums and libraries specialising in Military History. It also took me to half-remembered sights in the cantonment townships of Poona, Bangalore, Secunderabad, Ahmednagar and Mhow where friends old and new helped me tap into local memory for reassembling the past. In particular I should like to thank Dr. S. Ramaswamy of Bangalore, the late Meher Nagarwala, her husband Billy, and Grace Jacob of Ahmednagar, Principal M.V. Prasad and his colleague Mr. Kapasia of Daly College Indore. At Mhow I was assisted in gathering valuable information by the friendly Library staff at the College of Combat, Mr. P.M. Dinshaw of Simrole Road, Mr. Samaatwala of the Masonic Lodge, St. Paul, Mr.Dixit, the kindly foreman, and various railway employees at the Loco Shed. My special thanks go to Mrs. Eena Craven Threlfall of Basingstoke, England, for sharing with me vivid memories of her childhood in Mhow.

Finally, I would like to thank Pamela Richards, Michael Gannon, Marcia Buckley, Graham Buckley, Melanie Marden, Julia Pike, Adrian Hill, Chris Martin and Dick Nesbitt-Dufort for their enthusiastic support in producing this novel.

The beginning of everything was in a
railway train upon the road to
Mhow from Ajmir

The Man Who Would Be King
Kipling

... and the young Quentin Compson who
was still too young to deserve yet to be a
ghost but nevertheless having to be one for
all that

Absalom, Absalom!
Faulkner

GLOSSARY

anna	a small coin, no longer in use
ayah	nanny
badmash	crook/scoundrel
bandobast	order and discipline
baksheesh	tip
bania	a member of the trading caste
biddie	hand-rolled tobacco wrapped in dried leaf
bittia	daughter
boomla	bombay duck
boxwallah	British trader in India
bustee	shanty town
burra khanna	ceremonial dinner
byblows	illegitimate children
cantonment	British garrison township
chamcha	a sycophant
chi chi	a derogatory term for people of mixed caste
chotta hajeri	breakfast
chokraboy	errand boy
dak bungalow	guest house
dhobi	washerman
feni	a beverage made from cashew nuts
fishing fleeters	young British women who travelled by ship to India with the intention of finding a husband in the army or the Colonial Service.
funty	European gone native
gharry	horse-drawn carriage
griffin	young officer new to India

jeldi	hurry up
hakim	apothecary / chemist
havildar	Sergeant in Indian Army
kala jaga	a dark place
khansamah	housekeeper
khas khas tatties	dampened vetiver grass shades
khitmetgar	waiter
koi hai	literally a British Army Officer hailing a waiter
machan	raft-like tree-top platform
mofussil	rural district
mali	gardener
nabob	a Muslim ruler of a small state
nullah	culvert
peon	attendant
punkah	overhead fan
pongee	fabric made of undyed silk
sola	short for sola topi, a sun hat
shikar	hunt
syce	attendant in charge of horse
thakur	an aristocratic landowner
tommy	a private in the British Army
tonga	a one-horse buggy
zhat pat	rushing around

CAST OF KEY CHARACTERS

Any resemblance to actual persons, living or dead, and events is entirely coincidental. Local landmarks and street locations of the township of Mhow have been moved around to suit the general layout of the prototypical Indian cantonment

British Civilians and Army Officers   Mhow 1920-1945

Roger Chinnery	Retired Major, owner of Chinnery's Hotel
Amanda Chinnery	The Major's American wife
The Three Chinnery Children	Grace Robert (Bobby) Jo Anna
Miss Briscoe (The Dog-Lady)	A spinster who looks after dogs left behind by families who have left India
Gordon Robinson	District Superintendent of Police
The Sandersons	A socially active couple
Marjorie Sanderson	One of their five daughters
Mabel Figgis	Manages "Hungry Charley's" cafeteria

Lieutenant Adrian Ponsonby

76 Lancers (the Witch Doctors) – Grace's first love

Captain Jack Sullivan

127th Gurkhas – Grace's first husband

Anglo-Indians

Mr. Busby

Boiler mechanic

Carl Busby

Only son of the boiler mechanic

Mr. Gilbert

Elderly assistant stationmaster

Parsis

Sir Mancherjee Debu

Local philanthropist

Shirin Debu

Sir Mancherjee's elder daughter

Yasmin Debu

Sir Mancherjee's younger crippled daughter

Goan Catholics

Mrs.Roderigues

Ayah to the Chinnery children

Mrs.Fernandez
Eustace Fernandez

The Debu girls' ayah
Her son

Others	**Mhow 1920-1945**
Mr. David	The postmaster - member of the Bene Tribe of Israel
Mahamud	The Chinnery's driver
Thankoorani (Churail)	Spirit of a woman who has died during pregnancy
Khansamah	Housekeeper at Chinnery's
Mr.Munshi	Chief Accountant at Chinnery's

London 1945-1996	
Count Studjinsky (Stoodgy)	Grace Chinnery's second Husband
Camilla	Jo Anna Chinnery's daugher – raised by Grace
Jeremy	Camilla's first husband
Eddie	Camilla's second husband

Mhow 1989-1996

Bhola	An old retainer at Yasmin's villa
Noshir Ardeshir	Shirin's grown up son, Yasmin's nephew
Tehmi	Noshir's wife
General Grehwal	Head of the College of Combat in Mhow
Tejinder (Taji)	Elder daughter of the Grehwals
Col. Ross Harrison	A war hero
Rita Harrison	Ross's dead wife
Esmé	Their daughter
Olinda D'Souza	Middle aged daughter of Josephine Gilbert
Johar	A dashing trainee officer

UNDERSONG

Chinnery's Hotel was a manor house with the heart of a nest. Set in Mhow's red rocky soil where Corbett Road intersected the Mall, it opened itself up to guests. After tramping across squelchy forest floors or slag-filled shunting yards during inspection tours, if you needed a hot bath, warm food and comfortable bed, your horse would trot you down to Chinnery's without waiting for your signal. At the sight of that sycamore-lined driveway curving just short of the cream-washed façade, a web of intimacy descended on horse and rider. Here you could recover your sense of lost home.

Chinnery's avoided backwater banality by providing outdoor entertainment when the weather turned hot. Behind the main building, on summer nights, a band played slow music while guests danced on a wooden platform lit with wrought iron lamps. A few steps led down to the Italian fountain around which lay in horse-shoe pattern, twenty guest rooms, each with its own balcony at the top of the steps. Windblown spray from the fountain kept the lawn green even in summer. Behind the rooms stretched a mango orchard all the way to the hummocked hills that marched off into the distance.

Hidden from view by almond and pomegranate trees was a hoary-looking well. Little tubs swinging from a Ferris-wheel-like contraption scooped up water. When the moon came up above the hills, the fountain basin glistened and the squat palms around it looked like turbaned guards.

The Hotel catered to its guests' particular needs; each had a favourite room. It was nice to be greeted by the same bathtub with its familiar crack under the tap, the dusty old table lamp, tear in the mosquito net, and the chipped enamel of the wash-basin. The vaulted ceiling of the Dining Hall flattered their sense of station, but it was the cosy comfort of the room, with the irregular creak of the punkah, which they missed during their nights in mosquito-infested dak bungalows in the mofussil. At Chinnery's the walls of the rooms fell around them like protective armour.

In daytime the place was like a gigantic organism with a will of its own. Mornings began to the sound of scouring and scrubbing; the front gate swung open as Khansahib let in the dhobi's cycle rickshaw or the grocer's cart. Malis dug and planted in the garden to the muffled hoots of the pump clanking on the well. Chokraboys scurried to the rooms with morning tea or elevenses.

After lunch, all was quiet indoors while cicadas rasped in the hedges. Each chokraboy, when not busy cleaning or dusting, had a favourite niche on the verandah or under a banyan where he dozed until the Silver Ghost came up the driveway. As soon as Mahamud pulled the car up, the tiered steps leading to the hallway were dotted with grinning chokraboys, their joints hoisting in salaam as on wooden figurines at the prospect of baksheesh. While guests were registering at the reception desk under Mr. Munshi's kindly eye, luggage was carried to their rooms, windows opened, and the chokraboy in charge was ready to run the bathwater.

Chokraboys were everywhere, you could sense their presence in the smoke of biddies curling up behind hedges, feet padding down the corridor, snatches in alto of Hindi film songs wafting in from the garden. Only at night when they repaired to their quarters, with just a few on night duty, did the Hotel feel empty.

Recent arrivals from the darkened scenario of the northern hemisphere were blinded by the glare of the dusty towns of their posting. At first they were unable to judge the harmony between stone and moving figure. For them, Chinnery's was a real sanctuary, a harbourage for organised leisure. Till the monsoon broke over Mhow in late June, the dance floor was dotted every evening with men in fawn-coloured tropical suits, and women in chiffon and organdie; foliage washed in pastel light, milk-white tablecloths, tinkle of glasses, and someone jauntily calling the numbers at the game of housey housey.

Dirty knees thirty-three,
Bottom heavy number six,
Two fat maids eighty-eight.

Among its most frequent guests were the importers of British goods called the boxwallahs from the port cities of Bombay and Calcutta. After completing their rounds in the neighbouring cantonments of Jhansi and Neemuch the boxwallahs came bleating back for more of the succulent miracles conjured up by Chinnery's Goan chefs.

Over the years the hotel had learnt to adapt itself to a variety of needs. Winter brought members of various polo teams from upcountry stations for the Inter-Services Competition. Around the dining table were recalled memorable polo events of yesteryear. Someone talked of the great Hanutsingh whose equestrian skill had never been surpassed. A vision built itself slowly of men erect in their saddles, faces hooded by pith helmets, strong jaws jutting from chinstraps.

For all returning guests, Chinnery's was like a picture left intact, while the rest of the world grew old and fractious. When away from it they were part of a compact, a league of nomads. Strangers thrown together on trains winding through distant dusty plains, opened their thermos flasks and poured tea for fellow passengers who had spent a night or two at Chinnery's. Stretched out on the padded narrow bunks of night trains, they relived their days in far off Mhow till they heard the soft murmur of the fountain by the pomegranate trees and were gathered into the familiar shadows of their musty rooms at Chinnery's.

GHOSTLY PLAYBACKS

It is difficult to tell a small girl you are not her real mother. On the other hand it is even harder to wait till she is forty-three and has gone through two marriages.

Following her discharge from hospital Grace is dozing in her rocking chair. Clapham distilled to its basic autumnal grey, children's voices fading on the Common, and somewhere in the muted interior, a flare, a subaqueous stirring of a lost ship; there rises before her the cream and white facade of Chinnery's, trellised porch, red with clematis, bay windows shimmering in the wishy-washy drizzle of a receding monsoon.

When Camilla was old enough to be told, that is to say when she was nineteen and at Oxford, Stoodgy aborted Grace's confession on the brink. War had wiped out his entire family in Poland; to jeopardise another was unthinkable. "Let the sleeping dogs lie," he said in his lardy Polish voice, tipping a precarious memory that crumbled muddily in her eyes - a deluge. Part of Grace still lived in another world.

That afternoon as her mind enacts ghostly playbacks of Mhow, once again she sees those violet eyes staring out of her sister's mottled face. Strange sounds ripple in her throat, a scream as though her tongue is being slashed. Camilla finds Grace half-risen from bed, gagging and clutching at her heart.

Something rank has come unstuck within her mother.

Sobs and gulps follow as her sluggish mouth struggles to form words.

"The truth ... the truth is, you are my poor sister Jo Anna's child. Please don't hate your mother. That would kill me. Let God be my judge. You are my whole life."

Words tumble out, adding nothing to that distant dying in India. The moment passes; the rest of the story gets stuck in Grace's throat. Camilla holds her close as the sick woman disappears behind a strange mask. An emptiness spreads from Camilla's eyes down through her entire body, a stillness of truncated rail arms on a collapsed bridge.

She looks around. Nothing has changed: muffled pounding of the tube, Grace's gold-rimmed glasses staring up from the table, rumpled spread at the foot of the bed, clatter of a neighbour's typewriter, and out in the gloom, the quiet streets hastening towards blackness. Camilla looks at her watch. It's only three in the afternoon.

Photographs tell a story.

One hand resting on the withers of a horse, the young girl in jodhpurs smiles at her. Their eyes lock, but the word 'mother' trembles and dies on Camilla's lips.

At night Grace murmurs herself into a black stupor, but Jo Anna's eviscerated eyes continue to regard her through the iron bars behind which she'd died with no one by her side. For three decades Grace had clung to the official version of the story till her sister's face had petrified like corm in a water chestnut.

Something has disturbed that grave, halfway across the world.

That whispery voice has returned. When first heard by Grace it was a barely audible sigh from the library. In the light streaming through the windows, Jo Anna had looked so peaceful in death, a smile lingering on her bruised mouth.

Dr. Vansittart was upstairs with Mater taking her pulse while Grace dressed Pater's wound in the Lounge. In dire anguish he'd battered his head against one of the mahogany bookcases in the library.

Suddenly the voice was whispering directly in her ears. "Grace, Grace," it said, "give me my baby, let me hold her."

Grace had shadowed Pater for weeks after Jo Anna's funeral, leaving Mater in the Dog Lady's care. With the insane precision of a murderer she had buried her own grief. Only Dr. Vansittart and his orderly had witnessed that last hideous scene. It was put out that Jo Anna had succumbed to typhoid while in hiding at the Dayan's bungalow outside Mhow.

From its perch at the back of Grace's mind her grief had continued to leak.

Now suddenly Mhow is calling her back.

Camilla wouldn't hear of letting Grace travel alone in her condition. Overriding objections from her colleagues and friends, she decides to go to India with Grace. Joyce warns her that Alexis would throw a fit if she went

"You are too old to be clinging to your mum like that," she twits her. Camilla pins her hopes on Dr. Chaudhry's objection, but he says, "A few months in a warm climate might actually do your mother good."

Camilla was only two when the family moved to England, and the thread of her recollection doesn't unspool all the way to India. Mhow has always been a remote sepia region from which dusky figures of servants come alive, bowing and scraping when Grace talks; they are nothing like the immigrants beavering behind counters of corner shops.

ii

SHIPWRECK

Camilla is little more than a blur, dashing to Aldwych for Indian visas, shopping and finishing off her latest assignment at the firm. Grace's nightmares recede, illuminating her years in Mhow against the drudgery of the past three decades.

On her first day in England the neatly laid out pastures and streams sliding noiselessly past the boat train from Dover had seemed aloof. Since then she has carried her past like a pannier, one basket filled with memories of India, the other with promises soured in London. The dog-eared sheets of an old album keep hold of the flaking world of Grace's life in Mhow, the new smart one on the coffee table has coloured prints made by Stoodgy of Camilla in her school uniform and picnic frocks.

Instead of the sunlit London of Huntley & Palmer biscuit tins or Peak Frean Assorted, with bascules of Tower Bridge arched over a passing steamer, she had found a city traced in graphite. Everywhere behind smudged silhouettes of walls and listing façades of archways hovered ghosts of vanished buildings. Grace had dreamed of a table set for two, glowing in candlelight in Adrian's flat in Regent's Park or strolling through meadows and over the Downs, sitting together on the hump of a cobbled bridge in Dorset.

In India the word 'home' had been an icebreaker, a tentative beginning to a personal narrative. But after the War all but a handful of British had packed up and left as though their collective story had come to an end.

Life in Mhow was cushioned to soften hurts; simple pleasures outweighed a few passing setbacks. In the months following Jo Anna's death Mater sat staring at her plate and there was gin on Pater's breath even at breakfast. The three remaining Chinnerys felt like strangers in their own home, helped in and out of their clothes by chokraboys and maids before being put to bed.

Finally in the summer of 1946, they sailed home on a sea of sorrow.

On the ferry to Dover, Pater kept looking at the louring sky. His son's flaming plane had plunged into the Channel during the Battle of Britain. A week after the Chinnerys reached London Pater succumbed to acute kidney failure. As the coldest winter of the century hit Britain, bread was rationed and meat was short but foul-smelling whale meat was available on the open market. Mater refused to touch it.

The pipes froze, cold penetrated and blocked her lungs releasing her dormant asthma, and hiccups rocked her shrivelled body. One night with a strangulated cry she collapsed. The passing away of Grace's parents in London caused only a discreet ruffle on their neighbours' blinds; Grace felt like a refugee abandoned in a strange city. Save for the priest and three officers from the regiment of her husband, Jack, the funerals were bleak, formal affairs followed by limp handshakes.

A few months after Mater's death, the Gurkhas were transferred to Kuala Lumpur and Jack left with his men, like a schoolboy going home for the holidays. But before he could send for Camilla and Grace, he was killed in an ambush. Cremated by the Gurkhas, his ashes were flown home. Grace buried the urn next to his mother at Two Bridges.

The oblong Devonshire tableland of hedgerows, stone bridges across the Dart brought back the days when she had picnicked at Moonwater Lake during Bobby's last visit to India. The sheep grazing on the curving moor would have felt perfectly at home in the twisting paths leading to scattered farmsteads in the rugged countryside around Mhow.

Grace wanted to stay but she had just managed to land a

teaching job in London. Her widow's pension was barely adequate for their monthly grocery bills. Besides there was little Camilla's education to be considered.

While Grace fretted, war-battered London, busy picking itself up by its bootstraps, scarcely took any notice of her. Its embattled inhabitants felt no sympathy for this well-dressed young arrival from the colonies, with her scrubbed look and superior manner. They had no use for someone with whom they could not share painful wartime memories of loved ones who never made it to the crowded underground shelters and tube stations before being blown to smithereens.

Grace desperately needed cosseting. People were polite but preoccupied, salvaging from their gutted space a livable design. Everywhere the multiple fractures of the city were being mended, its broken bones slowly set by giant cranes to the beat of modern earth-moving machinery and whirling of cement mixers.

When she went shopping for clothes the bus would take her through certain posh parts of London. Catching sight of a cream-coloured building set in a garden, Grace would feel a stab of nostalgia, but she choked the impulse to tell anyone how it reminded her of Chinnery's. There were enough jokes on the television about blimps bragging about past glory.

One afternoon as Grace stepped out of Knightsbridge tube station, she noticed a plumpish woman struggling with three shopping bags on the pavement outside Harrods. It was one of the Sanderson girls. Grace's dammed-up hunger for Mhow suddenly exploded.

"Why if it isn't Marjorie Sanderson. How are you, my dear? Don't you remember me? I'm Grace Chinnery."

"But of course, how stupid of me. Do forgive me," Marjorie said freeing one hand to greet her. Grace noticed that her face still retained that childlike softness which typified all the Sanderson girls.

"It's been so long and I'm in something of a tizzy," Marjorie said. "There isn't a taxi in sight and I'm not used to all this jostling. How are you Grace?" she blurted out awkwardly.

Grace was thrilled and immediately began to ply Marjorie with questions about her parents and her sisters.

"You must come and visit us," Grace said, scribbling her address on a piece of paper.

Marjorie took it wordlessly but made no attempt to reciprocate. Grace was determined to find out more and asked Marje where her parents and sisters were. There were five Sanderson siblings, all girls.

"Pater and Mater moved to Belgaum and died there at my Aunt Sarah's place. It was all for the best, they couldn't have survived here on their pension," Marjorie said, frowning at the crowd of tourists surging out of the tube station. Grace suggested they go in and have tea but Marje was in a hurry to get back home before dinner. Grace gathered that she lived with her husband's family in Gloucestershire.

"I am afraid Cheltenham has spoiled me," Marjorie said. "I find the City too crammed, too much 'zhat pat' you know. Dear Cheltenham is quite like Mhow, an Indiahand in every other house. Most are Poonawallahs of course, and a few Bangalorians like my Harry. Last weekend Major Dobson paid a long overdue visit and after dinner we all sang 'I am looking for the Ogo-Pogo.' You remember,

One fine day in Hindustan
I met a funny little man
With googly eyes and lantern jaws
A new silk hat and some old plus fours,

Such fun, had tears in my eyes, " Marjorie tattled on. "Harry simply loves the Alphonso mangoes I buy for him at Harrods. Had them for 'chotta hajeri' in Bangalore. Ratnagiri variety you know, the very best."

Then before a taxi could barely let out its passenger Marjorie swooped into it like a giant bird, saying she had to catch the 3.10 from Paddington and was gone.

It was a brush off.

Grace couldn't understand why Marje had left without

bothering to give her her address. The two women had so much in common, heaps to talk about.

When sagging clouds hung over the Common and police sirens ripped through the lassitude induced by flickering neon over the off-licence, there was no one with whom Grace could share her memories of Mhow. How desperate she had been to compare notes, to find out if Marjorie's friends laughed at her for referring to her parents as Pater and Mater. To Grace's colleagues it sounded archaic, like something out of P. G. Wodehouse. They made fun of her behind her back and mimicked her slight colonial accent.

Marjorie had acted as though she had seen a ghost, not a long lost friend. Was it because the Sandersons, like all their friends in Mhow, still held the Chinnerys responsible for what had happened to Jo Anna?

Perhaps Marjorie had concluded from Grace's drab duffle coat and muddy shoes that she had come down in life. Perhaps she didn't want to make Grace feel small by flaunting her own obvious wealth. Marje had simply fled, opening up a painful chasm between what Grace thought herself to be and the way she was perceived by others.

The sound of riches and glitter of jewellery, glossy books on coffee tables, the tinkle of wine glasses around dinner tables had been unmistakable in Marjorie's bubbly voice. That encounter shook out memories crumpled like parchment maps at the bottom of a trunk, bringing to Grace's senses the smell, feel, and texture of her life in Mhow.

The more Grace was baffled by the way her life had turned out the further she retreated into Olympian loftiness. Even with Indians she met on the streets while shopping in London, she was awkward, patronising them with unsolicited advice.

Among them were matronly women in heavy cardigans over lumpy saris or greying men in dun-coloured winter coats, cowering under awnings, sheltering from drizzle, shrunken and lost, clutching bagfuls of groceries, flotsam of a sordid shipwreck. The women always looked forlorn like Grace's ayah, old Mrs. Roderigues waving tearfully from the receding platform at Mhow Railway Station.

Someone was always pontificating on the television about the so-called 'culture shock' immigrants had to cope with. None had the slightest notion of the difficulties British people in England for the first time faced trying to cope with the incessant rain, the paucity of funds, the patronising attitude of fellow teachers at school who considered those who had lived in the colonies to be culturally deprived, the sniggering creditors who thought her upper-crust accent an unwarranted affectation in a woman who toiled in a fish and chip shop with a foreign-sounding husband.

Grace knew as much about being an immigrant as any Indian or Pakistani.

Once witnessing a public humiliation of a bus conductor Grace had been very upset. He was so much like Khansahib, the leonine old watchman at Chinnery's.

She was on a double-decker going home. It was packed with men returning from work, a sullen-looking crowd with spanners sticking out of their pockets, crumbs of pork pie dotting frayed lapels, when a young woman with a peaked face came stomping down from the upper deck.

"Bloody Paki wog," she said with a venomous hiss, " why don't you go home?"

Then she pushed herself angrily between Grace and a schoolboy and continued to mutter racist abuse.

The conductor with the mien of a desert prophet came down and wordlessly started punching tickets. Grace's eyes met his, and in a sudden upsurge of kinship she urged him in Urdu to report the incident to the authorities, but he shrugged off her suggestion and replied stiffly in English that the woman was mistaken, he'd told her to go down because all the seats on the top were taken.

Despite the hurt in his large watery eyes he seemed even more embarrassed by Grace's well intentioned but misguided attempt to put such a public face on his distress. Unruffled, he went about the business of punching tickets, his set jaw indicating that he knew how to take care of himself. He had obviously decided from his very first migrant moments that to acknowledge such an incident was to get stigmatised as a pariah. To ignore it was to blot it out. It bespoke a strong instinct for survival, which Grace sadly lacked. Despite chastened stares and squirming in seats, the other passengers had acted as if nothing untoward had happened.

When Grace got off the bus, the defunct memsahib and the ex-native wordlessly passed out of each other's lives.

Even for the few Indians she met at Stoodgy's fish and chip shop she was just one more white face among others. They scarcely paid any attention to her. Anonymity pushed her further into internal exile. The sea of white faces bleached her to a point where she felt deprived of something bred in her bone, her uniqueness. She thought of that architect who, according to legend, was buried alive behind a brick wall by the Emperor in Agra so that he could not compromise the singularity of the Taj Mahal by replicating it. It was not until she met Stoodgy that Grace began to breathe freely. He shook her gently as a gardener shakes a rain-soaked tree to open clogged pores.

WHO ONLY ENGLAND KNOW

It was during her brief stint as saleswoman hawking the recently launched Collier's Encyclopaedia in the suburbs that Grace caught a fleeting glimpse of the England of comfortable homes set in tranquil countryside, white picket fence and flowering garden, of woodlands, moss and lichen. But that picture-postcard world was to remain perpetually beyond her means.

All sales agents were made to cram a patent speech, scripted by marketing specialists, extolling the encyclopaedia. It was utterly inane but out in the field it worked like magic, especially during the training period, when she was accompanied by a supervisor who did all the talking.

On the third day when she was on her own, she fetched up outside a beautiful old house with a gleaming brass handle on a carved wooden door like the one at Chinnery's. The garden was small but neat with trimmed rose bushes. Feeling extremely nervous, she rang the doorbell and immediately launched into her spiel.

"And what is this, Mrs. Jones?" she asked the lady of the house, whipping out a ballpoint pen.

"Why, it's a biro," the bewildered woman replied.

"There, you see Mrs. Jones," Grace continued, "that's what we want to achieve with our product. The moment you hear the word encyclopaedia we want you to say Collier's."

She started flipping through the glossy pages illustrating the spaceship's journey from 'count down' to 'touch down,' explaining how the word 'cranium' had gained wider currency since the assassination of President Kennedy.

"No household with growing children should be without Collier's," Grace concluded, snapping the demo copy shut.

But when she looked up triumphantly she was utterly horrified to discover that the young woman had started to cry. Through heart rending sobs came the stark words.

"I am a widow, a childless widow."

Mumbling an apology, Grace collected the display material and fled from the cottage. The next day she sent in her resignation. Never in her life had she felt so sickened with herself. She had violated one of the cardinal principles around which her life had been constructed, never to intrude brazenly on someone else's privacy.

That's what England had done to her; made her fall so far below her true self that she had very nearly tarnished the memory of Chinnery's.

Even though pampered at home, especially by her ayah, like all colonial children of her generation Grace was made to wear a prematurely adult face, to set an example to the natives and to show pluck and determination in the face of danger. But it took her a while to get accustomed to seeing British men and women doing work that in India was left to the Untouchables, of whom there were plenty in Mhow.

She had a soft spot for the Queen who not only shared her birthday, 21st April, with Jo Anna but also her equestrian skill. Grace had followed the Queen's progress in *The Illustrated London News* from the time she had been a small but graceful rider with bobbed hair and the erect carriage of a princess to a thoughtful and dignified monarch. Quite often Stoodgy and she were the only two left standing respectfully after all other picture-goers had scurried out of the local cinema house, while a scratchy record played 'God Save the Queen.'

Every November without fail, Grace joined the throng of pensioners and tourists outside Buckingham Palace, to cheer Her Majesty as she drove in her Irish State Coach, escorted by the Household Cavalry and Yeomen of the Guard, to open Parliament.

Sometime in the seventies, Mr. Edward Heath, for whom she had voted because he played the piano, rashly dragged Britain into that awful Common Market. A loaf of Mother's Pride bread or cod and chips for which one paid a mere 'one and six' now cost three or four times as much with the additional headache of having to count each tiny new 'p' when returning the change to customers. At one stroke their small fish and chip shop lost half its regulars. Practically no one bought plaice.

Grace fumed and fretted and was very cross with herself because she often bought more meat than she needed or the piece of cloth she had purchased turned out to be a few inches too short for her new curtains. She was congenitally incapable of converting pounds into kilos, and yards into metres, so she took to travelling by bus all the way to Newington Butts to buy meat by pounds from Sandy's Chopshop, which continued to defy the newly introduced 'metric only' regulation.

Around that time Grace came to the conclusion that England was not British enough anymore. Not only did they twist history on the television but even at Camilla's school they filled young minds with lies about the British in India. There were overzealous officers like Brigadier Dyer whose misbegotten sense of duty had resulted in the Massacre at Jallianwala Bag in Amritsar, not to mention bossy-boots like the Colonel's Lady in Mhow who during the trial of the Tommies for killing an innocent native said many uncharitable things about Indians.

However, for every foul tempered 'koi hai' and mem, there were several fair-minded men and women like Uncle Hulme and the Dog Lady who insisted on the Tommies being punished for their crime. By and large most British officers and soldiers Grace knew in Mhow were brave upright men like DSP Robinson. His very name struck terror in the hearts of the most fearsome dacoits terrorising the countryside.

She felt a stab of betrayal when those bright, ebullient and larger than life men and women were pilloried and reduced to garden gnomes.

"What do they know of England, who only England know."

Kipling's words, uttered with utmost solemnity by Uncle Hulme, would suddenly ring in her ears.

Gradually it dawned on her that there was no proper 'bandobast' in London, no mechanism to discipline rowdy elements menacing innocent people in public places.

Every year in November the Polish Cultural Centre hosted a dinner for War Veterans at their Club on Princes Gate. The year Stoodgy died Grace made it a point to attend. Although she didn't speak a word of Polish, as the widow of Count Studejinsky she was placed next to the President at dinner. Camilla had suggested a taxi for the return trip but Grace chose the tube.

The night was young, and stars blinked on the horizon. The carriage was practically empty when she boarded the southbound train at Stockwell. But when it made an unscheduled stop in a tunnel outside Clapham Common she was terrorised by skinheads. At Victoria where she had changed trains they had probably marked her down as an easy prey. The only other passenger, an old man in a seedy, threadbare overcoat, seemed to be too drunk to notice anything.

After vaulting into their seats at Stockwell just before the doors closed, laughing and screaming wildly, the boys were unnaturally quiet for a while. But the transfixed look of their pinhead eyes, waxen caved-in faces and the sheer arrogance of their sprawl was menacing. One with a wasted face flicked open a knife and stared at it vacantly. Grace felt a coffin lid close over her.

She stared in the dark avoiding their eyes. Then one of them said,

"I took Ginny to the pictures last night."

"Did you score?"

"What do you think - three times."

"Wo' was it like?"

" 'ot, very 'ot, the bitch ground me out of my seat."

"I mean the film, you git."

"Weird it was weird, a big 'airy bugger chasing this bird, round the bedroom and she going puck, puck, puck."

In the grossest parody of what Grace took to be a disco dance he landed right in front of her as the train began to move. Then he snatched her handbag from her hands, took out the two ten pound notes she had and threw the handbag back at her. As the train came to a stop they all ran down the platform, their feet clattering in the night.

Grace had not allowed herself to panic during her ordeal but the effort had wrested from deep within all her self-respect and dignity. They now lay in tatters, leaving her no energy to feel disgust or loathing for the skinheads. Camilla said she was lucky not to have suffered any injury. Gangs had been known to terrorise as well as beat up old people. That was small consolation. Never before in her life had Grace felt so degraded.

Her life had ebbed away during those terrifying moments in the dark tunnel; England had finally turned into a nightmare.

THE FLYING DUTCHMAN

A vexing delay at Heathrow rakes up a few more details: Jo Anna's brief romance in Poona with an American airman (certifiable lunacy according to Grace's first husband Jack), a sallow mustachioed smudge with a booming voice which had faded when Camilla was only three. The airman had a wife tucked away somewhere in Alabama; Jo Anna was terribly impressionable and so on. Then the pinched postwar years in England, queuing up for groceries. That still rankled. Camilla tells her to calm down, but Grace's neck muscles tighten, her voice grows shrill.

"You don't know how horrible it was, that first winter here, eating dried eggs."

Stoodgy had a shy brown-eyed smile in a gentle solitary face. He was in a Paris garret with a dying uncle when Hitler marched into Poland. During his exile in England, his father's mansion in the Warsaw suburb of Konstancin used to flicker like a mirage on windows of trains speeding into night till the Communists turned it into a low-rental tenement. In a picture sent by a cousin, its elegant sandstone facade looked like discarded theatre decor.

As Grace skulked, Stoodgy grew even more reticent, and spent all his spare time reading Conrad, but that sad smile never lost its late-breaking sweetness. It was like being sluiced with a cool flow of sparkling water.

In his youth Stoodgy had trekked in the footsteps of Pausanias with his archaeologist father. Those lost years were the salt and vinegar of a life trapped in the prosaic recipe of cod and chips. Thanks to him, Camilla's Latin was more than adequate when she decided to read Roman Archaeology for

Mods, but the Etonians had had an early start with Greek. The unseen translation proved to be her Achilles' heel so to speak. Nevertheless, she had more sense of antiquity than that hairless and toothy Algernon de May, now happily ensconced somewhere in the cavernous precincts of Oxford.

With Grace still in hospital, Camilla's second marriage began to unravel.

"Either come with me to America or set me free," Eddie said.

Each marriage lasted exactly ten years, as though it had an expiry date.

Her colleagues and friends were bewildered by Camilla's retreat into Clapham with its media image of tottering redbrick houses, gaping doors, and furtive whispers under sickly lamps on the Common. Her fashion designer friend, Penny, was frank in declining an invitation to a weekend lunch.

"Sorry to be so utterly *âme de boue*, darling. It used to be on my beat in the good old Fleet Street days remember? But now it's out, positively out."

Only Joyce Ahern came with flowers and chocolate chip cookies she had learned to bake during her assignment in New York. She suggested a special room for Grace at a retreat outside East Grinstead where her mother was Senior Nurse. Camilla shook her head.

"I'm afraid Mum will start a culture war there."

So she sold the South Kensington flat, put the money in stocks, and was just settling down to a comfortable suburban routine when India, till then just a tailfin sail on the horizon, suddenly docked into her life like the Flying Dutchman.

When she first entered the firm as a junior copywriter, Camilla's Latin proved astonishingly useful. She turned out pithy bites for American products; her copy for women's cosmetics was a subtle nod to jet-set materialism without losing the British sense of aloofness. She could also jack up male ego with a "Marcus Aurelius in Armani" brand of redemptive message.

From crispy cereals ("Put a Song in Little Debby's Mouth") to aftershave lotions ("Start Each Day With a New Bloomin' Face"), products under her imprimatur doubled and tripled sales. The quartet of Tacitus and Tiberius, Cicero and Catiline always came through with useful hints, although it also helped to have blue-eyed Debby covered in golden ringlets and the slouching, bleary-eyed chap transformed into a square-jawed animal with a predatory smile.

When Alexis sent her to New York, Camilla spent most of her time window-shopping, deciphering unspoken desires on the faces of lunch-hour crowds. No one had an inkling of her secret. Once she merely twisted an old chestnut into a brilliant advertising coup for an advanced formula beauty cream by loosely translating *faber est quisque fortunae suae* into "With sunshine, you can devise the face of your choice."

"But why India?" Alexis asked, looking like a miffed managing director, which he was. Circles were beginning to form under his eyes. He drove himself too hard. Camilla was fond of him and it would please her mother if she married a real toff like Alexis. Mistaking her smile for willingness to comply, Alexis pressed on.

"If you need a holiday, go to Paris or Monte, somewhere you can be reached in case of emergency. Why go all the way to India, for god's sake?"

"I was born there, remember?"

"But that was in a different clime, when the place was a bloody Jewel in the Crown and so on. Why this sudden urge now?"

"Family obligations."

"Rubbish. What about your obligations here? We are about to clinch this deal with Gabe. Gabe is American, remember. The Yanks don't understand stuff like family obligations. They are not like us. Besides, you are not the right age for India."

"Don't be ridiculous Alexis, there's no such thing as the

right age for anywhere."

"Oh yes there is, believe you me, especially for India." Alexis said stroking his chin with a donnish air and leaning back in his chair.

"If one must go to India, it should be when one is young enough for some elegant slumming across the burning ghats of Benares, as I did after Oxford, smoking biddies and roughing it up in some fly-blown joint so that later on you could use the experience to pep up a bestseller or something useful like that. Or you should be old, like your dear mother, and be fussed over by some doddering waiter in milkwhite uniform, complete with blue sash and red turban, mixing you a gimlet in some mouldy club for sahibs, and nattering away about the good old days. But you, my misguided Lalla Rookh, do not fit the bill. Someone of your age and taste would be bored stiff within a couple of days, that is if you do manage to find a quiet corner after dodging all the beggars."

"Darling, I am touched by your concern," Camilla said giving him a parting peck on his quivering cheek. "Don't worry, I shall find a way to amuse myself."

Through the glass partition she caught a glimpse of his frantic gestures as Alexis talked to Joyce. He was proud of his ability to make fritters of pretences, but with Camilla he always felt helpless. Later, a smiling Joyce came into her office to wish her *bon voyage.*

V

THE GRAND TOUR

Grace looks out of the window as the 737 takes off from Santa Cruz Airport and Bombay disappears behind fleecy clouds. In less than an hour she would be back in dear old Mhow. Pater was convinced that M.H.O.W. was an acronym for Main Headquarters of War during the Sepoy Mutiny, but Shirin always disputed that.

"Really, Major, you know that's not true," she would say, sounding like a bored Vicereine. "Daddy tells me it was already there when we snatched it from the Maharaja in 1818."

One year at Auckland House in Simla, and Shirin had become snootier than ever. "At Aucky we do this and we do that."

In India, escaping from the bustle of crowd to your own private seat on a plane can lull you into a false sense of well being. Past scenes begin to unfold frame by frame like a silent era film. Grace's mind drifts back to a lush green post-monsoon day just before the War.

She is on a train from Poona to Mhow.

Such a languid, voluptuous affair; mist-blue carriages of the Deccan Queen, egressing from tunnels like a row of dancers from the wings, brushing a hut hanging by its teeth on a rock face, hills sweeping down like naked thighs into water-logged paddy fields. Then the night mail from Bombay, crimson flames from the engine shaft and screeching rails. Next evening, Bhusawal Junction, Mhow still lurks far in the night, roast chicken and caramel custard in the 'Europeans Only' Refreshment Room. Out of bounds for our fine Miss Parsi brat, Shirin Debu, never mind those blue eyes, ivory complexion, and la-di-da Simla manner. Pushing the screen door, Grace steps into a moving wall of people, chain couplings rattle on a passing goods train. Almost fourteen, Jo doesn't mind the seethe of smelly bodies, smoke from vendors' pans and buzz of flies, as she strolls up and down the platform like Garbo in *Anna Karenina,* looking for her Vronsky.

Wheeler's Stall for an Agatha Christie. Three hours to kill before Khandwa, then seven to Mhow.

The shunting yard at Bhusawal which in daytime is a spaghetti of tracks is now barely visible. Jo wonders if that 'poor old choo choo engine' is still there? Turned turtle, wheels lying in a tangle of loop lines, it had looked so forlorn when they passed this way last month.

From Khandwa it is metre gauge. There's that red and blue baby engine releasing chuffs of smoke under criss-cross girderwork, pulling out without jinking, sliding gracefully round bends, purring over bridges, plunging smartly across ravines. A low pale moon at a wayside station peers in anxiously, looking for a vacant seat. The train is suspended in a timeless moment. One wakes up in time to see the grass roll smoothly up the hummocked hills of Kalakund. The entire journey is not unlike The Grand Tour. A warning whistle at the outer signal where the line curves gently, they gather their belongings with a touch of sadness. First the bungalows of Mhow Railway Colony - roofs decked with pretty red Mangalore tiles - come into sight, then the station canopy. End of picnic.

The fasten seat-belt sign goes on with a ping as the aircraft banks for descent and the cone-shaped Malwa hills disappear like tents of a battalion striking camp. Her 'bandobast' skills are rusty, Camilla is in charge.

Bandobast! Those old cantonment phrases!

A storm of industrial shafts darkens the outskirts of Indore.

It's been barely an hour since they left Bombay.

In the airport lounge, Captain Noshir Ardeshir comes walking briskly towards them, a wiry, garden mongoose of a man with quick round darting eyes and moist, blood-red mouth under a thin moustache. His crisp manner smacks of drills on dusty parade grounds.

"Good flight?" he asks, honking his way through the meddling rickshaws to the Bombay-Agra Road, one of the two arteries of the Empire along with Kim's Grand Trunk.

"Not bad, except for the Huns and Japs bivouacked in the aisles."

Camilla smiles. How effortlessly has Mum's voice slipped into a different register! In that moment, all sorts of local quirks, manner of speaking, habits of mind come together; she feels like an actor's child at a performance when parents step seamlessly back into the interrupted memory of a stage character.

"Sorry about that," says the Captain, dodging painted lorries that bulge like Mongolian yurts. "Technical crew. Jolly smart lot actually. Run the industrial show up at Pithampore. Very keen on golf."

At Villa Shiphidol, Yasmin's hazel eyes stare out of a face too large for her wraithlike limbs. The two older women hug and kiss tear-smudged faces, Camilla watches from the door.

Three months have gone by since Grace's confession but they still cannot look the thing in the face or give it a decent burial. For one harrowing week Camilla's desire to know more had waged a constant battle with the fear of losing Grace to a relapse. There were enormous things to say to each other but with a child's hurt expression Grace had begged that no one should ever know she wasn't her real mother. Camilla had replied truthfully that the thought of revealing their secret to anyone had not even crossed her mind.

But its shadow lies between them; they tiptoe around it, act as though nothing has changed. There is still awkwardness between them, wariness about each other's true feelings so that every exchange is an evasion. Sometime Camilla finds her mother scrutinising her face like someone trying to read a difficult script. But both of them are locked in its dumb solitude.

The surprise on Yasmin's face and the moaning of the old servant make Camilla uneasy, she feels herself changing into that girl in the photograph back home.

Yasmin is temporarily confined to bed with a bad cold. Her girlish voice greets Camilla from the folds of a beige counterpane, hankering mouth opens in a smile.

In a glass cabinet stand absurd hairless celluloid dolls with frilly, immodestly rolled-up skirts. A faint odour of urine and rosewater rises from the crib-like bed, a sickening smell of decay clings to the draperies. An acrid whiff of tobacco fills the air. Camilla turns around. The old man with Milk of Magnesia eyes is sniffing her out.

"I've put you in my old bedroom," Yasmin says to Grace. "You'll find that Shiphidol is just the same, nothing has changed."

The old man leads them to their room. He moves slowly like a dog, a dog in a dream with unseeing liquid motions.

vi

THE DAK BUNGALOW

Roadside hedges are lurid with bougainvillea, as Grace cycles down to the Prince of Wales Park. Jo and Yasmin are at the bandstand. The Drum Major raises his baton. Bugles, trombones and frenchhorns swing into *The 3 D.G.'s*. Its jaunty beat fades into Stoodgy's low, lumpy intoning of his favourite passage from *Nostromo*.

The vague consciousness of a misdirected life given up to impulses whose memory left a bitter taste in his mouth ...

"How strange, that even after nearly three decades in England he has been unable to get rid of that Polish accent," Grace says.

"Maybe he doesn't want to," Camilla says. "It's his only link to the past."

Grace has some of those passages by heart.

"My dear, why bother to read it, why?"

The mongrel pack is at it again; sleep is ripped from her eyes.

It is distressing to find yourself asleep across two worlds, not quite knowing where you are.

The lead is a cur from the direction of what would be the Maidan across the road. Footsteps recede, growling subsides, then a cough in the dark sets off another frenzy.

Mongrels shudder through the clear night, web-footed wails go crawling over the pleats and folds of Grace's brain. Camilla murmurs in sleep, lies spread-eagled, pale skin sodden with moonlight, like Desdemona smothered in bed. With her second marriage over, fat has begun to coil around the waist; her long eyelashes twitch and from the rushes of thick honey-blond hair, slowly streams forth Jo Anna's face.

Grace had to invent that American pilot; it seems to have worked.

Unable to sleep, she slips into a cardigan and lets herself out. In the driveway, the gravel is damp with dew, cyclamen leaves glisten in the grey light. With some difficulty she lifts the stopper on the heavy wrought iron gate, then crosses the road along with a mixed group of construction workers. Women in homespun magenta saris slow down to let her catch up with them, the held-up lorry driver honks impatiently. She thanks them in Hindi; they giggle, covering their mouths with calloused hands.

With vegetation pushing through windows, abandoned bungalows crouch in obeisance. Exhausted mongrels lie like duncoloured mail bags. Grace slinks past them, bears right, comes face to face with The Orpheum. On the hoarding a buxom starlet leans against a doorpost, a hirsute thug twists a cat-o'-nine-tails. Faded elegance still clings to the ashen gateway arch.

Post Office Road is stark like a promontory at hightide, on the left looms the massive portside of St. Mary's Convent.

An olive-green army car sporting a tiny flag comes bearing down on her. A swarthy officer in a smart dark green tunic and black turban stares at her. He sees a withered old white woman chased off the road by his driver. She tries to retain her balance. The car stops and starts backing up. The chauffeur jumps out and holds the door open and out steps the tall Sikh officer.

"Good Morning Madam," he says with a slight bow. "I must apologise for the rudeness of my driver. Generally no one is about this early in the morning. But that's no excuse. I am General Grehwal. May I offer you a lift?"

"No, thank you. I am out for my morning walk. I hope I am not trespassing. Civilians may walk here I hope?"

"Indeed they may, Madam."

A graceful bow, a polite smile through his beard, and he is gone, leaving behind a vision of two golden oak-leaf chains on the front of his turban. She stares at the receding car. Such civility and grace. A splendid upright officer. Just like old times.

Dustier and ramshackle, the town is spared the industrial squalor gripping the once beautiful city of Indore. Not all her past has been rinsed out, things familiar begin to return with a mild flap of wings.

There behind the grassy knoll in the Old British Cemetery are the graves of John and Clarissa Lilley.

Even then it was a furtive sort of place.

Grace can still see the soft undercurves of clouds and Maude Aspel's tall, gaunt figure in black lace over white tulle dress crouching by those twin graves. The faded lobster shell of sola was unmistakably Jo's. Grace remembers standing up on the pedals and toiling up the road, perspiration running down her nose. But at the top of the hill, there was only the dry tinderbox of the Chowkidar's hut and a white shirt on a clothesline fluttering with outstretched arms. Down below on the other side, Wodehouse Road was utterly deserted.

"I saw you this afternoon with that horrible woman," Grace said to Jo Anna at dinner that night.

"Where? What woman?" Hint of smile in Jo Anna's eyes.

"Don't lie. I distinctly saw Mrs. Aspel and you in the Old Cemetery."

"When?"

"Twoish, I should think."

"You must have dreamt it. Ask Yasmin. I was with her the whole afternoon listening to the new recording of *Tales of Hoffmann* Pestan sent from Bombay."

Poor Yasmin, she would have sworn to anything.

A whitewashed building with red tiles and green jalousies is held back by a detachment of bougainvillea.

It's the Dak Bungalow, of course!

How could she have forgotten it? Jack's friends from Bombay stayed there the night before their wedding.

Further up must be the Dog Lady's place. Kuttawala

Memsahib, the servants used to call old Miss Briscoe. The tilted shaggy roof is screened by a clump of persimmon. The derelict bungalow stands alone in what used to be the Dog Lady's garden. Tiles burned black, living room filled with languid creepers and gabled porch sagging dreamily to the ground, it looks like a very old basset hound put to sleep. It seems astonishingly peaceful and empty as though it had expelled all its ghosts and closed in upon itself.

They were the best-behaved dogs in town, obedient and eager to please. The beauty of its garden and the good manners of its kennel determined a family's social standing in Mhow. The Dog Lady could take any fractious pup and within days turn it into a house-broken marvel who fetched slippers and stood to attention on hind legs at her command. The Cantonment doctors were no longer able to treat the Dog Lady because most of her afflictions were believed to be not human. So deeply was she said to empathise with her charges that their maladies often found their way into her frail body.

"And how are our canine friends today?" Revd. Todd would inquire after Sunday Morning Service at Christ Church.

"Quite well, thank you, Vicar, except little Krems here that poor Mrs. Tanner left behind when she died, bless her soul," the Dog Lady would say picking up the Lhasa Apso keening behind its shock of white cascading shag. "He didn't eat his breakfast today, poor mite. Do pray for him, won't you?"

"I shall indeed," Revd. Todd would say with a kindly smile.

You could tell a recent addition to the kennel by the occasional garrulous whining during a longish sermon. They sat patiently in a circle around the marble baptismal fount at the rear of the nave and it was wonderful to watch the entire Pooch Squad rise with yelps of joy at the end of the service and metamorphose into one gigantic wag. The Dog Lady spoke to each of them as they filed out one by one. "So watch your step," she would caution the frisky Corgi, explaining the highlights of that day's sermon. Then, her bonnet bobbing in the air, she would set off in the direction of her bungalow, followed by her troop, single file in order of seniority, without breaking rank.

"If you 'ad 'arf the bleeding turn for discipline o' Miss Briscoe's Pooch Squad, you'd be by far 'n away the smartest regiment in the British Empire," the Sergeant-Major was often heard to remark loudly on parade.

Grace's past is still there, but her step falters. Up on Mall Road Chinnery's waits. The mist has lifted, the sun is out, and, in the refracted light of the bougainvillea, the Dak Bungalow has gone almost blood red. It takes on the aspect of her own longing; she feels a stab in her old flesh as she remembers her wedding day, and stops for a minute to savour the moment. She must not be morbid, her first day back in her beloved Mhow. Today must belong to the Dak Bungalow.

A RIGHT GOOD CREW

When the Chinnerys came to Mhow in 1918, the British had been there exactly one hundred years.

Picture a dreamy sunlit room behind French windows with a varnished desk, rows of quills standing "at attention," blotting paper stretched like a parade ground, prim memsahib of a vase sporting fresh flowers from the garden. Below the desk, helter skelter like merchandise in a bazaar lie pieces of overturned furniture, broken toys, books and clothes amidst other forgotten incunabula. A smell of decay rises from abandoned dishes and calm, in the midst of that chaos, stands the snickety desk - prototype of a British cantonment in India.

When the Sepoy Mutiny floundered on blood-soaked plains, Mhow ceased to be a garrison dotted with pillbox hats, and Red Coats smelling of horse piss. In its place grew a township of Midlands sobriety and unbuttonedness. One by one moneylenders, grocers, bakers, tailors, doctors, chemists and hakims opened their premises along Main and High Streets. A century old Cantonment trade displayed its trophies in the baroque edifices of Parsi villas lining Simrole Road. The rest of the town lay higgledy-piggledy beyond the mud-caked river where the progeny of Gunga Din eked out a living.

Squishy with crushed marigold and wilted jasmine lay the Red-light District in a maze of gullies in the town's southern reach. Past the Railway Crossing were low mangers fringing a hushed forest wherein squatted the Bhut Bungalow or Ghost House, as the locals called the Masonic Lodge.

In the weather-beaten Station yard were tethered colourful tongas to spare, fly-swatting horses. From a small bakery wafted the appetising smell of freshly baked loaves.

In the mud and wattle bustees beyond the river were pictures of a scrawny man in loincloth, ridiculously spinning cotton on a rustic wheel. In the barracks, east of Mall Road, well-fed men oiled their rifles for target practice, and the Union Jack whipped and snapped from the top of Flagstaff House.

On 29th September, there was Michaelmas Goose for dinner.

On All Souls in November, "drink for the dead" was left outside British homes.

On 1st December, rehearsals began for the Nativity Play at St.Mary's Convent, followed by the annual Gilbert and Sullivan Evening in the New Year.

On 2nd February candles were consecrated at Sacred Heart Church.

On Shrove Tuesday in March, thoroughbreds lined up for the Commander-in-Chief's Cup.

In April and May, Mhow malingered behind khas-khas tatties till the subdued intensities of Malwa evenings and distant hills striped in red afterglow drew forth withered old Anglo-Indian and Goan Catholic pensioners from the Railway Colony, the down-and-out subsisting on the charity of fellow Parsis, and the town's only Jewish resident Mr. David, the Postmaster, who never took a holiday. They sat on wooden benches around the empty bandstand, leaning on walking sticks, chin on hand. Meanwhile, at the Orpheum and the Vaudette, Mary Pickford and Lillian Gish reigned supreme.

Towards the end of June, the monsoon arrived, beating an uneven tattoo on corrugated barrack roofs, pounding mud huts beyond the river into sludgy ground, leaving crows around the Parsi Tower of Silence shivering and dishevelled. But life marched on to the precise beat of a platoon on parade.

In July and August holy rivers in the mofussil swallowed

their quota of pilgrim ferries, nervous ford-elephants shook their heads before raging rivers, culverts foamed, nullahs gurgled, but there was no let up in whist-drives at the Club, or Saturday Dances at the Railway Institute and, at the bandstand, a few stragglers clutching their umbrellas promenaded to the rousing strains of mazurkas.

Such was Mhow's yearly calendar, with all the seductions of solitude and silence, giving shape and meaning to a variety of creeds that assembled at the Ghost House. They had no use for ideas that first quivered innocently like a horse's flank, then tossed the rider off with a vicious flick. Here, order and wisdom went hand in hand and the Captain of the Pinafore commanded a right good crew.

viii

OH, ROSE MARIE I LOVE YOU

"Waist down I am all crab."
Yasmin throws the soughing Pashmina shawl across her
legs. It descends daintily in slow motion - a whispering mist
- on her naked tubular calves.
"Due to inbreeding among Parsis they say. Look at Aunt
Parvez, matriarch of our Nagar branch, mien of sphinx, but
hands like dangling weaverbird nests."
A scrabble at the door, a swish of curtains and Bhola enters
pushing the trolley with her morning tea, followed by
Sitaram. She must get ready for breakfast with Grace and her
daughter. The parrot flaps in like a miniature vampire in a
green cloak and clambers up to his usual perch by her
bedside. "Aunt Yasmin is a Dodo," he says cheerfully, cracking
a nut. Sitaram can render her nephew Noshir's words in his
crisp gravelly voice - a parrot for a nephew. She leans forward
to stroke the bird, but he hops away on the bar. A tiny draft
sneaks in and tickles her feet. Though the place is damp she
prefers it to her bedroom. It used to be the nursery and has
lots of natural light. The past lingers in its walls of faded
pink, curtains sprigged softly with violets, and a bevy of puff-
cheeked blue-eyed celluloid dolls going bald in their glass
cabinets. The day she moved in, the under-sized bed hugged
her as though it had no memory of emptiness.
Unlike Aunt Parvez, she had begun to go quite early, aged
sixteen to be exact. Till then she had been the gorgeous one.
Hazel eyes in pale face, skin soft "as the inside of an angel's
wings" - Daddy used to say. She looks at him. The portrait
has gone a bit wonky on the wall. She must speak to Bhola
about it.

35

As her limbs whittled, breasts and head amplified and eyes elongated all the way to the ears. Gradually her cheekbones spread sideways, flattening her face "like the dish that ran away with the spoon." Only this dish did not - unlike Barkis, the spoon wasn't willing. Instead, she stayed in bed and read through her youth and midlife, becoming the wisest woman in Mhow with alert, assessing eyes. Nuns from St. Mary's Convent bunched around her to be enlightened on matters concerning chemistry, literature, and geography. The Parsi Panchayat commissioned her to write the history of their community. The encyclopaedia of Mhow they called her. But the childlike limbs attached to a face with hot come-hither eyes troubled men. Her voice acquired a nursery lisp and wafted up in moist squishy syllables.

As a child her sister Shirin had been skinny, too, angular in shoulders, but with those blue eyes, much coveted by the Parsis. Yasmin shivers. Bhola hands her a cup and stumps across to the door muttering through wheezes and bangs it shut.

"Shirin was pretty, but I, let's face it, I was absolutely it."

Until that August of stretched monsoon, arteries zigzagging through clouds, elephants of dust snouting skywards. She had swayed, was airborne and deposited in a nearby bougainvillea bush.

A summer of bougainvillea. There were poinsettia, roses, hibiscus, chrysanthemums and creamy yellow blossoms on the Mahua trees in British gardens all over the Cantonment, but whole brigades of livid bougainvillea outflanked them everywhere. Jo Anna Chinnery was put out over Sister Miriam's umpiring. "Foul is not fair," she had muttered and stalked out of the hockey game. That was the time when Jo had turned funny and started sneaking into the Old Cemetery in the company of Maude Aspel.

Other girls had rushed to help Yasmin, brushing purple bracts from her school uniform the impact had shaken off the bush. But Jo had just stood there, squinting at a drooping peepul bough where crows scuffled over the day's pickings. Half a century had trundled by and yet . . .

Bhola fumbles with the picture frame. To the British Resident at Indore, Daddy was always 'Sir Mancherjee.'

Bhola's lungs are working overtime; his memory has dimmed with his sight. Those long-gone afternoons when he used to sneak in to be with her seemed to have crawled away from his crumbling mind like ants looking for a new home. He was past fifty even then, with dog's eyes in a man's face. Thirty years ago. He must be over eighty now. He could go any day, the last of the old guard. She is prepared for that. Blind as a bat, he is what's left of the old house; its past is lodged within him like an ornate ship in a dusty bottle.

A scrabble in the portico. The sun has turned buttery that early October morning.

Why did Grace have to come back? Why couldn't she let the sleeping . . !

Her chest heaves and suddenly she brings up tea and lets it dribble into the bedside spittoon Bhola holds up for her.

His old hands hover protectively over her head as he stoops to adjust the pillow. Yasmin smiles at him gratefully.

Good thing Ross is not around at the moment. Yasmin has never understood why he always seems so lukewarm towards the British. In the old days, lighter-skinned Anglos went to ridiculous lengths to pass themselves off as British. Ross can be easily mistaken for a sunburnt Englishman but he takes care to nip any such impression in the bud.

She closes her eyes and waits for the maid.

What's that dribbling sound out on the Maidan? There are no parades in Mhow these days, no horses with rippling flanks, only scrawny ponies that pull the tongas in town and those overloaded lorries spewing diesel fumes. Lorries and mongrels vie with each other at night to ruin her sleep. She must speak to Noshir and get rid of that pack. In times gone by the Dog Lady's Pooch battalion could smell any mongrel from half a mile and blocked its entrance to the Cantonment.

She dozes off.

Buggy wheels crunch gravel, there's a whiff of sandalwood from the Fire Temple, Nelson Eddy serenades Jeannette Macdonald - "O Rose Marie, I love you" - and at dusk the distant wail of the Last Post.

She could have drawn Grace from memory, cotton candy hair, puckered forehead, wrinkles and all. But every time that violet shimmer in Camilla's eyes sends a paper boat bobbing down a stream.

Baby Camilla was a tidy bundle on Grace's lap at the Railway Station the day the Chinnerys left for England while Daddy, in his starched white trousers, long brown silk coat, and round black Parsi cap, talked to Major Chinnery. It was such a shock to see the usually dapper Major nodding his head listlessly, with unseeing watery eyes, face buried under a nine-month-old growth. Yasmin leaned against a pillar as she watched Grace brush flies off the baby's face. The Europeans Only Waiting Room was crowded with Italian POWs from Abyssinia awaiting transportation.

In small knots, some of them weeping openly, stood the entire staff of Chinnery's Hotel. Mrs. Roderigues, their Ayah, was too weak to stand and Grace made her sit down on a footlocker. Old d'Quodros, the Hotel Chef, his white suit glossy with age, straw hat in hand, spoke to Ayah in that mixture of English, Portuguese and Konkani which Goan Catholic elders used when discussing family matters. Chalk-white in a crumpled black silk dress, Mrs. Chinnery sat on a trunk, clutching her inhaler, staring at the shunting rake of a goods train. She hadn't spoken since the day Jo Anna's mangled body was brought home from the Dayan's house. One by one the old servants edged forward and went down on their knees, crying all the time. Mrs. Chinnery patted each head mechanically, only stopping to pull on her inhaler. Without the manorial backdrop of the Hotel, the Chinnerys seemed more destitute than the poor peasants huddled around their bundles.

Sir Mancherjee drew some solace from the fact that Mrs. Chinnery was not true-blue British like dear Miss Elton, his adored Governess, but after all an "American" who had reinvented herself as a stylish English lady. Captain Chinnery had gone to Mesopotamia with the Poona Brigade, and was wounded defending Kut against the Turks while fighting under Major General Townshend. The girl he had been courting in Poona had taken one look at the broken leg, the livid scar on his cheek, and caught the next ship home. To all appearances your average fishing-fleeter, she drew a line at limping captains. He was promoted to Major but couldn't see himself toiling behind a desk the rest of his life, and had obtained an honourable discharge from the army at the end of the War.

Amanda claimed to have been a schoolteacher summoned to India by her uncle at the Methodist Mission in Poona. "School teacher, my eye," Mrs. Talbutt, the Colonel's lady would snort. "More like a music hall floozy, if you ask me." In the winter of 1917 when the Major was convalescing at Sassoon Hospital, Amanda had come in with a group from the Mission to sing carols to the patients. The Major had taken one look at her and instantly lost his warrior's heart.

THE CHERRY ORCHARD

"Grace be reasonable," Yasmin says. "It's been a long time since you were here last."

"But nothing seems to have changed much. I'd not venture out alone in Poona or Indore. All those crowds, I should be soon run over by one of those auto-rickshaws, I believe they call them. The din they make! But dear old Mhow is still the same. A little scruffy, a bit untidy perhaps, but still the same. And I met this nice General Greywala. A handsome Sikh officer and a thorough gentleman. He was most polite."

"You must mean General Grehwal," Noshir says, handing her a cup of tea. "He is in charge of the College of Combat. A fine shot. Would you care to join us tonight for dinner at the Club with the Grehwals? Burra Khana is still the finest quality. I'll pick you up at 1800 hours."

At the Club there is that great assortment of shields, lances and old Enfield rifles on the walls, and in the Billiards Room a dull thud of cue hitting the ball. Axe cutting into trees at the end of *The Cherry Orchard*. In the Men's Bar, Club Presidents on the wainscot change pigment halfway down the line, but have the same gimlet eye. The place is ringed with echoes that flutter in like nesting sparrows. Grace wants to nurse that feeling of recoupment, to stroke its feathers.

Through the window she can see a peepul leaning against the verandah. It waves a friendly branch at her.

One day when the trial involving the Tommies was in its last phase, Jo Anna and Yasmin accosted Grace outside the Club.

"We think Auntie Maude is having an affair with Captain Rowlins." Jo's voice was breathy with excitement.

"Don't be silly," Grace said, getting down from her bike.

"It's true," said snoopy-eyed Yasmin, "We saw them in the library, they thought they were alone. She was kissing him."

"So what? She may have been saying goodbye. You know how she blubs when someone is transferred to another station."

"It was on the mouth. A long lingering kiss," Jo said, "like Marlene Dietrich kissing Charles Boyer in *The Garden of Allah*. And his Regiment is not due to leave for Umballa till next month."

Mhow used to cup its hand to hide its smile when new peccadilloes from Simla were reported. Even young Shirin down for the holidays could offer a lively retrospective to her friends of last season's dalliances. Spartan Mhow was proud of its blot-free escutcheon. One heard awful stories about the Anglos, of course. But they were Eurasian, half-breed, chi chi, eight annas. And to the cabal of thakurs and nabobs that gathered at Chinnery's every Saturday, a well-stocked harem was proof of manliness. When the men died, their funeral processions included, besides their legitimate brood, a sizeable number of byblows. When let off the leash, the Sahibs in Simla could teach the Rajas a lesson or two, but the compact Mhow community made up mostly of hardy soldier types and ex-boxwallahs, was solidly puritanical. A serious breach of social protocol would at most dredge up the 'touch of the tar' insinuation.

At St. Mary's girls openly rooted for the dashing Captain. With a brooding Ronald Coleman brow, he looked as though he had stepped off the set of *Bulldog Drummond*. Despite his weak eyes, old Major Aspel had continued to practice medicine after his retirement from the army. In his small surgery at the corner of High Street and Simrole Road he tended to his patients, British and Indian, with the same courteous care. He was something of an anachronism. During a surprise raid by outlaws on the North West Frontier, when the officer commanding his unit was shot dead, the Doctor had rallied the men and held the position till reinforcement arrived.

One evening, waving a revolver at Captain Rowlins, the Doctor charged into the Club. Colonel Vansittart F.R.C.S., the new Medical Officer, adroitly saved the situation and sent him home with an escort. The Army had not yet recovered from its humiliation over that wretched Bhagwan Case during which Doctor Aspel had testified against the Tommies accused of beating Postmaster David's old servant to death, pitting the resident British against their countrymen in the Barracks. The soldiers were transients, lacking the strong ties to the place of those who had made Mhow their home. Mostly they hung about at Hungry Charley's. The trial had dragged on for days, its echoes were heard in Westminster. Not since the infamous Crawley Affair of the last century, which had left in its wake the beautiful graves of Sergeant Major Lilley and his beloved wife Clarissa, tended by unseen hands to this day, had the British Community in Mhow been torn asunder by such a civil war situation. Even Edward's decision to abdicate did not heal the rift and on Coronation Day, the Chinnerys and their friends made only a token appearance at the Club to drink to the health of King George VI.

The day after the incident with the revolver the Doctor was declared persona non grata at the Club. Next day the poor man blew his brains out. The entire township turned up at his funeral. Women in Purdah wailed "Doctorsahib who will look after our little ones now?" Old retired havildars walked shoulder to shoulder with rich Baniyas, Parsis and Catholics. After sitting on the fence during the trial, even the Anglos joined the procession.

Grace looks around; the Lounge is filling up. Old men, still ramrod straight, play rummy while their spouses sip gimlets. Some of the women have taken to wearing jeans which bulge in the wrong places.

Noshir's wife Tehmi, who was raised in Hong Kong,

considers them a bit stuffy.

"That's the Signal Vihar crowd," Tehmi whispers. "Retired armywallahs who live in their exclusive Housing Colony, chewing the fat over how the country is going to the dogs."

The General in his blue serge jacket looks younger but Sandra Grehwal's equipoise suggests a trained rider, her gait more glide than walk. Even the most cross-grained foal that whinnied, scratching the ground, used to calm down when Jo Anna crooned, stroking its withers, breathing up its nose. When she raced in the Ladies' Plate, every little movement of her hand and heel had a meaning for the horse. How Pater's eyes used to glow with pride when she galloped, her cheeks flushed by the exercise.

Man's pathway to glory
Is strewn with the bones of a horse,
he used to quote. Despite his gammy leg, Pater rode his roan even after Mater bought the Silver Ghost at such great expense. There was always the smell of horses on his clothes.

That's it, Grace thinks. It's the horses. They are gone and along with them that paddocky whiff of horse sweat, the sweet smell of hay chaff, and roughage.

"How do you happen to have such an English name?" she asks Mrs. Grehwal.

"You mean Sandra? Oh, that's short for Surinder. My name got anglicised at the Convent in Poona. In that respect we are still very British you know. My husband is called Monty by friends, but his real name is Monteksingh."

"Of course, how stupid of me," Grace says. " We knew someone called Pat who later became the Maharaja of Kesarpore after his father the Old Highness died. His name was Pratap Singh. His son Vikram was called Vicky. He was such a beautiful child, always very polite. He was absolutely devastated when Miss Bailey, his governess, went back to England."

Sandra and Grace have Poona in common. In those distant days the only window on the world was provided by

Movietone reports from the Front and trailers of coming attractions at West End Cinema with its garden restaurant. In its place stands a hulking eyeless malformation in solid concrete. The land has shrunk; the eye is hostage to tedium. Their distress is palpable.

Camilla sails in with Noshir. She is laughing at some mishap on the dance floor.

"You cut a pretty mean rug, Batman," she says to Noshir with a friendly nudge. An easy confederacy has blossomed between Camilla and the Parsi couple.

"You're not so bad yourself, Catwoman."

"Your husband is too kind," she says to Tehmi. "I was thrashing about like a windmill."

" You two were great," Tehmi says, " it was a real treat. I am bored stiff with all that 'You are my sunshine, my only sunshine,' kind of shuffling that passes for dancing here." Looking defiantly at the cardplayers she adds, "This place has grown too antiseptic for my taste anyway."

A sudden hush falls on the lounge as two young girls in designer jeans come in, leading a very tall man with light blue eyes in a terracotta face, and hard muscular body.

"Look who's here, Daddy," one of the girls says to the General.

"We caught him in the act of giving us the slip, " says the elder of the two.

The newcomer has a slight limp. Chairs are pushed back as he is accorded a hero's welcome. The General gets up to shake hands, Noshir hugs him like a long lost brother, and Surinder pulls up a chair for him. The two Grehwal girls arrange themselves around him like cherubs.

"I must apologise for not changing, Sir," he says to the General in a clipped baritone. "Needed a drink before Khana. Packed the kit off with my man to the Guest House and came here straight from the airport."

Sandra, who has known Grace for just a few minutes, notices the way she freezes at the sight of Colonel Ross

Harrison.

"Ross has collected more gallantry awards than any other officer I know," the General says introducing him to Grace. "The latest was for conducting a highly risky mopping up operation in the hills of Assam against separatist insurgents. Luckily for us he'll be here for a while on a new assignment."

"That's all very well," Grace muses, "but why does he look like, . . . like?"

Her bosom still heaving with the exertion of dancing, Camilla stares at Harrison with trancelike immobility. "That's Camilla for you, easy meat for a bit of dash. Poor girl has had a rough time fending off hawkers and beggars in Bombay. But that's no excuse for acting like a schoolgirl. At her age too!"

Grace is embarrassed. He is an attractive devil with that trim moustache and quicksilver manner, but quite obviously an Anglo-Indian mix-breed, probably of the worst strutting sort.

Grace's illness has made her somewhat ghost-prone. Her pent up bitterness against Anglos suddenly comes welling up. Grace had not only inherited the unconscious elitism of the British ruling class but also imbibed certain arcane notions of caste purity from her upper-crust Indian friends. After Jo Anna's tragic end she'd readily succumbed to theories of amateur geneticists who claimed that the Anglo-Indian was mean and vicious because he carried the inferior genes of some ill-bred Tommy and a low-caste, black-as-coal biddy from the Untouchable community.

The fairer among the Anglos claimed that on the Indian side they were descended from pale-skinned Rajput warrior women, but only the silliest and most gullible subaltern from England would buy such a story. Rajput women indeed. No outsider, whatever his rank could ever get within hailing distance of those high caste women who generally led a solitary life in purdah, not showing their face to any men except husbands and brothers.

Grace always gave a wide berth to that 'grovelling Strickland woman' in her Clapham haberdashery in London, who pathetically tried to pass herself off as true blue British, whereas anyone could tell from her first squawk that the wretched creature was a 'chi chi.'

She looks at Harrison but is unable to locate any plebeian traces in his finely chiselled features. And she is quite rattled by the way he returns Camilla's admiring gaze, fixing her with those pale blue, meat-appraiser's eyes - so very familiar.

A paper boat capsizes and disappears in the foam.

"Mhow too has changed considerably, don't you think Mrs. Studegynski," Sandra says to Grace.

"Yes, but fortunately not quite as dreadfully as Poona. Although I must confess, now that I am here, I don't know if I shall have the courage to visit our old home."

"Really, and where's that?" Sandra asks.

"On Corbett Road. Yasmin tells me it's a hospital now. My parents ran a hotel there. You may have heard of Chinnery's Hotel."

The Colonel's hands begin to shake, his eyelids quiver and like a wound-up toy soldier he gets up stiffly, excuses himself and marches off. Everyone is taken aback.

"It must be something really important," Tejinder, the older Grehwal girl, says, pouting with obvious disappointment. "We must ring later and find out what's bothering him."

"Something about Esmé," Sandra says. "She is in the dorms at the Convent."

"All the same," says the General slowly, "it's very odd that Ross should take off like that."

That night while undressing Camilla says, "Tehmi tells me the Colonel and Noshir were at school together. Wasn't it odd the way he suddenly got up and left without saying goodbye?"

Grace is brushing her teeth in the bathroom.

"I am sure some of the women I know in London would

go quite ga ga over him," Camilla says. "He is very good-looking and reminds me of someone."

"Whom?" Grace asks shutting the bathroom door behind her.

"Oh, I know, he looks a lot like that chap from the old film on the telly a few days back. I watched some of it because it was set in Africa. *King Solomon's Mines* it was called."

"That's Rider Haggard, of course."

"Of course. Full of big game hunters in khaki, ordering the natives about. Not my cup of tea, I'm afraid. Granger played the lead."

"Don't be ridiculous darling, Stewart Granger is British. This man is quite obviously an Anglo, a half breed."

"How do you know? He has a tan but he looks white enough to me."

"Some of them do dear, quite like us as a matter of fact. But I can always spot that chilli-cracker accent for miles, though I must admit, in his case it's not very pronounced."

X

THE CRACKED MIRROR

All the blood shed by Ross on the battlefield has not washed off the stain of his father's tail-between-his-legs exit from Mhow. With the arrival of this Chinnery woman, overnight Mhow has become the dark house where his father had been crabbed in youth. God, how they sucked up to the British, the Anglos of that generation. Till the very end Dad would talk of going "home" some day.

After being chased out of Mhow by the Chinnerys, Carl Busby had re-emerged in Calcutta. Tommies had beaten him, he said, burned him with cigarettes, broken his ankle with a hockey stick. Condemned to hobble, he'd accepted the lowly job of a toy-train driver in the Amusement Park, become a Catholic to marry his uncle's widowed daughter, and adopted his last name, Harrison. But when it was time to choose the right school for Ross, the couple had opted for the expensive St.Paul's in Darjeeling, instead of the Jesuit administered St. Xavier's High School in Calcutta.

Dad used to take him for a run with other children and pretended to be driving the Frontier Mail. He would speak of the legendary driver, Mr. Kelly. Cautioned by the Guard to take extra care because the Viceroy was travelling one night, Kelly asked that a silver rupee be placed on the footplate of the Burra Sahib's luxury saloon which was always at the rear of the rake, before pulling out of Colaba Station in Bombay. He wagered that the coin would not move an inch during its nearly five hundred mile run up the line where his shift ended. The coin was still there, resting on the footplate, when they stopped at Ratlam. By the end of the story his father would have tears in his eyes. Then he would cheerfully toot the whistle and tell them to get aboard.

The image of his father's tormentors Ross has carried in his mind doesn't tally with this pale-faced, shrivelled Chinnery woman. He is confused because his instinct for revenge is thwarted by that frail solitary figure. The formidable ogre of his childhood has turned out to be a pathetic bundle of skin and bones.

He is angry with himself for letting the old crone make a shambles of his much longed-for visit to Mhow. After five years of dodging bullets and attempted ambushes by the rebels, he has been looking forward to spending a few peaceful months in Mhow with his child. It had taken all his savings plus the money from the sale of his wife's jewellery to construct his little bungalow in Signal Vihar. Ross is now ready to put down his roots in the soil which had nurtured his father.

That Chinnery woman had reacted the way old tea planters do at the Saturday Club in Calcutta on meeting him for the first time. Their own skin burned biscuit brown by the hillside sun in Assam, they can immediately sniff out the Anglo lurking in his speech. Unlike his classmates at St. Paul's, Ross has never bothered to tailor his speech to that of BBC newsreaders, but his prolonged exposure to the soldiers' Hindustani has not pidginised his English.

The message in that woman's probing eyes was unmistakable. 'You can't fool me,' it seemed to say, peeling off the scab and exposing the pariah under his skin.

In cities and towns Ross is an Anglo, an object of derision and awe at the same time. His English heritage grants him a certain reflected glory, a whiff of the past, especially with officers like General Grehwal who had trained under British Commanders of Indian Regiments. Widowed in his thirties, Ross still has difficulty fending off bored army wives. He has managed to keep their teenage daughters at bay by producing from his wallet Esmé's picture with her frank "Keep your hands off my Daddy" smile. But when you spend the better part of each year tramping through sniper-infested jungles in

Assam, a pair of nubile breasts can fetch you blossomingly back to life.

The pink rotunda of Lutyens' Connaught Place in New Delhi was like an expanding bracelet of light when he ran into Tejinder Grehwal and took her to the New Year's Eve Ball at a friend's place in Green Park. Things got a bit out of hand at the stroke of midnight. As the lights dimmed, she kissed him on the mouth. It was the fourth Christmas without Rita and he had been drinking steadily all evening. His friend Bunty Rajpal would not hear of his driving back to the Guest House in his condition. Events following that kiss were hazy, but a scraping noise woke him up. Taji stood in the connecting doorway, dressed only in her pyjama shirt. He pushed her back into her room and bolted his door.

But Major Dhaliwal returning to Assam after a holiday in Delhi gave him a long searching look after conveying Miss Grehwal's "fondest regards." Since then, Ross has been on the ragged edge, wondering how that scene in Delhi was going to play out. God, what was he thinking of? The daughter of his dear friend and mentor!

It was during the Bangladesh War that the then Colonel Grehwal had asked him, instead of a senior officer who was fearless but fought by the book, to take charge of a platoon defending a bridgehead.

"Captain Baxi is brave and solid as a rock; he'd do a fine job," he had told Ross, "but rocks can breathe. What we need here is steel."

Ross's platoon had come under heavy fire, the entire forward observation party had been decimated, and he'd taken a hit in the leg. Barely able to walk, he had crawled around on his belly directing fire. When a machine gunner collapsed, he'd pulled him away and propping himself on one leg worked the gun, shouting encouragement to his men who had fought hand-to-hand to repulse the attack. That first act of casual valour had given rise to the cult that made the men fighting under his command feel they were invincible. He owed it all to the General.

Ross carries his wife's photograph everywhere, but never actually looks at it. Like a moth trapped in a flame, she had perished in their burning kitchen. The young sweeper who had been the chief suspect had disappeared after the fire, probably killed or spirited away by insurgents.

He has put all that behind him and started planning for Esmé's future. She has always been slightly frail, and boarding a bus in Calcutta to go to college requires survival skills of a trained commando. But in a letter from Vancouver, his cousin had bluntly stated that Canada wanted doctors and engineers. Professional warriors had really nowhere to go.

Ross would always love the army; it's the only institution the politicians have not been able to drive to the dogs. The regiments of the day are less caste-and creed-based, but they continue to draw their officers from old army families. His cousins in Calcutta are content to sweat it out in Loco Sheds, clock in long hours behind reception desks in hotels, or toil as cabin crew on international flights. Only a few have followed the trail of Captain James Skinner, the Anglo founder of Skinner's Horse. Along with Probyn's, Gardener's, Watson's, Sam Brown's and Poona Horse, Skinner's had been the backbone of the army when a cavalry charge could turn the scale.

The army is his true family, where regimental pride makes the crack in the mirror fade away - the crack that hyphenates the Anglo from Indian.

The year after the British abandoned them, most of his relatives dissolved like raindrops in the sea of anonymity. His aunt's children, including those with dusky skins, disappeared almost seamlessly into Australia or Canada. He often wonders what he would have done had he been a few shades darker. Would he have felt more Indian then? That sense of doubleness does not allow his two faces to come into any sort of lasting alignment.

To be an Anglo is to be forever reflected in a cracked mirror.

II

i

FILES-ON-PARADE

When the Chinnerys came to Mhow, the First World War was winding down towards Versailles.

In those five years, the town had changed more than it realised. Old sawbones at the Cantonment Club could only glare and thump the table causing the upturned points of their Wilhelmines to quiver when Indian Officers, who were awarded the King's Commission, went for a splash in the Swimming Pool. And after Kitchener ushered in the "Khaki" era, and cavalry regiments were converted into armoured units, even old-timers had difficulty identifying them at ceremonial parades.

But before the War, when the 6th Inniskilling Dragoons marched with their officers' dark green-and-red horse furniture, their cocked white-over-red plumed hats, laces, loops and gold-embroidered epaulettes, crimson silk waist-sashes and red breeches, yellow cuffs and housings, it was as though unseen hands had poured from huge vats brilliant dyes all across the burning landscape.

Pensioners remembered how on 24th May, Queen Victoria's Birthday, which later became Empire Day, the Parade Ground exploded like a giant peacock fan and from its churning centre buoyed up red Zouave tunics with yellow sashes, gold-and-blue-striped turbans of Infantry Regiments, and red facings on the green jackets of the 125th Napier's Rifles. Like great surfs breaking in measured rolls came the blue-and-gold-tasselled turbans of the 16th Rajputs and the red-laced dark green tunics of the Bombay Native Infantry. They were matched in splendour only by the black plastron and piping adorning the orange-yellow lancers' tunics of Skinner's Horse.

Then the piked helmets of the Duke of Connaught's officers rose in the air like rows of shiny miniature pagodas, with their fetchingly-laced fronts, cord loops and olivets, followed by the orange fringes of Sikh turbans, discreet fly-swatting and polite neighing of well-groomed horses and the angulating and straightening passage of red trim on blue trousers on hundreds of feet marching in unison to the "oompha, oompha" of drums and trombones.

By the end of the Great War, khaki became the base colour of Mhow. The coming of Amanda Chinnery was thus timely. The day she arrived the town was salvaged from pointless space and wrapped in a blue ribbon.

The boxwallahs from Bombay who supplied goods to the Cantonment had to commute from Khandwa or Ratlam and spend the nights in bug-infested retiring rooms at railway stations. A modest 'Bed and Breakfast' establishment where a boxwallah might doss down for the night seemed to promise a decent living. But as the Major and his friends were to soon find out, in Amanda's reckoning, Chinnery's Hotel was to be what Raffles was to Singapore or the New Stanley to Nairobi.

Among frumpy old women of Mhow, whose taste in clothes ran from drab to dowdy, Amanda, who was still in the first stages of pregnancy, cut an elegant figure. She invented a genteel persona, acquired a Mayfair accent, gave a Garbo arch to her eyebrows and, on the day Chinnery's opened, she made a stunning appearance in the subdued light on the staircase, white face, throat and hands breaking out as separate entities from a long, flowing black evening gown. A collective gasp was heard all the way to Neemuch. The ill-digested bits of knowledge about art and literature served her well in a garrison town like Mhow, which was to Simla what Jane Austen's Highbury was to London. And there seemed to be a private treasure trove of radiance tucked away inside her tall full figure, which lent splendour to the occasion. The Major smiled proudly and poured Scotch for his guests.

Nothing as dramatic had happened in Mhow since the Crawley Affair of the last century. From the smelly bylanes crisscrossing the native bustee to the dim interiors of Goan tailoring shops on Main Street, rockers squeaking on Parsi verandahs on Simrole Road, and scissors snipping at hairdressers on Plowdon, inhabitants of Mhow felt a pleasant jolt like passengers of a stranded train recoupled to a new engine.

The building was leased from a wealthy Parsi called Daruwala, a direct descendant of the liquor merchant who was induced by General Crawley in 1862 to go with him to London to testify against John Lilley. The RSM was falsely charged with drunkenness while on duty because, in a letter to the Governor of Bombay, Lilley had exposed Crawley's attempt to conceal the record of his absences from parade. By saving the General's skin through brazen perjury, the wretched Parsi had cornered all the trade with the Cantonment. Over the years his progeny had made amends for the perfidy of their dynastic founder by contributing generously to the Sakhawat, as the Parsi Charitable Trust was known. Then Mancherjee Debu, the scion of the most distinguished Zoroastrian family in Mhow, married one of the Daruwala girls whose extraordinary beauty and charm diluted the stigma, and brought together the two oldest and wealthiest Parsi houses of Mhow. However the odour of The Crawley Affair never quite evaporated and to the local Parsis a Daruwala always seemed to be looking at the world with sly basilisk eyes.

The advent of the Chinnerys coincided with the elevation of Mhow to District Headquarters for Civil Administration, and with it arrived several senior varsity-trained British officers like the Collector, the Magistrate, the Superintendent of Police, and sundry staff of the Public Works Department.

Mhow was no longer a town of uprooted soldiery, a transit camp for a line of marching feet. The Masonic Lodge lost its pukka character and brought under its roof all creeds, spawning a lifestyle neither British nor Indian, and between the wars, the town blossomed exotically. Bangalore and Poona were restive, incendiary cities with cantonments attached to them. At Mhow the native township was incidental, a minor accessory tucked away in the capacious bosom of the military machine.

For some the social day began with breakfast at Chinnery's and for others it ended in its lounge with after-dinner coffee. One could get lost in its grounds. There you could intrigue, dream, plot, and suffer heartbreaks and hope. Above all it allowed proximity to Indians without the awkwardness of entertaining them at home.

AN ENGLISHMAN'S HOME

Returning one evening from a birthday party when she was six, Grace told Mater that Sylvia's family lived in an outhouse.

"An outhouse?"

"Oh yes, ask Ayah, she was there."

"No, no, Grace Baba," said old Mrs. Roderigues, "It was their house onlee, no?"

Grace wasn't convinced.

"But there's no garden, and they serve food in the kitchen."

How could that patch of green in front of Sylvia's house be a garden? Even their bungalow was no bigger than the outhouse at Chinnery's where Khansahib, the night watchman lived with his family by the wrought-iron gate. The Bickleys didn't even have a call box on the gatepost with the inscription "Not At Home" where newcomers from England left their calling cards. Mr. Bickley was a Mechanical Engineer on the Rajputana Malwa Railway, better known as RMR. His bungalow in the Officers' Colony was tiny compared with Chinnery's.

Besides, how could it be a real house if there wasn't enough room to play hide and seek and no staircase to duck under? At Chinnery's there were so many nooks and crannies in the hall, the library, the dressing rooms and the nursery. Grace's house had voices that whispered in the night, the sycamores nodded their heads and went woosh-sh-sh-sh. Sometimes the wind whistled frantically through them like an engine approaching an unmanned crossing. Late in the afternoon, shadows of clematis leaves cast by the fanlight over the front door danced on the floor. After a heavy downpour at night, the smell of mildew wafted out of the cupboards, calendars on the walls scrolled up, and pages in the book of nursery rhymes got stuck.

"An Englishman's home is his castle," Pater used to say.

Chinnery's was indeed a fairy castle, with brass polished doorknobs that burned in the night like the eyes of a tiger. During a rainstorm, there rose from within the large hall a sound as if a trumpeting baby elephant was splashing in a river. The house had eyes as well as ears. Sometimes it was so quiet; it seemed to be listening to the voices of tree people in the banyans behind the guest rooms.

At night, moonlight streaming through the stained glass Union Jack made red and blue stripes on her white nightgown. Sometimes she saw a shadow cross the window and heard taps on the pane followed by a whisper. It was only the grandfather clock that stood in an alcove upstairs, clearing its throat and chuckling before croaking out the opening bars of Brahms' Lullaby at twenty past. Grace could already play it on the piano, but she was scared all the same and ran down to the drawing room where Pater sat chatting with friends. She would kiss the palm of his dangling hand, he would pull her up and let her doze on his gently heaving stomach listening to Uncle 'Woom' talk. Woom was Isambard Hulme who'd retired as Principal of the public school at Indore and lived with his Muslim wife in an old bungalow away from the Cantonment in the western section of Mhow, not far from the Bhut Bungalow. The Principal was touchy about the way memsahibs at the Club poked fun at his wife's lack of English.

Grace even began to talk like Hulme, using big words, the meaning of which was not quite clear to her. She would say, "It is 'imperative' that I have a new dress for my birthday." Expressions like, "exquisite," "immaculate" and "ineptitude" came tumbling out of her tiny mouth in the unlikeliest contexts, and made Uncle Shikari, who ran the Army and

Navy Store on Main Street, laugh under his drooping, walrus moustache.

A few years later, an angle formed by a pair of potted aspidistra flanking a window seat in the library was to be Grace's favourite reading nook. One day she dozed off with Henty's *Rujub the Juggler* on her lap and was awakened by the heavy library door being shut followed by whispers and giggles. Peeking around the bookcase she could see the big sofa rocking violently. A swollen bottom, red like a Dutch cheese, rose and fell over a tangle of black legs. Then a woman cried out in pain. Grace was too terrified to move. It was Uncle Fred who had come down from Ajmer, and Josephine, the daughter of Mr. d'Quodros the chef. Uncle Fred, who was the Deputy Manager of RMR, was on an inspection tour.

To Grace's surprise, Josephine was married to the assistant stationmaster, Mr. Gilbert. But the wedding was held at Sacred Heart Church. That was odd because Mr. Gilbert was a regular member of the congregation at Christ Church and sang in the choir. But Josephine was a Goan Catholic and he had to convert in order to marry her. After the wedding he stopped attending the service at Christ Church. Mr. Gilbert was promoted to stationmaster and Mr. Pandey, his predecessor, was transferred to Ratlam.

The wedding was a strange Anglo-Goan affair. The guests foxtrotted and did the rumba but then some of the women started singing in Konkani, the Goan language. One song in particular produced a frenzy of giggles,

Dad is black
So is Mum
The daughter's white
Hey, how come?

Although being an Anglo, Mr. Gilbert was not quite as dark as Josephine was; everybody grinned and nudged each other. When their daughter Olinda was born, she turned out to be so fair people said she took after Mr. Gilbert's father who had come down from Bareilly for the wedding, and whose skin was like an ivory box lightly tinged with snuff. Mr. Gilbert was already in his fifties when he married Josephine, but she was happy because he was an Anglo, which was the next best thing to being British.

Mrs. Menezes, the wife of the Goan Catholic Bank Manager who was a Brahmin, declared that such an alliance would never be tolerated in her circle. Her own daughter had married Mr. Fonseca of the PWD who, like the Menezes, was a Brahmin. Five hundred years of Catholicism had not made the slightest dent in Goan caste consciousness.

iii

THE SILVER GHOST

The girls' Ayahs were often drawn into their wards' competition.

Ayah Fernandez: our Shirin Baba's eyes are bluest in Mhow.

Ayah Roderigues: Ish - sh, but she's so thin man, like a boomla only, Mrs. Fernandez. Our Grace Baba came first in her class.

When Jo Anna arrived, Grace suffered a slight demotion as the whims of the newly born took precedence over everything. Curiously she felt none of that resentment which had accompanied the arrival of Bobby five years before. When Mrs. Roderigues took Grace to Amanda's room, the baby was asleep, and then she opened her eyes and looked up with round violet eyes. Leaning over the infant, Grace felt a sudden wave of love that had only waited till that moment to well up from somewhere deep inside her. She also knew it would always be there.

The interior of Chinnery's was all aureoles of light from lampshades and echoing corridors. Everywhere were Chinese vases filled with flowers in soft arrangements and regency chairs grouped comfortably around sofas. Hands clasped over his stomach, the Major watched helplessly as carved wooden screens, gilt-framed paintings depicting the Battles of Seringapatam and Waterloo, prints of famous race horses, leather-bound books, luxurious couches and settees, mahogany wine tables and sideboards came in and were billeted in spots reserved for them by Amanda.

One day there appeared on the streets of Mhow a brand new Buick that belonged to Shirin's father, and made the

Chinnerys' buggy look like an elderly aunt. Amanda took yet another loan from Daruwala and acquired a Rolls Royce before the month was out. Though a used one, it was a Silver Ghost of which the Maharani of Indore had tired.

Attached to the front of the dashboard was a plate on which were engraved the words The Silver Ghost and on its prow stood its mascot, the Spirit of Ecstasy, a figurehead with her arms spread like wings below its fluttering draperies. With a smart wooden toolbox on the driverside running board, shining spokes of a spare wheel, a beige folding roof and silver-plated lamps the Ghost shimmered with bluish streams.

It brought with it a chauffeur, Mahamud, who was dressed in livery with polished brass buttons on his white tunic, and a gold aiguillette over his right shoulder, black trousers with orange welt, and a white hat with the insignia CH for Chinnery's Hotel embroidered on its front. Every evening, with baby Jo Anna in Amanda's arms, Bobby on Mrs. Roderigues' lap and Grace in the passenger seat, the Ghost purred softly through the streets of Mhow.

Amanda waved back to passers-by like the Queen acknowledging her subjects. On Mall Road where army officers lived in their spacious red brick bungalows, the greetings were a bit perfunctory, but tailors, bakers and grocers on Main Street, cobblers and their families on Plowden Road, cheered from the plinths of shops, and pedestrians on the road parted respectfully as the Ghost glided majestically through High Street.

iv

PALE HANDS I LOVED

The first to speak her mind was the Dog Lady.

"Do be careful, dear. It never helps to set yourself above your station."

People tended to forget that to Amanda's American mind, wealth and its trappings defined station.

Grace noticed that the boom was gone from Pater's laughter and his moustache, which always reminded her of a cowcatcher on a locomotive, drooped over his mouth making him look funny and sad. Eyes glued to his feet, he paced up and down the garden like an apparition trying to remember from which direction it had come, while water gurgled down perpetually from the mouths of dolphins at the base of Minerva's statue. All around him the freshly mowed grass was green from porch to gate, trying to become an undulating velvet lake.

On Sundays the Commandant and his wife arrived at Christ Church in their black Morris. Their driver wore a regimental uniform, but a tiny flag with red and gold stripes fluttered from its hood-ornament. It was one of the very few times in their marriage that the Major overruled Amanda's decision and prevented the Ghost from acquiring a flag of its own.

"But, Roger, dear look how incomplete the Ghost looks without a flag," Amanda pleaded. " It was custom-made for Her Highness Indore, remember?"

"I am sorry, Mandy, I cannot let you have a flag," said the Major. "Don't ask me why," he added, "it's a matter of ... er ... er, tradition and etiquette and that sort of thing."

By now almost all traces of an American accent had

disappeared from Amanda's speech, but the English code of conduct still confused her. She could only laugh at the pother when Pat's father, the Maharaja of Kesarpore, got his official letterhead printed with an arched instead of an open crown, an insult to the King Emperor according to the Resident Sahib.

For decades Mrs. Talbutt, the Colonel's Lady, had been the dowager queen of Mhow. Out of deference to her husband, who had laid down his life on the Northwest Frontier, the Major was polite to her at Church. She was in her seventies and lived in a bungalow on Michael Road surrounded by her husband's trophies, ordering her servants to polish them every day. But dwindling numbers at her weekly soirées drove her to ridiculous acts of desperation.

It was conceivable that in her youth she had met Lawrence Hope, the author of *Indian Love Songs,* during the poet's brief residence in Mhow with her husband Major Nicolson. But the Colonel's Lady claimed that she had been Hope's confidant, and knew the true identity of the Kashmere Prince for whom the poet was believed to have written,

"Pale Hands I loved Beside the Shalimar."

Courting her displeasure the Sandersons began to attend New Year's Eve Balls at Chinnery's when all the griffins were there in force. The Sandersons were known as the Goose Family, because their five buxom daughters always waddled after their mother in a descending order of age and height. Mrs. Sanderson herself was built like a sideboard but she scrimped, sewed, and baked cakes for church sales to provide them with new dresses for the Ball. The Sanderson girls were stiff competition to the fishing fleeters. They had superior knowledge of local picnic spots, but more importantly, they had plump bodies and sweet, dimpled, angelic faces which held promise of sturdy and loyal companionship for upstation types looking for security in marriage. They did everything well, they swam, rode, and played tennis with superb skill. Their third daughter, Marjorie, who was fond of

Jo Anna, helped design a doll's house for her and taught the little girl how to furnish it and make dresses for the tiny figures. The Sanderson girls epitomised order, living life according to a plan. They would have been successful in Hong Kong, Sydney, Kampala or Bath. They attended church regularly, loved long walks, went duck shooting and, when the time came, they married.

Despite the fulmination of the Colonel's Lady, the resident British continued to flock to Chinnery's Hotel on Sunday evenings to hear Principal Hulme hold forth and recite poems by Walter de le Mare. The Countess read their palms and Amanda played the piano, entertaining the guests with spicy rhythms of Broadway hits like "Goodbye, Molly Brown" or "Turn off your Light, Mr. Moon-Man."

THE LOCO SHED

Mhow is no longer the miniature town of Grace's memory, around which ran a toy train. The soot-covered arches of the water tower and blackened windows of the foreman's office have a terrifying intimacy. She can still picture the dingy interior, the heavy bow-legged desk covered with green oilcloth, two telephones, one of which was red. The tepid milk-thickened tea, served by Mr. McGregor's peon had almost made her vomit.

After the foreman had excused himself before disappearing in the arabesques of steam from locomotive pipes, she'd read the slogans on the wall. One said *Safety has no holiday.*

Shiva, the mali's ten-year-old son gestures her to follow him through the pair of stone posts into the New Cemetery. Yasmin has warned her that most old gravestones are badly in need of repair.

Although Mhow still appears to be a secretive, tight-mouthed place not given to telling stories, Grace has warned Yasmin that all precautions must be taken not to stray from the edited version of Jo Anna's death. Yasmin idolised Jo. It was unnatural, Shirin used to say, for one girl to love another with such passion. It went beyond friendship. She had seen such compacts at Auckland House, girls bestowing on other girls their total trust. All sorts of noises were heard at night from the dorms, hands caressing skins soft as silk.

Who knows what Yasmin would do if she knew Camilla was Jo Anna's child? She has noticed how Bhola's stone-cold divining eyes snowblink at the sound of Camilla's voice. Grace is determined to spare the poor girl further pain.

Shiva sticks his head in the door of the chowkidar's hut,

but no one is around. A naked potbellied boy of five or six is chasing a clucking hen in the muddy front yard. Shiva climbs the wrought iron gate behind the house, knocks the rusty stopper up with a brick, and beckons her to follow. Like the living, the dead of Mhow also have little elbowroom judging by the congestion in the new cemetery which seems to have moved closer to the railway station. Only the very recent graves lie further apart in the "annex." Do cemeteries have annexes?

Each banyan is a forest unto itself, with thick buntlines of roots cascading into the ground. Improvising a broom with a broken branch, Shiva begins to brush the soggy leaves off the stones. Jo's grave is nowhere in sight. Suddenly, Grace panics, stumbles through fallen twigs, wild creepers tug at her skirt like grubby street urchins, a dappled cobra skin lies in her path like a translucent stocking. She is breathless with all that walking. Her legs buckle and, despite the faint fetid smell rising from the damp soil, she removes her shoes and lowers herself on the thick dark cushion of leaves between forking roots. A beetle with a red velvety back clambers onto a half-eaten leaf. A weaving column of ants sets into relief the inscription on the nearest pair of headstones, highlighting the name Dinkins. The boxwallahs were generally reunited in death; the solitary grave almost always belonged to some forgotten regimental.

A pungent smell of leaves rotting around a crumbly termite hill on her right tickles her nostrils but she does not move away. Has the grave simply disappeared? In her nightmares, Jo's voice always sounded like a piece of cloth ripping from a bale. "Grace," it said, "Grace, let me hold my baby, let me kiss my little girl just once, just once, please Grace."

For the first time in the past six months, her giddiness has returned. She must find the grave before something happens to her. Like an old elephant she has come back to die. Poor Camilla would have to bear the brunt. Yasmin would certainly help her to clear the mess. But she seems to have one foot in the grave herself, Tower of Silence rather, in Yasmin's case. Gratefully digging her toes in the mulch, Grace wonders if they still do that.

Soon her eyelids droop, and she is back in time in the foreman's old office.

The flap door swings open and Carl's father, Mr. Busby, the boiler mechanic, comes in mopping his sweaty face with a grimy handkerchief.

"Please, Grace Baba, please go home. No harm will come to Jo Baba. My Carl, he is a good chap. A bit wild but inside a good boy."

Grace glares at him, then in a voice trembling with rage says,

"I am sure Mr. McGregor will see to it that she is safely returned to us. I am leaving for Bombay tonight to join my WAC(I) unit. There's a war on. No time to waste."

"McGregor Sahib has just telephoned Kalakund," Busby grovels. "They are on 31 down. She'll be here very soon. I'll personally escort Jo Baba home," he says, his lilting Anglo voice cracking with jitters.

Grace fears the worst. What if Jo did something stupid? She is alone there with Carl and his cronies. Since Bobby's death, Jo has become utterly reckless. Kalakund without the picnic crowd is so deserted. It's all Maude Aspel's fault; that woman ought to be shot. One would have thought that after her husband's suicide she would mend her ways. Grace has no choice but to wait for Jo to come back.

She is in a tunnel and hears the hiss of the locomotive, its pistons working hard. Green valleys jump out of the dark as the steam engine clanks out of the tunnel and chugs along, past the flanks of hills, careening over plunging valleys. Smoke-puffing chimneys of aborigine huts cluster around stunted, gnarled trees. And there is Jo clinging to Carl, buttons of her frock undone. The leering sooty fireman grunts, shovelling coal into the burning maw of the furnace. Grace sees the blanched face of Mater, Pater's drooping mouth.

Suddenly the ground shakes and an engine comes bearing down upon her. Her scream dies in the throat. She straightens up, bright round medallions of light bounce off her skirt.

How they switch tracks, those nomadic memories? Not the precise remembrance of an accident on playground or the first betrayal in life, but memories that start in those interminable shunting yards where tracks proliferate, where in the watches of the night, the ghost of an engine chugs dementedly, back and forth, back and forth, shrouded in its own smoke.

The boy is munching wild berries. To reach them he has had to climb the mound that has been someone's resting-place. Grace feels too weak to protest. Besides, what's the use? They probably do that all the time. Has Jo's grave been crushed under the feet of berry-picking lads? She rises determinedly. A faint inner beam directs her to the spot where the grave is buried under a pile of leaves. She hails the boy and together they brush aside a heap of brambles and weeds. There it is at last, split in half. The inscription has eroded but she can still make out the dates. *Born Indore 1926 - Died Mhow 1945.*

They go so quietly, the very young, when their time is up! We only remember the fear in their eyes when they first realise it's all over. We forget their courage at the end. How splendidly had Jo Anna lured the beast away from her child and forfeited her own life.

The footstone has caved in and slithered down the long narrow ditch beyond the fence that marks the boundary between the graveyard and the Loco Shed. Forty-three years of moisture has caused the base to crumble.

Dim spectres writhe in the sun. What Grace remembers most is the sudden ageing of Pater after Jo Anna was laid to rest. When Bobby's Spitfire was shot down over the Channel, the whole of Mhow had mourned with the Chinnerys. Even the Colonel's Lady had attended the memorial service at

Christ Church, and shops on High and Main Streets had downed their shutters for one day. Messages of condolence had poured in from all over India. Grace, in the second year of her marriage was devastated, but slowly her robust appetite had muted her grief, and within a year Jack had weaned her back to life.

The week after Jo Anna's funeral Maude Aspel had accosted Grace at the Post Office and with dilated eyes and palpitating voice invited her to the Dayan's place for a seance.

"We have had a visitation from poor Jo Anna already. She wants me to have her baby. Come and see for yourself. The dead do not always stay put where they are buried you know."

There had been a strong smell of laudanum on Maude's breath. Everyone knew how batty she had grown after Doctor Aspel's untimely death but Grace was quite startled by that wild look in her eyes. She'd rushed to the Dog Lady for advice and that arch enemy of any sort of mumbo jumbo had prodded DSP Robinson to act with dispatch. Within three days Maude Aspel was bundled off to Bombay and put on a boat to England. The DSP had threatened to charge her with the abduction of Jo Anna and her baby. The Dog Lady who had always been a great source of comfort in times of crisis, had reacted with characteristic testiness to Grace's account of the whispering voice, dismissing it as 'mummery flummery' not at all worthy of someone brought up in sound Low Church tradition.

But the horror of Jo Anna's end had scorched the Chinnerys, branding them murderers, shutting them off from all but their closest allies. Although Dr.Vansittart had carefully orchestrated the story that Jo had died of typhoid at the Dayan's bungalow, Mhow had gone into a deep hush, leaving the Chinnerys to fend for themselves against the buzz and tattle of bazaar gossip, forcing them into the crypt of their own guilt. Mater who had begun to come to terms with

Bobby's death, supervising Burra Khana and going to Church on Sundays, had gone still as a painting, and Pater had simply wilted away, wrinkled skin lolling under his chin, his suit hanging over his frame like the grey tarpaulin on Jo Anna's bicycle.

BEDSORE CASSANDRA

"Why this sudden interest in Jo Anna's grave after so many years? "

Lately Yasmin has taken to talking to her father as she used to when he was alive. It helps her unburden a lot of disturbing thoughts. She pretends that he is still within earshot, pottering about the villa.

"My nerves are in shreds but I am glad she has brought Camilla with her. Perhaps my mind's been playing tricks, but truly, Daddy, looking at her even you would say Jo Anna has come back to visit after a long absence. There I've said it. Camilla is the spitting image of Jo. Now you tell me how that comes about?"

In the hall the grandfather clock emits a frenzied sigh, then strikes two. Yasmin stares expectantly at the portrait of Sir Mancherjee.

His eyes probe hers. Before she was struck down by polio Yasmin was quite a handful, as Sir Mancherjee recalls. Now playing the dispassionate and wry observer of life she can still raise the devil.

"There's one other thing," Yasmin says, taking advantage of the lull in barking outside on Simrole Road. "Tehmi seems quite taken with Camilla. There's that look in her eyes again, the sort that says she is hatching something. She has long wanted Ross to settle down with one of the war widows. Remember how brazenly she schemed to get him hooked with Shirin's anthropologist friend from the States last year? I shouldn't be surprised if she tries to set him up with Camilla. Just imagine what that would do to Grace, Daddy."

As far as the Chinnerys were concerned the entire Anglo community collectively shared responsibility for Jo Anna's gruesome end. Grace in particular had been relentless in her denunciation of Anglos and cut off all contact with their childhood friends like Irene Popjoy and Sylvia Buckley.

"You were the only one besides the Chinnerys who knew what really happened at the Dayan's. What was Jo Anna doing out there in the first place with Grace's baby? Did she die of typhoid, or was it something even more hideous? Why did Dr. Vansittart shoot the Dayan's bitch dead? I had only a passing glimpse when they brought Jo in. Couldn't bear to look at her, all blue and trussed up like a fowl. When it came to defending the honour of the British even mortal enemies closed rank. The entire resident British community sealed their lips and so did you Daddy."

Sir Mancherjee is standing on top of a ladder as though looking for something to read.

"Tehmi can be heavy-handed at times especially when she tries to get Ross married. Don't you think, Daddy, it's time to let by-gones be by-gone? I don't want Ross to stop visiting us. He has been in town for nearly three weeks and hasn't come to see me yet. You know I love him like a son. There's Noshir, of course, but let me tell you, he is only waiting for me to croak."

Pince-nez clipped to the tip of his aquiline nose, Sir Mancherjee now looks up from the book in his hand. That was his standard posture at night when he was alive. Now he sits hunched in the rocker in his Parsi "kasti," head covered in white handkerchief, eyes closed, lips moving in prayer. Yasmin yearns to go and kneel by his side.

A scrabble at the front door . . . .

All those years ago it was she who had raised the alarm. But no one had listened.

Really speaking, Maude Aspel was to blame for everything. She had filled Jo Anna's young mind with that lunatic notion about her being a reincarnation of Clarissa Lilley. She was a dangerous woman Maude Aspel was. Ostracised after Dr. Aspel's suicide, she had turned to the Dayan for companionship. The sorceress lived alone outside town, beyond the Dairy Farm. Some said she was an Iranian gypsy who had been left a bungalow by the Nabob of Bhastipore. She had been his favourite concubine. The Dayan barely spoke any English, but people went to her in secret to get amulets made for their children. Some Parsi, Goan and Anglo families were also among her furtive visitors.

Yasmin had felt like an insufficiently hatched life unable to crack open its shell. Over her objections Shirin had made a disastrous marriage with their cousin, Kayzad Ardeshir, when it was obvious that he would never stop philandering. He had tried to fondle Yasmin one afternoon when everyone was away. She had suffered the indignity because no one would have believed that the handsome Kayzad, who could have any girl he wanted, would molest a human cockroach like herself. Shirin had dismissed it as fantasy of her sexually starved sister. Within two months of her marriage, she had found out how unfairly she had treated Yasmin.

"Bedsore Cassandra," Noshir once called her in a fit of pique when Yasmin refused to sign away her share of their property for one of his speculative ventures.

No one ever looked beyond her grotesque sibyl's body, but for days her nipples had ached, and the lolling skin on her thighs hummed at the recollection of that attempted seduction by Kayzad. Then one day while Bhola was tucking in the blanket during a particularly chilly day, her hand had gripped his fingers and dug them between her legs. The old retainer had retracted his hand as though bitten by a snake. Even his tribal mind with its instinctive knowledge of animal imperatives had received a severe jolt. But then his dimming sight had caught the helpless pleading in her eyes.

When Yasmin was a baby Bhola had changed her nappies. With tears streaming into his beard, the old man had sat down and, like a father cleansing a child's wound before dressing it, he had tried to assuage her pain. She had outgrown the need for it well before that phase of his life had

toppled into the abyss, to rest among other forgotten debris.
When she was young and footloose she had met Pestan in
Bombay. Still in high school, he was already playing for the
Parsi Gymkhana and opened their innings at the Pentagular
Cricket Tournament. Had she not been struck down by polio,
she would have been Mrs. Pestan Godrej instead of being
cased up like a relic in this villa.

In Jo Anna's case not fate but British snootiness had
intervened. Yasmin knew that despite her unconventional
ways, Mrs. Chinnery would never tolerate an Anglo for a
son-in-law. A prince from one of India's major royal houses
might have passed muster, but for the British the Anglos were
an embarrassment. You never said it in so many words but
there was a running assumption that even Anglos with very
fair complexions were somehow tainted, like flesh-coloured
fruit gone bad.

"Well, Daddy," Yasmin says to Sir Mancherjee, "I know
family likeness is an elusive affair and one may resemble an
aunt more than one's mother, but if you saw Camilla now,
you'd think Jo had risen from the grave."

Yasmin's father is standing outside on a garden stool,
framed by his favourite rose arch. He has put his soul into it.
Beard peppered with grey, bare arms sticking out of his white
Parsi vest, face misty in the fanning spray from the upturned
sprinkler, he stares blindly at her like a statue on a Roman
fountain.

THE NYMPHET

The last few days in Mhow, Camilla has had this sensation of being watched, as if a face were looking at her through water streaming down a windowpane; quite different from the feeling of *déjà vu* she had in the Berber town of Lambaesis, founded by homesick legionaries where ghosts of Rome are piled up in stones from local quarries. No, this is different. Jo Anna's breath still lingers in the air. A threshold awaits her, and there's tenderness in the collective eye.

Is it her imagination, given to encapsulating other people's fantasy working its magic, or has Jo Anna been really waiting for her all these years?

Now back in her room at the Dak Bungalow, she has finished dressing for dinner, but the General's daughters are fussing over their jeans and shirts. She can hear them talk in the adjoining room. Both have a tremendous crush on Ross and seem to have persuaded their father to arrange this trip just to be near him.

"It's a toss up," Tejinder says to her sister, "how many scars on Ross's body are from field action and how many from shikar."

"Hey, how do you know that Taji?" Jasbir asks, her voice brimming with mischief.

"What do you mean?"

" I mean, how . . .do . . .you . . . know he has scars on his body?"

There is an awkward pause. Camilla stops at the door and listens.

"Well one can surely make an educated guess, judging from all the campaigns he has been in."

"What rotten luck he's an Anglo,' Jasbir says, "I would have simply gone on a hunger strike till he agreed to marry me."

Anglo! That word again!

Grace always makes it sound like some toxic pollutant. Once when coming out of Mrs. Strickland's haberdashery across the road from the tube station, she had said,

"I am pretty sure, that woman's an Anglo. That chi chi tone is unmistakable."

For some reason her mother had seemed very keen on sending her to Mandu. What would she do if she knew that Colonel Ross Harrison was to dine with the General's party that night?

"He may be a colonel but you cannot be too careful with these Anglos," she'd said the night of their very first meeting with Ross. "It's the low-caste blood on the Indian side of their family that makes them so untrustworthy."

Camilla cannot help smiling. What is the source of her mother's skewed sociology, her irrational spitefulness towards the hapless Anglos? When she was younger Camilla used to think the term referred to British officers with a long record of service in India. But thanks to her mother it has mysteriously come to represent a fallen state. And yet with his big-game-hunter tan which sets off the cerulean blue of his eyes, few men Camilla knows in London have such a distinct air of the bulldog breed that Grace finds so appealing in her heroes like Henry Lawrence, the defender of Lucknow during the Sepoy Mutiny. Why should a few drops of Indian blood in Ross set her mother quavering like a vengeful fury?

Surely, some festering soreness has peaked.

At a time when their neighbours were getting squeamish about the influx of immigrants in Clapham Common, Mum never said anything remotely distasteful about them. On the contrary she always fawned on the few Indians who came to the fish and chip shop.

Camilla had hoped that this trip to Mhow would prove

therapeutic for Grace, that amidst these familiar landmarks she would hear once again the unspoiled laughter of her childhood and youth. Instead a crumpled old road map points to the site of her self-inflicted martyrdom. Far from providing relief, Mhow seems to have stoked a long simmering animus towards the Anglos into a raging fire.

Camilla feels let down. She had risked job security in coming to India at a critical time for her firm, to give her mother a new lease on life. But instead of a parent-child bonding adventure, their trip seems to be headed for a fiasco. She is annoyed with herself for not realising that like a zealot her mother would refuse to be cut down from the stake. Whingeing was a kind of tonic for her.

Camilla wonders why she shouldn't put what's left of her vacation to better use, have some fun, get to know the land, travel a bit, go to Agra and Jaipore, do the touristy thing, perhaps even try writing a bestseller as Alexis had suggested half-mockingly. A deft nudge in the right direction to her considerable copy-writing skill and 'voila' a bestseller.

Her mother would be driven out of her mind if she knew how much her daughter looks forward to meeting the colonel that evening. The last two years of her marriage had been arid, Eddie coming home too late and too tired to fulfil what her solicitor friend Clementine called conjugal obligations.

A fling with a decorated war hero may be just what she needs to break the tedium of life. No permanent commitment, no long-term relationship. At the very least it'd be something to tout when Clementine, Joyce and she got together for their weekly 'Tea-at-the-Ritz' girl talk.

There's no denying that this chap Ross has by his sensuous presence tapped some hitherto unknown reserves of passion in her. That he is a forbidden 'Anglo' of her mother's worst nightmares makes him even more alluring.

Her ex-husbands Jeremy and Eddie were barely tolerated by Grace because one was a hippie, and the other a money-grubbing commoner.

"Maybe it's destiny," she thinks. "Maybe I am predisposed to the type of man Mum has a fatal aversion to."

Their visit to Chinnery's has to wait because the doctor in charge of the Hospital is away, and his wife is not ready to receive them. According to Yasmin, the graveyard is overgrown with weeds and needs clearing. But in Grace's tone urging Camilla to go to Mandu, there were hints of something more to be told. Camilla doesn't mind waiting; the prospect of suddenly confronting Jo Anna's grave makes her spine tingle with unknown dread.

As evening approaches, her mind is in a whirl. All day she has tried to cope with the alternate bursts of light and colour in the medieval city of Mandu, now gone utterly still under pink brushstrokes of hurrying clouds. At sunrise the minarets were doused in crimson, and by the time they reached the ramparts later that morning, the burnished domes had turned from apricot to pink. Now the moss-covered surface of a distant dome turns green in the fading light of the sun.

Standing in the shadows of arches in Rome, Camilla had felt the same breath of the past wash over her. She could never resist the spell of lost cities, the candle ends of centuries. Here in Mandu you may be walking down a dusty barren street, haunted by mangy pie dogs, and suddenly a minaret pokes its jewelled finger up like an aficionado, shushing you to listen. Those ruined walls and courtyards are filled with echoes that are not drowned by the loudspeakers blaring in the marketplace. The chaffering bazaar with a banyan-shielded shrine at its centre is not unlike the agora with its temples and bustling shops.

After taking possession of Greek citadels like Brindisi and Rimini, the Romans had transformed the agora into a forum. British Mhow with its garrison fort at one end and a clocktower in the centre of town, had obviously been a Canute-like gesture to stop the tide of native hurly-burly and regulate its ebb and flow by the carillons of Big Ben.

What does she know about India? Students of Classics stop

at Greece. Some go to Egypt but rarely venture beyond the Middle East. India only attracts hippies looking for spiritual kicks. She has never been inside an Indian home in London, only caught a glimpse of it in films like *My Beautiful Launderette.* Unless she strikes out on her own, Yasmin and her friends would never let her see what lies beyond the sanitised world of the Cantonment.

Above all there's Ross, eyes glued to the floor like someone looking into a pond, waiting for a splintered reflection to coalesce. Early in the week when Camilla was having a drink in the lounge with Tehmi, Ross had come to apologise for his rude exit from the Club the day of his arrival in Mhow.

There hasn't been anyone like him in her experience of men before, unless you counted the distant sound of boots tramping across Chelsea Barracks she sometimes heard on her way to Sloane Square.

That evening at Mandu, Ross had obviously not expected to find Camilla and Tehmi playing badminton in the forecourt of the Dak Bungalow with the General's daughters. Tehmi had tried to make him laugh but failed to limber his parade-ground stiffness. He was camping in nearby hills to select a possible site for staging war games or something like that, and the General had sent a messenger inviting him to dinner. After a belated hippie of a husband and his tie-tugging, soft-bellied successor, this gunmetal being in khaki was filling her mind with the most egregious fantasies.

At dinner Ross is quiet. Young Jasbir tries to tease him.

"Are the Khasi girls as pretty as some say? I bet Ross has a regular harem tucked away in the hills of Assam."

Both Tejinder and their mother look uncomfortable.

"That's enough," the General snaps.

"No, no, it doesn't matter really," Ross says. "Yes, they are very pretty, with high cheekbones and figures that your models in Bombay and Delhi can only dream of."

Despite his gallant effort, a chill descends on the group and dinner ends in strained silence.

Jasbir mimics the guide's broken English,
"And Roopmati is telling Sultan, my bones with you are resting here."

Everyone laughs, but the evening has gone sour.

Camilla remembers how the group of tourists from South India had listened to the guide with dilated eyes. The women wrapped in filigreed mists of billowy silken saris had looked like giant exotic butterflies.

They move out to the verandah where coffee is being served. Tehmi whispers to Camilla that separatist rebels in Assam had killed Ross's young wife.

The General is seated in a wicker chair while Ross leans against the post, his face blurred by the flickering light of the lantern. Behind them in the darkness are silhouetted two peaks where a fingernail moon is deepening into a smiling crescent. Ross's mind seems far away. His alienation from his surroundings has nothing to do with that sculpted look or blue eyes. Tehmi herself could easily pass for an Italian with her broad Umbrian face, long lashes, and slightly hooked nose. It's the way the others relate to the place that is different. The girls drool over the legendary lovers, the Muslim Sultan of Mandu who had passionately loved his Hindu wife, the beautiful Queen Roopmati, and built a Summer Palace for her, complete with a luxury bath and concealed drainage.

Ross listens to them with polite interest. He is that oddity, a foreigner in his own land. The word Anglo, uttered with that mixture of acceptance and rejection, "one of us, but not quite," sets him apart even from Tehmi and Noshir who are Parsis. And he seems to know how much he might claim.

"Do these hills remind you of home?" Camilla asks him as they walk down to his jeep.

"You mean Assam. No, not really. This is the rearguard of the Vindhyas. For me home is Cal. Calcutta that is. Are you planning a visit? That's where it all began you know, the Empire."

"Indeed, I'd love to, but I am afraid we may have just enough time to do the Taj and Jaipore."

"Pity, it's certainly worth a visit."

"But what about the poverty; Mother Teresa and so on?"

"All that's true, but the place has something, I don't know why I feel at home there as nowhere else. Perhaps it's like me, like us, I mean." There's a thin edge to his voice. "It has the same mongrel pedigree as we Anglos."

"You mean the architecture . . ."

Tejinder steps between them and cuts off his reply

"Tell me Ross, how is Major Dhaliwal? I saw him in Delhi last month before he left for Assam."

"He is well, as far as I can tell."

He turns abruptly to salute the General and climbs into his jeep.

In an upward plummet the crescent moon scales the peaks and is soon adrift like a skiff.

Camilla's insides churn and she can barely sleep that night. Joyce would be shocked but Camilla has no doubt that if Ross were to walk into her room that moment she would grab him by the hand and pull him into bed.

Next morning they stop at a ruined temple. The invading Mughal army, which had attacked Mandu because the Sultan refused to surrender, had desecrated the place where Rani Roopmati used to worship. But even after her marble image had been hacked to pieces, the Goddess continued to cure sick people and grant everyone their wish. The place now is nothing but a graveyard of broken statuary. Their incompleteness is harrowing.

Somewhere in Thucydides, there is an account of how the Athenians reconstructed their ruined city, stone by stone after the Persians had sacked it. They took broken pieces and fragments of statues and' built them into a new wall. This, too, must have been a scene of bloody carnage, rape, pillage, plunder, dismemberment, and all people remembered was the love story of the Rani and her Sultan.

In the midst of that rubble there is one figure, a dancer perhaps, judging by her pose, which has miraculously escaped mutilation. As though the spirit of the Goddess had taken refuge in her, she erupts from a column, supporting her undulating form on one comely leg, and almost seems to float above her base, body arched like a taut bow, face tilted in a saucy smile, arrested in perpetual maidenhood. Her story, too, seems to have no closure.

Camilla is deeply moved by that one nymphet who has escaped the despoiler's glinting steel. These stones lack the majesty of Rome and the dense colouring and sumptuousness of Tuscan art, but there is a delicacy of feeling here, of something branching sensuously like a dance that might enthral a passing Lar.

LITTLE RED RIDING HOOD

Grace loved the flowing white kimono she wore as Peep-Bo in *The Mikado.* Shirin playing the lead smiled bashfully behind the fan, and fluttered her eyes on
"One little maid is a bride Yum-Yum."
With Sylvia as Pitti-Sing, they were a great hit, but the more Grace was pushed into competition with Shirin, the further she withdrew into herself. "Why can't you be more like Shirin?" was Mater's constant refrain, causing her to run away to the paddock with a young girl's tempestuous agony.

Under Mother Colombier's tutelage Grace was already outplaying Amanda. "Schumann," Mother Colombier said, "makes it easier for a beginner to tackle pieces like First Sorrow." Played *legato* it allowed Grace to use the pedal at her level of skill and the wistful chords from *Album for the Young* rose on Sunday afternoons, to the swashing of light and shadow on the wainscotted walls of Chinnery's.

It was the time of day between post-lunch siesta and tea at four, when the hotel noises subsided, guests napped in their rooms at the back of the house, the kitchen fell silent save for an occasional tinkle of cutlery, the chokraboys dozed in their usual corners on the verandah, the reception room was so quiet that you could hear the faint scratching of Mr Munshi's pen as he did the accounts, the dog Napoleon was out chasing birds, and the Chinnerys were alone for the first time since that morning as a family and not as boats heaving by the side of a mighty ship. Mater sat with Baby Jo Anna in her lap and Bobby, with his arms around her neck, stood behind the sofa. Pater, in his rocker, tapped his knee with the shank of his pipe and Ayah squatted on the rug, her old eyes brimming with pride.

"Our Grace Baba is going to be a big big concert pianist in London onlee," she would say.

Shirin's Ayah, Mrs. Fonseca, tried to match her ward's skill with Grace's, but really there was no contest. Shirin's beauty made people stop and stare, and it caused an upsurge of jealousy in Grace, but as the girls moved into their teens, they became inseparable. At twelve, Shirin already had an air of self-possession that a growing awareness of her power over men gives an exceptionally beautiful girl. In her wine-coloured dress setting off the smooth pallor of her exquisite face with delicately shaped upturned nose, pouting red lips and clear blue eyes, she always entered the room and stood in the doorway assessing the impact her entrance made. While Grace continued to grow taller and, consequently, flatter in her chest, Shirin who had been bony began to fill out. Boys were confused and enslaved by her flirtatious manner and imperious tone of voice. To Grace's despair, even Bobby, who was barely ten, seemed to come under her spell and sought her company under one pretext or another. There was no trace of that unconscious cruelty she showed towards other boys when Shirin spoke to Bobby. At first, Grace resented his attachment to Shirin and even complained to her mother about it, but Amanda cut her short,

"What a fuss-budget you are, young lady. Don't you realise the Debu girls have no brother?"

During picnics to Kalakund, when boys scrambled for a place next to Shirin on the train, she would always push them aside and make Bobby sit with her. At tennis, it was Bobby on whom her choice of partner fell. And while it was Grace who played the piano when Bobby presented his favourite, *Alone in the Pirate's Lair* on the tiny stage of his toy theatre, it was Shirin who moved the cardboard cutouts of the crew of the good ship *Titania* and gave Bobby the feed lines as midshipman, blew the boatswain's whistle and played first mate, while he doubled as Captain and narrator.

Having spent hours in the company of the rough and

tumble inmates of "Admiral Benbow," Bobby's language was peppered with nautical terms. And, as it happened, *Alone in the Pirate's Lair* was studded with tar lingo.

Captain: Wind Mr. Rushton?

Midshipman: Aye, aye sir. Northwest by north sir.

Captain: Good! Tell Mr. Dale to heave anchor at once; I'll be on deck in a few minutes.'

Narrator: Soon the boatswain's whistle rung shrilly along the quiet deck, the crew came tumbling up the hatchway and forty sturdy tars tramp, tramp, tramped around.

Grace's fingers made the piano rumble like a tall wave crashing against the bulwark. DSP Robinson and the Countess applauded Shirin's articulation, but Hulme insisted that it was Grace's keyboard simulation of the storm that lent the presentation a sense of drama. Such kind gestures softened the competitiveness she felt towards Shirin.

Bobby's passion for the toy theatre was so infectious that Shirin, who was sometimes bored by the juvenile quality of the dialogue, continued to help him backstage. Grace was happy to assist because it gave her an opportunity to improvise. She sat closer to the keyboard than she did while playing proper music and, using both pedals she tried to produce sounds that gave atmospheric value through a sudden shift from a diminishing tempo to purling. Eyes widening with exertion, her hands fluttered over the keys like agitated doves.

Hulme also helped Bobby's friend, Carl, to cut figures of Shylock, Bassanio and Portia from *The Merchant of Venice*. Carl was good at drawing, and had already made a sketch of the Rialto Bridge from an old illustration of a performance at Drury Lane. However before he could paint it to suggest the bustle of life on the Grand Canal, it was decided to send Bobby to England, and the entire project fell through.

But it was such fun while it lasted! You worked the wings by manipulating wires attached to both sides, and a roller curtain descended from the top. Cut-out characters suspended on strings were lowered from the back of the theatre, and Carl, who was quite handy with tools even at the age of ten, wielded his torch like a travelling spotlight. Tossing back black curls falling over slightly protruding green eyes and long eyelashes, pale face glowing in torchlight, he crouched in the makeshift prompter's box. Despite the Dog Lady's warnings, he often relapsed into his brand of Anglo patois, strongly laced with expressions like "bloody" and "damn," if he failed to produce the desired effect. When asked by Amanda to stay for cocoa and biscuits after the performance, he would say,

"Thank you, Missis, but I'll be 'buggered' if I'm not home when my Dad returns from the Railway Institute."

His father, Mr. Busby, the boiler mechanic at the Loco Shed, whose wife had run away with his assistant, was notorious for his foul temper.

When the lights were turned off, and Bobby rattled the metal sheet to suggest the crackle of lightning, and Grace began to worry the base keys on the piano, Carl's beam would pick up the cutout figure of Little Red Riding Hood, standing by a stream with her basket, in front of the painted cottage of Grandma, with menacing silhouettes of mountains in the background. As Shirin's Wolf smacked his chops in anticipation of a good meal, the tiny toy stage took on a mystery that brought the guests nodding over their brandy to the library, lured the d'Quodroses from the kitchen, and Khansahib's wife and children from the main gate. Ayah Roderigues squatted on the carpet, right in front of the stage, with Jo Anna on her lap. When the Wolf pretending to be Grandma sprang from the bed, Jo Anna buried her face in Ayah's ample bosom. But at the end, when the lights were turned on, she always wanted to see it again. Adult world merging into childhood, the library became a haunt of dreams for all those gathered at Chinnery's.

III

i

THE LANCASHIRE WITCHES

Shirin's dresses came from Bombay where the modistes were skilful enough to adapt patterns from London and Paris. Grace's frocks were made by Mr. Suvarez, the Goan tailor on Main Street, who was justly celebrated for his workmanship in army uniforms. But even his most daring creations could never match the elegance of Shirin's blouses with semi-raglan sleeves and square necklines, skirts with cartridge pleats and charming low belts. Mr. Suvarez came to Chinnery's, with his eyeglass and a pencil stuck behind his ear, to take down measurements. He wore an enormous sola, too big for his head.

On Saturday afternoons Mhow cheered regimental units marching down Post Office Road to bivouacs. A mule carrying a huge leather waterbag followed each unit. On Field Days, a couple of companies of infantry filed past St. Mary's, accompanied by field batteries, sweat running down their pommy faces. When the girls spotted their favourite batsmen or polo players among the officers of the 10th Royal Hussars, 102nd Grenadiers or the East Surrey Regiment, they cheered them with "Hip, Hip Hooray."

Among Indian Regiments like the 123rd Outram Rifles or the Royal Mountain Artillery, there were some fine fast bowlers, but the skill of Bhopal Lancers and men of Skinner's Horse at Inter-Regimental tent-pegging left you gaping. They tipped their caps to cheering onlookers and marched smartly looking straight ahead.

But the children's particular favourite was the Torchlight Tattoo, held in the evening at about half past nine. Each soldier held a lighted torch and the whole parade ground was like a sea of light as the men marched up and down to *The Lancashire Witches,* or *God Bless the Prince of Wales.* Sometimes the Tattoo ended in a magnificent representation of *Napoleon's Retreat from Moscow in 1814.*

The only place forbidden to the children was that mysterious Red Light District, about three quarters of a mile to the south of town. No one would tell them what went on there, but every time it was mentioned, Shirin hid her face behind her hankie and giggled, rolling her blue eyes.

"That's where Tommies go to get clapped," she said.

It remained a dark place till the end, like the Bhut Bungalow. The latter was typical of Masonic Lodges scattered across the country in every major cantonment township. It was in the best tradition of Pax Britannica and exuded an aura of imperial brotherhood. The likes of DSP Robinson, the Collector Sahib, senior army officers as well as Crown Prince Pratapsingh, and the girls' own fathers congregated there every Tuesday evening. The Red Light District on the other hand seemed a lurid blot on the benign face of Mhow. Grace imagined a dark forsaken place under a red pall of signal lights, glimpsed from midnight trains where lurked hunched shadowy figures, white eyes staring out of soot-covered faces.

ii

THE MAVERICK

The white chrysanthemums in Yasmin's garden have the texture of infant flesh and along with the reflexed pinkish petals of the cyclamen, they make the crisp bougainvillea look like paperwork mongrels, only good enough to screen from public view the floral élite in their nappy beds. Bougainvillea bushes proliferate outside dank-looking government buildings, and serve to obscure the creeping squalor with their tarty purple. In a hot country like India, even shadows of trees have a velvety texture, and propose a happy ending to a troubled journey.

Tehmi gets up and waves Ross over to the lawn behind the arbour. The Debu women are having tea in the garden with three young nuns from St.Mary's who want Yasmin to identify for them African nations from the new atlas. The older sisters at the Convent still think of Zaire as Belgian Congo, and Zimbabwe as Rhodesia. Their order has run schools and hospitals for over a century in those remote regions of the world.

Even before Ross bends down to kiss Yasmin's cheek, her manner becomes flirtatious. She lovingly strokes his hair and, with a sudden spasm of body, her fingers close around his neck. Two of the nuns sit silently, staring at the tea things, but the bright fluttery eyes of the youngest cruise over Ross's deep chest, strong hands and neck. Tehmi smiles. When receiving visitors, Aunt Yasmin dresses mostly in black to enhance her pallor.

"Well, what took you so long?" Yasmin says, as soon as Ross sits down. Sitaram, who is perched on the arm of her chair, repeats the question, fixing Ross with one orbicular eye.

"I have been out in the field," Ross says to the parrot.

"Stuff and nonsense," Yasmin says. The parrot manages that, but stumbles when Yasmin's mock petulance explodes in rapid fire French. *"Plus ca change, plus c'est la meme chose. I am very cross with Tehmi for keeping you to herself."*

In disgust, Sitaram picks up a cashew nut from the plate and withdraws into the world of parrots.

"Don't sulk, Auntie," Tehmi says. "Ross has been busy touring the countryside. He hasn't had a chance to spend time with his own child. Poor Esmé rang to complain yesterday. He has been to see her only once."

"That's true. By the time I finish lecturing at the School of Combat, it's too late to do anything. I am going to stop at St.Mary's on my way back today," Ross says. "Besides," he adds, looking meaningfully at Yasmin, "you know very well I cannot intrude when you have visitors from abroad. Incidentally, where are they?"

"They are at church," Tehmi says.

"Really, I didn't know they were religious."

There is an awkward pause.

"They've gone to the new cemetery where Mrs. Studejinski's sister is buried. Later they will go to church for the evening service," Tehmi tells him.

Ross is silent. It was on account of that sister that his father had to leave Mhow.

"Why, they are exquisite," Yasmin says. She has opened the box Ross has brought. A pair of beautifully crafted wooden rhinos from Tripura. Ross always remembers to bring her something. The young nun caresses the single horn of the rhino, then suddenly brushes it against her lips. The older nuns frown in their seats.

"Shall you be back from the field for the School Day? Esmé will be very cross if you miss her performance this time," Tehmi says.

"That's true," says the young nun. "She is playing Portia in the trial scene from *The Merchant of Venice*."

"I've promised her you'll be there," Tehmi says.

91

"How long are you staying this time?" Yasmin asks suddenly. "You must come and dine with us next Sunday. Do tell Mother Gabriella," she says to the nuns, "we want Esmé here for a day. Her father will bring her back in the evening."

"I shall pick her up on Saturday after classes," Tehmi tells Ross.

"All will be forgiven if you show up on Sunday," Yasmin says to Ross, as he gets up to leave. "Don't you dare stand me up again. Noshir has invited the Grehwals."

"Don't worry, Auntie Yasmin, I guarantee that Ross will be here. He won't let us down this time," Tehmi says in a teasing voice. "His chamchas Jessy and Taji will come with their parents. But now there's someone else he wouldn't want to miss."

"Whom are you talking about?" Yasmin asks.

"Why Auntie I told you, a lady who goes by the beautiful name of Camilla."

"Are you sure?" Yasmin says, "Why, she is much older than he."

"She doesn't look it," Tehmi says.

Pulling the jeep out of the driveway, Ross almost knocks down an old pedlar. He stops at the speedbreaker and watches the man shamble across to the other side of the road. The past two weeks in Mhow have left him feeling scraped out from inside. He had walked into the Club the day of his arrival to a hero's welcome, and fled like a scalded cat.

He was already tense from having to keep a straight face while brushing off Taji's hand from his knee under the table, when he had caught the startled eyes of the older English woman. To see a cruel image lick itself into flesh and blood was harrowing. At the same time the creased photograph he had found in his father's trunk had pulsed across her daughter's face. It was like walking straight into a cobweb. He had to make a dash to the Guest House and take a shower.

At Mandu part of his mind had tried to hold him back

from Camilla. But now he wouldn't mind getting her into what his men call a "little *kala jaga*." Standing by her at the swimming pool last evening his neck muscles had relaxed and the inadvertent brushing of their hands had opened up his nasal passage; he had felt light in the head and had this insane urge to grab her. Her nearness had almost made him forget that it was her grandparents, the high-nosed Chinnerys, who had made his father flee from Mhow whimpering like a mangy dog.

His friends in the army think he is afflicted with a passion to win. They don't know that with each risky mission he has tried to salvage his old man's dignity. When classmates at St.Paul's, including Noshir, went picnicking at Eden Falls or hung around the bandstand at Larkin's Folly in Darjeeling, he would torture his body in the gym, till every muscle stood out like a rivet.

After years of combat he is now eager to put the boys through their paces and is looking forward to grooming that born warrior, usually the most self-effacing chap in any unit, whose silence is tipped like a pair of acute sensors. Twenty years before, the alert eyes of Major Grehwal had marked him, the only Anglo cadet in the unit, as a leader.

It has become something of an established law that the true maverick never says much, but the jungle is mapped in his veins. He can tell at the crack of a twig whether it's man or animal. Patrolling no man's land is rather like slow seduction, and requires an ear sharp enough to pick up the slightest quickening of pulse in the quarry. Perhaps, being exiled from the mainstream in a deeply wounding way sharpens one's tracking skills.

The past few evenings he has been going to bed needing no drink to induce sleep. Since the gruesome assassination of Rita, ignoring his own warning about a drunk being an easy target, he had been getting really tight - very bad for discipline. He used to feel like a fraud when warning his cadets during the assault course how drinking placed a soldier in personal danger, rendering him incapable of dodging guerrilla snipers, shooting straight, or comprehending combat situations nearly as well as when he is sober.

The ugliness of his father's Mhow is considerably relieved by this vibrancy of spirit in the new cadets. His only regret is that he won't be able to spend enough time alone with his little girl. The weekend seems to be all planned out for him by Yasmin. He has to be careful not to let his daughter see his agitation when he meets that Chinnery woman again. Esmé is a sensitive child and can catch the faintest drip of a tap in the night of his wretchedness.

iii

THE DAIRY MAID

Camilla finds it difficult to reconcile the arid, slightly melancholic town of today with the colourful, haunting place of her mother's memory. Still there's enough left over of the old feudal sense of personal worth here. Her mother always let everyone in London know, through not very subtle hints, that she belonged to a better class than the men and women with whom her circumstances compelled her to associate. Mhow seems to have retained in more than vestigial sense, a way of life not defined by wealth alone.

Every time Grace and Yasmin are alone, an esoteric language surfaces, and there is a sense of three-way conversation with shadowy figures hovering around them. It's the language of Grandfather Chinnery, the tone generally imperative, and the voice unfettered by adjectives, springing from verb to verb, as those two remote and despairing women pick their way back into their shady kingdom that was graceful, and dismal, at the same time.

Camilla has never seen a place so chock-full of out-moded paraphernalia; Trafalgar chairs, Sheraton sideboards in the dining room, Wilton carpets in the drawing room and adding to the clutter are huge room-size wardrobes in gleaming mahogany smelling mothballish, and tables of every sort. In the spacious bedroom Camilla shares with Grace, there are two elegant writing tables, one with a roll-top desk, a bridge table in rosewood, a drop leaf tea table, and photos in faded sepia of bearded Parsis and their wives in brocaded saris with embroidered hems.

There is an old victrola in the drawing room, and four old grandfather clocks merrily tick away in different sections of the villa. Before going to bed, Camilla has to shut the door against their incessant ruckle. At the end of the hour they knock you senseless with loud bangs.

The servants treat Camilla as though she were made of expensive china. She only has to step out to the verandah and old Bhola comes scampering after her like a sheepdog, and stands there panting with his tongue hanging out.

Yasmin doesn't seem to know that she came into this world a little late. The best is over. The army by sealing off its borders against all encroachment has preserved the trappings of a lost civilisation in Mhow, which should have crumbled under the commercial juggernaut that has pulverised the once sleepy little princely capital of Indore. In its place pullulates a seething metropolis.

Tehmi and Noshir want to get out, but Yasmin would not let go. According to Tehmi, she has even accused Noshir of trying to poison her. The shining parquet floors, the china wiped by servants every morning, the linen curtains in pastel, keep out the heat and dust. Though Yasmin seems ready for the knacker's yard, her language has a prissiness that strangely reminds Camilla of Stoodgy who, despite his scuffed Polish accent, had a fastidious ear for English.

Like his hero, Conrad, he had reinvented himself; said "box of matches" instead of matchbox. Every time Grace got into one of her moods, Stoodgy would push his chair back with a wink, and go out to buy a paper.

Jo Anna would have probably felt more at home in today's world. Camilla imagines her gazing calmly from the pool of light on the verandah. The following afternoon Camilla stands by her mutilated grave and senses eyes opening beneath the rubble seeking her own. Shadows gather around and she feels as though she were peeking through parted curtains at a vast emptiness surrounding a retreating figure, its white dress wrapped tightly around it. She stares at the spot where Jo Anna was laid to rest. A refreshing cold gust whips past Camilla's face, briefly dispersing the odour of tiny lives teeming under the sodden peat, the squashing of translucent things. She feels drugged by the thick syrupy smell of long-fermenting rot. Grace is brushing off the leaves. There is the inscription with dates. Camilla is now well over twice the age her poor mother was at the time of her death, barely nineteen.

All this whilst she had lain alone in this remote corner, under those vast, lonely starlit nights, the lash of monsoon, the wrath of sun. Camilla looks up. The graveyard is like the verdigrised inside of a battleship, sunk up to its forecastle in deep sleep, but over in the west are round hills backlit by the setting sun.

Though rendered in Hindi, Camilla recognises the hymn, "*Guide me, O Thou Great Redeemer,*" and sings with the congregation in English. The service gives tidiness to grief. Later they stroll to Christ Church, which has lost its flock and is now the haunt of spiders and cockroaches. Grace is unable to go past the octagonal marble font at the rear of the nave where Bobby and Jo Anna were baptized, and slumps into the nearest mildewed pew. From the far side of the shrouded transept comes the sound of flapping, followed by a great cloudburst of white feathers, like thousands of snowflakes volleying from alpine windrows. They tickle Camilla's nostrils but behind the high altar the stained glass window is bright like a summer garden.

She is able to make out the inscriptions on tablets in the purple light bouncing off the ambulatory walls past the chancel rail. Erected by brother officers of The Suffolk Regiment, 76th Hussars, The Gloucestershire 28th Foot, 6th Bengal Cavalry, 102nd King Edwards Own Grenadiers, they carry laconic tales of hard knocks, of remote dying in strange places. Other aborted stories on bronze plates and tablets lurk unread on the walls behind the arcades, each a tiny spot of unclaimed memory, refugees stranded at a defunct station clutching bundles of aimless sorrow.

That night, on Yasmin's instructions, Bhola pulls out a

manila envelope from a battered old suitcase. It has a photograph of Jo Anna in a long high-waisted flared skirt, head covered in an old-fashioned bonnet.

"Shirin took that picture during the dress rehearsal of *Patience*," Yasmin says, handing it to Camilla. "Jo played the Dairy Maid."

The young woman has a radiant look, and even the black and white photograph cannot conceal the bloom of youth on her tanned cheeks. There is a feeling inside Camilla of something softly unstitching as Jo Anna's deep gaze settles on her face. While the invalid in her bed, the old retainer, and the woman she calls her mother look on silently, the face in the picture levitates like the dancer from the ruined temple, flutters before Camilla's startled eyes, and dips sideways out of the window - a butterfly caught in a sudden gust.

iv

PROTECTOR OF COWS

When Grace and her friends played cricket behind the Dog
Lady's bungalow, Peppermint, the agile beagle manning silly-
mid-on, never strayed to square point which was guarded by
Pronto the long-necked Spanish greyhound with a tapering
body who could slew and twist sideways to stop the ball.

Hulme found the well-mannered Pooch Squad to be like
the natives who willingly served the British. He resented
anyone calling his wife Begum or Sahiba and always referred
to her as Mrs. Hulme. His tall angular figure, tapering beard
and whiskers, gold-rimmed glasses on a large hooked nose,
gave him the appearance of a near-sighted elderly goat.
Among the conventionally dressed British residents and
uniformed army personnel, his delicately tinted cravat,
creamy bosky shirt with golden cufflinks and buttons, his
long silken jacket with cutaway front and striped trousers
made him look like a character from Oscar Wilde's
Importance of Being Ernest which the Stallybrasses, a touring
group of Thespians from London, had performed at St.
Mary's.

The politics at Chinnery's Hotel covered the entire
spectrum from the esoteric to anarchic. With the Countess's
tirade against the Catholics, the Shikari's imperial rhetoric,
Doctor Aspel's concern about the growing incidents of
venereal diseases among the Tommies, the Major's caveat on
the lack of leadership quality in the new officers of regiments
and their dependence on the railways for field marches, and
Hulme's brand of liberal Fabianism which would grant India
freedom the very next day, the guests at Chinnery's were
assured of a stimulating evening. Among them were regulars

like Fred Thompson who travelled to Mhow once every three months, Mr. Tiplow of Badham, Pile & Company who sold Argosy Braces and was always immaculately dressed in white twill, and the rumple-suited, ginger-haired and whiskered Mr. McBride who supplied Lowrie's Whisky to Chinnery's.

Sometimes the discussion would turn to the relative merits of the new Viceroy Linlithgow, and his predecessor Willingdon. Prince Pratap Singh dubbed Linlithgow, the organiser of the All India Cattle Show, "a protector of cows". He preferred Willingdon to Linlithgow because the former was a thorough gentleman who treated his father with a courtesy commensurate with his royal status. Pratap had reservations about the new Viceroy because he cosied up to the Congresswallas who wanted to strip the princes of their power. Shikari, who was always pleasantly tippled, retorted that Willingdon was henpecked. He preferred the new man because he was an accomplished shot and went tiger hunting in the Terai forest with Jim Corbett.

Occasionally a boxwallah might bring disturbing news from the real world about events such as Gandhi's Salt March or some of the impish things he did like meeting the Viceroy dressed like a 'half naked fakir,' to the annoyance of Winston Churchill. When an English reporter asked him whether he would visit Buckingham Palace during the Round Table Conference in his usual loincloth, the old man replied,

"Some go in plus fours, I'll go in minus fours."

"Bloody cheek," roly-poly Mr. Arblast of Brown & Polson's Custard Powder would bristle.

Shikari, who would by then be deep in his cups, would shout, "These wretched banias, do you really think they'd know how to run the country? What do you say Pat, you are like us, the same breed? We know how to rule, eh?"

Pratap Singh, heir to the Rajput throne of Kesarpore and a crack shot to boot would nod his head thoughtfully and say, "You are quite right old man. Rulers don't grow on trees. These jokers don't even know how to load a simple 303."

"And what's more," Shikari would add, "reality is much different. The moment we leave, the Muslims and Hindus would carve each other up."

Hulme would listen quietly for a while with closed eyes, then clear his throat, and open his eyes. His peroration, when it came, had practically no direct connection to what was being discussed.

No, no, no. Come, let's away to prison;
We two alone will sing like birds i'the cage.
When thou dost ask me blessing I'll kneel down
And ask of thee forgiveness. So we'll live
And pray, and sing, and tell old tales, and laugh
At gilded butterflies, and hear poor rogues
Talk of court news; who's in, who's out –
And take upon's the mystery of things
As if we were God's spies.

Shakespeare gave that shy, slow man who dreamed of one world, a running start. He moved from one topic to another, ransacking the history of the world, the journey of the Buddha to the Tree of Knowledge, Christ debating the Pharisees, the sacrifice of Hassan and Hussein, the martyrdom of saints of all ages, the nobility of Michaelangelo's David, the majesty of Lear's suffering, the magnificence of the 9th Symphony, the Humanism of Kant, Voltaire on Freedom, the insights of Jalaluddin Rumi, the wisdom of Confucius.

The speech had a calming effect on those assembled in the lounge, making them feel that all was well with the world and that Gandhi was not such a bad sort after all if Hulme said so.

During the ensuing silence when everyone replenished their glasses, beady-eyed Mr. Tillotson of Favre-Leuba Watches might bring up the bombing of the Viceroy's train outside Delhi.

"The old boy might have been killed, blown to bits. Where was your precious Gandhi then, eh?"

"If we have to leave," Hulme would say, "and we will have to sooner or later, it'd be better to hand over power to Gandhi. Otherwise we'll have to contend with that Bose fellow and his revolutionary cohorts who want to throw us into the Arabian Sea."

Grace was happy that her Uncle Woom was so wise. He was Grace's only confederate when she was devastated over Bobby's going to England. Bobby had just turned ten when it was decided to send him to Marlborough. Grace was beside herself with grief and there was a melancholy that haunted those last few months. But Amanda was adamant and the Major, too, seemed to agree with her. He had attended the local school at Colne in Lancashire before coming to India, and all his life found himself at a disadvantage with the public school network with its codes and in-jokes. He'd seen much younger fellows superseding him. He did not regret the sacrifices he'd made for King and Country, but he'd had to work twice as hard as those with posh accents to advance in the army.

Besides, Amanda had set her heart on it, and was prepared to endure the inevitable pangs of separation. She had never been to England and looked forward to the trip. Jo Anna had turned four and, after much discussion, it was decided to leave her in the charge of The Ayah.

V

THE LADIES OF CALCUTTA

Bobby was excited at the prospect of sailing to England, but Grace's eyes would begin to moisten while reading to Jo Anna from the *Jungle Books*. She was unable to fight back her tears when it was time for Mowgli to take leave of his wolf mother.

"Now, he said, I will go to men. But first I must say farewell to my mother; and he went to the cave where she lived with father wolf, and he cried on her coat, while the four cubs howled miserably.

"Come soon, said Mother Wolf, little naked son of mine; for listen child of man, I loved thee more than ever I loved the cubs."

Baby Jo Anna sobbed disconsolately.

Amanda was very cross with Grace and said she was being selfish. How was it selfish to cry when she couldn't help it? Uncle Woom was the only one who seemed to understand her agony. He, too, was against sending Bobby to England when there were so many good British public schools in India, like Lawrence School at Sanawar and St.Paul's, Darjeeling. But he understood why certain British and princely Indians were impelled to send their boys to study at one of the famous schools in England. Hulme himself had been at Harrow and had known the misery of being uprooted from his family in Dorset.

Even the Countess, who was once married to a Russian aristocrat was all for it. Her second husband Major Dunsterville, had been in the Army Bearer Corps, a mostly Indian outfit commanded by British Officers. She said Marlborough would make a man out of Bobby. She was given to reciting *If* by Rudyard Kipling in her slightly nasal voice.

At dinner Grace fished out liver from her bowl of chicken curry for Bobby. Ayah shadowed him everywhere, fetching and carrying his shoes and clothes. There was no longer any dispute as to who should take the front seat by Mahamud when they went out for a drive. Bobby's slightest wish became their command.

Grace couldn't understand how others went about their business as though nothing terrible was happening. She felt turning within her a spring of suffering that had no parallel. There was Ayah, of course, but then Ayahs were supposed to cry anyway. The numbness and hopelessness she felt had no name. She couldn't talk to anybody about it.

In the evening when friends gathered at Chinnery's, they gave advice to Bobby on how to protect himself against the cold.

"Always wear your scarf when you go out. Protect your throat, I say, and the rest will take care of itself."

Uncle Shikari must have repeated that advice ten times. He'd never gone back since the time he'd first come out as a young man of eighteen, some thirty years before. Someone drew a map and explained to Bobby how to get to the Tower of London. The boy's forthcoming trip to England released within them a whole flood of nostalgia.

One evening, Uncle Fred, who was in town, got up and started singing *Burlington Bertie*.

Soon everyone, including the boxwallahs, joined in and the Countess was seen dabbing her eyes. There was a big applause when Hulme rose to his feet and proceeded to recite,

"Oh to be in England
Now that April's there."

But they were taken aback when Grace suddenly ran out of the lounge shouting,

"I hate you, I hate you all."

She was shaking with hurt as she ran and stumbled blindly into the library.

A few minutes later Hulme found her standing by the window. After pulling a volume from the shelf, he sat down on the sofa and pretended to read. Grace was afraid to turn around because she was sure she wouldn't be able to hold back her tears. She felt betrayed because Hulme had joined those who were taking Bobby away from her.

"Even if it hurts, you must be brave. For Bobby's sake," Hulme said from the sofa. "You know I do not approve of his going to England, but now the decision is made, you mustn't let Bobby see you cry. Besides," he added, "someday we'll all have to go back."

"Go back where?" Her voice was still hoarse from crying.

"To England, of course. After all, there's no place like home, as they say."

"But why?"

"Because," he said, slowly going to her, "we are all guests here. Mhow is only a temporary home as Chinnery's is to guests like Freddy Thompson, Pat Kesarpore and Giles Tiplow."

"But don't you see, Chinnery's is our home," Grace said stamping her foot.

"It certainly is, now at this moment and a very nice home it is too, but ...er... er... but soon it'll be time for you to go to Simla with Shirin. I am sure you won't even remember Chinnery's when you are in those beautiful Himalayan hills. I've been there, several times. You can actually see some of the great peaks, extending into other peaks on a clear day."

She was silent for a while.

Then she looked up.

"Never, I shall never forget Chinnery's."

There was such mad passion in her grey eyes as she whispered those words, that Hulme was speechless for a moment.

"Anyway, Bobby will come home for the summer holidays, like young Jonathan, the Farleighs' boy. Then we'll all be together again."

Grace felt much better after that. But she was still puzzled by what Hulme had said. What would happen to Chinnery's, who'd run it if everyone left? And what would the Dog Lady do? You are not allowed to take dogs to England because of some law. That's why people left their dogs with her.

"And what about Ayah?" Grace's throat suddenly contracted in alarm. "She's so old. Even now she can hardly see in the dark."

"Don't you worry about Mrs. Roderigues. She is Indian after all, even though a Catholic. The Goans have large families with uncles and aunts all living together. She'll go to Panjim to be with her brother or someone else. Come, let us go back to the lounge. I should be going home and it's well past your bedtime."

Hulme was perturbed by the intensity of little Grace's feeling. There was so much love sloshing about in that frail frame. He recognised himself in her, there was the same fragility, a malady really, that dire urge to give yourself to others completely. All right, perhaps, when you were a child. Quite touching actually when you come to think of it. Warms one's cockles and that sort of thing. But it can become a chronic condition, this terror of losing those you love. Then where are you?

Grace lay awake for a long time. She was from Mhow like Shirin, no matter what anyone said. Every summer when they went to Matheran, even the Parsi lady who ran the Hotel referred to Mater as Mhow Memsahib. "Put those towels the dhobi brought back yesterday in Mhow Memsahib's bathroom," she would tell the servants. Mrs. Fleming was Nagpore Memsahib and Mrs. Gavin, Bhusawal Memsahib. And when her friend Irene Popjoy sang

The Spanish girls are lovely,
Oh yes indeed they are
But the Ladies of Calcutta are fairest by far,
there was never any doubt; those 'ladies of Calcutta' were British.

vi

AN OLD NAG

Grace sticks her head through the door and finds Yasmin sitting upright in her bed, scribbling something on a pad. She looks up and their eyes meet. "Oh, do come in Grace," she says putting the pad down on her lap.

"Hope I am not intruding," Grace says, sitting on the chair by the window.

"Not at all. I am just jotting down a few points. I have been asked by our Panchayat to write about the Parsis of Mhow. The place is changing so fast, someone has to document the contribution of Parsis, especially our father's."

"How very interesting. Will there be a place for the Chinnerys in it?"

"Why, certainly. Everyone who was important will find a place into it. Mhow minus the Chinnerys would be like *Hamlet* without the Prince of Denmark, as Sister Benedicta would have said. Remember Sister Benedicta?"

"I certainly do, and that awful row when she caught Jo doing an impression of her in class."

Grace and Yasmin share so many memories that gradually the initial awkwardness between them has given way to an easy camaraderie. They have fallen into the habit of taking their afternoon tea together. In Yasmin, Grace senses a familiar isolation, a kinship of those exiled from the company of the living. And Yasmin has found an ally in Grace against raids from the ugly world outside, a world where her nephew hatches nefarious plots to evict her from Mhow. Noshir is intent on demolishing the most precious remnant of her past, her dear Shiphidol. The villa is to Yasmin what Chinnery's is to Grace, a real refuge although it too exists only as a memorial to a vanished past.

The two of them have noticed an increasing togetherness between Camilla and Tehmi. Often a conspiratorial wink followed by a knowing smile passes between them, especially when Grace and Yasmin get carried away, talking about long-dead acquaintances as though they were beings of flesh and blood who might any moment pop in for a chat or a game of bridge. The younger women find it spooky and leave the room with bored looks as if to say "Oh dear, they are at it again, the old crones, each one dottier than the other."

Of course the younger women know nothing of the wonderful friendship between Major Chinnery and Yasmin's father, an alliance that extended to their respective communities, the British and the Parsis. It was their teamwork, which had made Mhow such a model of good manners and cultivated taste. When Yasmin's book, *The Chronicles of Mhow,* is published, the world will no longer see the Parsis as mere camp followers of the British, but rather as co-founders of the town. It is a debt of honour she must fulfil before the sound of wing-beat fills her tower of silence.

In an old country like India, history is a snob. Monuments from Ajanta, Madurai, Delhi, Jaipore and Benares move effortlessly from coffee tables, tourist brochures to films. Mhow lays no claim to hoary antiquity, has been part of no country, having been many countries and many peoples. Living there was like having two passports. Grace still remembers the vans that used to sprinkle water every afternoon on roads, tamping down dust.

Yasmin tells Grace that the Daruwala virus has infected her nephew.

"One evening last week when you were taking your constitutional, my nephew gave a tour of this property to one of his builder friends. They couldn't see me because I was hidden behind the hedge. The builder said the villa along with the garden could easily fetch two crore of rupees. When my nephew complained I was a real thorn in his flesh, you know what that horrid man said to him? If he had an old interfering aunt in his household, he would put her to sleep like an old nag."

Grace is stunned.

"And what did Noshir say to that?"

"He said it wasn't possible to get rid of me because it would upset Tehmi. Besides, nothing could be done while the guests, that is Camilla and you, were here. To which the wretch of a builder said something so terribly cruel in Hindi that I am ashamed to repeat it."

"Go on, let me hear it," Grace says.

"I don't know how good your Hindi is. Let me translate it for you," Yasmin tells Grace, closing her moistening eyes. "He said I reminded him of one of these eternally grumbling Hindu widows forever probing with hands their tonsured heads for missing tresses. Oh Grace that really hurt. I had half a mind to ring Shirin and report it to her."

Grace is speechless. The builder's evil-sounding words are like a whiplash. Only a perverted and cold-blooded man could bring himself to say something so vicious about an elderly and defenceless person. Grace finds it hard to believe that Noshir is the son of her longtime friend and Yasmin's older sister Shirin who lives in the States with her daughter.

"My wretched nephew wants to sell Shiphidol to this developer and bury me in a two-room flat of a housing colony for super-annuated Parsis in Parel, a dingy little suburb of Bombay," Yasmin says wiping her eyes. "Haven't you noticed those black Fiats with tinted windows parked outside Noshir's wing night after night? From your bedroom window you might have noticed that fat, pot-bellied man completely gone in the teeth getting out of the car. That's the odious builder fellow himself. The Mali's wife keeps me informed of the goings on. How Tehmi can stand those badmashes is absolutely beyond me! Some of them have bulldozed old farmers out of their lands in order to build housing colonies. They have blood on their hands that lot. That is not just rumour; local papers from Indore and Bhopal have openly accused them of running crime syndicates. I tell you, Grace, with such fine, safari-suited friends, Noshir would have no trouble having me filleted and hung up to dry like a bombay duck, and no questions asked. Only fear of Tehmi has prevented him from lacing my bedtime Horlicks with arsenic. You know what that Sitaram said to me this morning?" Yasmin asks glaring at the parrot.

"No, tell me," Grace says suppressing an impulse to smile.

"That goonda of a parrot said clear as a bell, 'Wish the old bag would croak.' I don't have to tell you where that comes from? Why until Camilla and you arrived, Bhola first tasted my food. Now that I eat with you at the table I feel much safer."

Grace is too shocked for words. Outwardly Mhow seems as calm and orderly as ever, but Yasmin's words evoke squalor so outrageously hideous that her voice cracks when she speaks.

"My dear, how do you explain such ruthlessness in Shirin's son?"

"I don't really know," Yasmin tells her. "But listen to this. Last July on utterly flimsy grounds, old servants from my father's company, Mazda Chemicals, were sacked."

Grace remembers the Pharmaceutical Company, which was located on the outskirts of Indore.

"But how does Noshir get away with it?" Grace inquires.

Yasmin's eyes go misty; she dabs them with a paper napkin.

"He and his sort can get away with anything in this country. Everybody is corrupt including the magistrates in court. You see, in Dad's time, there was no such thing as a service contract. Everything was done on trust. Noshir calls such notions of loyalty old-fashioned. Would you believe it, our accountant, Mr. Nanavati, who had dandled Noshir on his knees, came to see me with tears in his eyes. The poor chap was summarily dismissed. But what can a cripple like me do? And now this nephew of mine is simply waiting for me to die."

For a minute or two neither woman speaks.

Everywhere in Mhow there are still many reminders of Sir Mancherjee's philanthropy: the local Vernacular High School, the Dharamsala (Travellers' Inn), the Vegetable Market, the Public Park by the railway station at the centre of which, on a pedestal, sits Yasmin's great grandfather, Sir Jamshedjee Debu, in white marble.

"Do you know, Grace," Yasmin says, speaking with fervour, "at first when you wrote to say you wanted to visit Mhow, I didn't think it was such a good idea. But now that you are here let me tell you what a comfort it is to me. My father could never find another friend like Major Chinnery. When the Major died, Dad cried as though he had lost his own brother. He even stopped attending the meetings at the Lodge. I plan to write a whole chapter on Chinnery's Hotel," Yasmin says flipping through her pad.

"That's splendid. I can't wait to read the book," Grace says, quite moved by Yasmin's account.

"Our Parsi-British friendship dates from the time when my great-grandfather burst on Mhow with a soda-water machine, which he carried around on the back of mules. He wangled permission to follow British battalions to the firing ranges and, during 1857, marched with the troops as far north as Jhansi. Instead of tramping around the dusty plains in the heat, with the money his father had left him, his son, that is my Grandfather Jamshedjee, set up the first pharmaceutical company in India, manufacturing quinine and cough syrups. After you left Mhow, big chemical factories began to crowd out smaller units, but our good old Mazda Chemicals continued to break even. That wasn't enough for Noshir. You remember our famous Linctus with its logo copied from Nasarwanjee Debu's old soda water machine?"

"Of course I do," Grace says, smiling happily at the memory. The Linctus left a wonderfully tangy sensation and girls often resorted to sham, unladylike hawking, in order to wheedle the sweet syrupy linctus from the Matron.

"Why, the Infirmary at St.Mary's was always well stocked with Jamshedjee's Linctus," Grace says."Couple of spoons and your cough was gone."

"Well, go and ask for it at any chemist, and they wouldn't even know what you were talking about. Noshir stopped production because the profit margin was not big enough or something like that. But I haven't got the heart to tell you about his worst act of vandalism. You remember the two lakes at Kalakund?"

"Yes, of course," Grace says, "who can forget The Sun Water and Moon Water. Why, I am so looking forward to a dip."

" Well, you can still have a dip but not in the lakes. They have been blasted off and reduced to one horrid swimming pool, all cement and green mucky water."

"What?" Grace, who has got up to put her cup down on a nearby table, freezes.

"Noshir and his thug partners persuaded the Commissioner of Tourism, Mr. Jindal, to turn the place into a tourist resort. So now there's a Guest House, a row of dingy rooms that people can rent from the Government and then swim in that pool where the water is never changed for months on end. There's no Moon Water any more," Yasmin says, her voice quivering with infinite sadness.

Hurried footsteps and Camilla appears in the doorway.

"Let's go before the light fades, Mum. I want to take a few pictures of the famous Chinnery's," she says.

Still bewildered, Grace picks up her handbag saying she must go and have a look at what's left of Chinnery's.

"Do take Shiva with you," Yasmin tells Grace. "There are too many mangy pariahs on the road these days. Noshir has already lodged a complaint with the Municipal Office, but they are very careless. Also the men in charge are reluctant to use poison. The officials are mostly Hindus these days, you know."

"I shall carry a walking stick from the hall," Grace says. "One can't run away from them all the time. Besides, I need my constitutional."

"I rang to say you were coming," Yasmin says. "Doctor Das is back but he likes to be alerted. The nurses might think you were sent to inspect the place by the World Health Organization. Dr. Das gets quite rattled when someone shows up without warning."

"Don't you go fretting about me, dear. I might not have the courage to go in," Grace says. "Just a quick dekko from the road perhaps, to get reacquainted with it slowly, if you know what I mean."

As a child Yasmin used to let her fingers glissade lovingly down the balustrade of the great staircase at Chinnery's! Perhaps she should have warned Grace not to expect too much? On the other hand the visit might finally open her eyes to what Yasmin has known all along, that memory kept alive by touch is the Braille of ghosts.

CHINNERY'S

And there it is at last. Without the lawns, flowerbeds and trees subtending its plinth and columns, the façade wears a smirchy look of something excavated. The fretwork of its wooden lattice has rotted away and the entrance porch, in a suspended wobble, gapes in the harsh light of a naked bulb. The pediments over the bay windows are askew and in danger of falling. Stoodgy would have appreciated its lime and mortar frontage; it still gives off an air of slightly soiled majesty.

Her life before Stoodgy had been one long trip to and from Golders Green, cooking and washing up. He ran the 'Fish And Chips' because there were very few jobs in Britain for war-scarred Polish aristocrats with their quaint English. On Saturdays, too tired to cook, Grace had fallen into the habit of buying plaice and chips. Then Stoodgy introduced her to Joseph Conrad.

In the pages of *Almayer's Folly* lurked Grace's own lost world. Dain Maroola could have been her Uncle Pat, the proud prince of Kesarpore who had immolated himself in his palace rather than be deprived of his royal privileges after Independence. And like Lingard, Pater knew every servant on his estate by name and was loved by all.

Stoodgy and Grace soon became a familiar sight in the reading room of the ivy-covered redbrick Clapham Public Library on Northside. It was there amidst shelves filled with the latest novels with sleekly designed covers that she stumbled one day upon an old edition of Kipling's *Plain Tales from the Hills*. The Librarian, Mrs. Danby, who never spoke to anyone, told her that Grace was the first member to borrow it since 1938.

"Practically no one reads him these days. Because of his political views, you know. But I cannot recommend him enough. None of these so called modern writers can hold a candle to Kipling."

Like every colonial child Grace had grown up singing *'Mandalay'*, but she had forgotten the almost wickerwork texture of Kipling's prose, which could set her life in Mhow on foot to the skirl of bagpipes, flash of sporran and checkered gaiters. It was like walking into a friendly bakery and being greeted by familiar aromas.

Across the road from the Library was The Parish Church of Holy Trinity where Stoodgy and she were married, and subsequently she moved into his flat at the far end of Orlando Street which was still within walking distance of the tube station. She wasn't particularly religious, but with its stucco facade, white Ionian columns, dome-crowned tower at its west end, its memorial tablets and cenotaph 'To The Men Of Clapham' who had fallen in distant lands during the Great War, Holy Trinity stood in ghostly alliance with Christ Church in Mhow. After Evensong she went down to Grove Road to help Stoodgy.

Camilla snaps pictures while Grace hovers over the ditch where once stood the Italian fountain in the garden at Chinnery's. It is now part of an atrium in a five-star hotel in some distant city. The pit of its uprooting is filled with jagged red bricks, a mouthful of broken teeth. The mango orchards, almond and pomegranate trees are images scattered across a blind sea.

"The Taj in Bombay and Raffles in Singapore are bigger but they lack this charming setting," Mr. Barker of Whiteway Laidlaw used to say.

Grace is awakened from the reverie by the sound of water splashing down. Through an open window a maidservant is emptying a bucket without so much as a "Gardy loo." Camilla had stood directly under the window while loading another film in her camera. Dr. Das and his gynaecologist wife seem to have taken extra care, the nurses are dressed in milk-white uniform and a refreshing tang of floor polish is in the air. There are solid wooden benches for patients to wait in the hall. To the left, now carpetless, stands the great staircase, and a diagonal crack, like the flight path of a stricken aircraft, zigzags through the stained glass Union Jack.

Under the watchful eyes of women lying in bed, Camilla follows Grace, clicking away on her camera. Cold, stiff looking chairs with scald marks are abandoned in the centre of the lounge where Amanda's furniture, arranged in graceful patterns, used to be. The doctor is obviously on the fiddle, trying to be helpful and rich at the same time. In place of Grace's piano, a hulking steel medicine cabinet stands cockily. Traces of her existence have been carefully wiped out, as though years of her living there had never happened. Did she think that the moment she walked in, all her dead would hobble in, clutching poppies like retired servicemen on Armistice Day?

A dozen or so women with infants in their arms come stumbling out of their beds and surround Grace with cries of "Memsahib." She stands there with the shy dignity of visiting royalty.

"Such a small town and what a lot of babies are being born here," Camilla says.

"As they say, life goes on," Grace says wistfully.

Camilla is relieved to see the car from Shiphidol parked close by. The driver who is waiting for them in the porch says Yasmin was worried about their walking back in the dark. As they follow him down the steps they come face to face with a large, motherly woman of sixty or thereabouts. Her paleness carries faint coffee traces and her large bulbous brown eyes are set in a round chubby face. She is gasping for breath and dabbing her forehead. She looks vaguely familiar but Grace is unable to place her.

"Onlee just now I heard you were visiting. When message

came from hospital I was at Church."

"How do you do," says Camilla. "I am Camilla and this is my mother, Mrs. Studejinski."

"Yes, yes, Madam knows me from early childhood. I am Olinda, Madam. You do not remember? I am Josephine's daughter. You used to let me ride your pony. My grandad was head cook at the Hotel. You remember Mr. and Mrs. d'Quodros, naturallee."

"Good Gracious. You are little Olinda. Of course, I remember you," Grace says with amazement.

"No longer little, Madam," the woman says tapping her ample waist. "I work here as Head Nurse and will now gladee show you your old home."

"Thank you, but we've seen everything. We have to go now. We shall come again," Grace says hurriedly.

The woman looks crestfallen and waddles after them all the way to the car, panting for breath.

"The moment I saw you I said, that's our Grace Baba, come back after so many years."

Her cowlike gaze is trained on Grace's face, seeking some urgent sign of special relationship. But Grace keeps her eyes averted and abruptly gets into the car. Camilla stops and turns around to say "Nice meeting you," with a parting smile.

"I will come to Shiphidol on my day off to pay my respects," the woman shouts after the car.

This woman, this Olinda, could be a nuisance. Grace is not sure how old she might have been at the time of Jo's death. Twelve or fourteen perhaps. Old enough to remember things. Anyway she must check with Yasmin. She'd know. Yasmin knows everything. Grace wonders how far she could rely on Yasmin herself? All her servants; the Mali, the Cook, the sweepers and Bhola spy for her. She doesn't even spare the nuns, pumping them for tidbits about their pupils' families. What if she still hates us secretly for what happened to Jo Anna? It hasn't escaped Grace that every time Jo's name comes up in conversation, Yasmin's eyes glaze, and a condescending smile appears on her face. Shirin was effervescent, but Yasmin was a slyboots even as a child.

"But wasn't Josephine away at the time somewhere in Ajmer," Yasmin says. "I remember her husband was transferred there sometime before the war."

Grace feels relieved. One of dear Stoodgy's favourite scenes in Conrad was when, after his fellow officers abandon the ship, Jim stands baffled before jumping down to safety.

"In *Lord Jim* Conrad was reliving the moment of his own exile before boarding the Vienna Express for the last time at Cracow Station," Stoodgy used to say. "Even as he leaps, Jim knows there's no turning back."

Until that day, Grace had never quite understood what Stoodgy had meant by that. One day before his death, interrupting her with that sad apologetic smile, he had said,

" You know, I'd never want to go back to Warsaw. Not only because of what the Nazis did to my parents. To me, Poland is my past. When the past dies and leaves no live tissue with which to rebuild life, the place also goes with it, and the road back disappears like a brief furrow cut by a passing breeze in the Serpentine. Going back is no longer a choice, it's self-indulgence."

IV

i

THE GOOD EGG

As everyone knows, Bombay was part of Catherine of Braganza's dowry and became British when she married Charles II. But what was the reason for the Parsi exodus from Surat to Mhow?

Well, after a period of dithering, not knowing what to do with it, the King palmed Bombay off to John Company in 1668. But that upstart little island, with its pervasive smell of fish drying in the sun, had a deep natural harbour and it began to edge the old city of Surat out of the trade. The mighty river that once rolled by its ancient ramparts was now clogged with the silt of the Mughal Empire. Enterprise demanded a quieter place where the rule of law prevailed. Mhow signalled and the Parsis came. Some were good - some were not.

The warrior Princess of Indore fought bravely, but was finally overpowered, not by the hardware of superior guns and drums, but the software of drill. Huge Indian armies were one-trick ponies. Charge! That was it, and if it failed, regroup and attack. With a drill, a small British force could cut down to the centre of the larger Indian force and pour fire upon it at the most vulnerable point. The new software allowed one to cease fire at will, march or counter march.

Yasmin's paternal ancestors, the Debus, had dealings only with the good Parsis. They always smiled and were happy, even as Zarathustra himself, who arrived into this world laughing instead of crying. Like him, they strove to be good and shared what they had with others. Hence, the idea of Sakhawat, which doesn't quite translate into Christian charity. As Sir Mancherjee used to say, "The Parsi gives because he cannot be happy alone." However, at the "Agiyari," the Fire Temple on High Street, the good and the bad worshipped together.

The bad Parsis of Mhow were the ones who had strayed from the path of "Asha," revealed by Ahur Mazda to Zarathustra, and emulated the bad British. Yes, among those Olympians, too, there were the good and the bad, and the first Daruwala of Mhow had run with the wrong pack. All that was in the past when Mhow, like all other up-country cantonments, was limping back from the depredations of the Sepoy Mutiny.

But some said that in the scorching heat of May 1862, as Clarissa lay dying in her one room barracks to which the irascible General Crawley had confined the Lilleys, she uttered a curse on Daruwala of the Cantonment Liquor Store for brazenly testifying that her teetotaller husband was an alcoholic.

When Lilley's brother officers of the 6th Inniskilling Dragoons raised their voice against Crawley, the General was summoned to England and court-martialled at Aldershot. There, too, the wicked Parsi whose passage was paid by Crawley repeated his charge against the RSM.

"The RSM come everyday to drink. Many times I refuse. He drink too much. Then he threaten to kill me. So I give him gin."

By the time Daruwala returned from England, Clarissa Lilley's curse had taken root and the storekeeper's evil had been passed down to each successive generation. The Daruwala gene had continued to evolve in a manner that confirmed the duality of good and evil, which was central to Parsi faith. As Dasturji, the elderly priest at the Fire Temple used to say, it had to do with the bad egg produced by Ahriman, the evil son of Light, who knocked it against the egg containing the good genie made by his brother Ormuzd, forever scrambling good and evil.

Yasmin never knew her mother, who had died of complications during her birth. Lady Mancherjee had the mark of Daruwala on her and liked to be squired around town by dashing polo players from British regiments. Only the high esteem in which Sir Mancherjee was held, especially for his charitable work in Mhow, put the lid on speculation about Shirin's deep blue eyes. Despite pressure from his family, Sir Mancherjee refused to marry again. Instead, he personally supervised his daughters' education and started attending the Fire Temple. The two little girls went with him.

When her limbs began to shrivel, and fat gathered in her middle as on a duck, Yasmin's envy of her sister's good looks slowly waned. And after Jo Anna started bunking classes to be with Carl, the nuns at St. Mary's came to look upon Yasmin as their number one pupil. At the same time, her secret yearning for carnal embrace set the good and evil eggs of Dasturji's sermons on a powerful collision course.

One day in Bombay, her cousin Pestan's fingers stroking her thighs suddenly darted up like a lizard's tongue and she was blown open inside out like an umbrella caught in a gale. Pestan accompanied all the assembled cousins on his piano when they sang *Red River Valley* or *I've got spurs that jingle, jangle jingle,* but when alone with Yasmin, he held her captive in a luscious web of operatic arias. During his visit to Mhow, they sampled the pain of Violetta and Alfredo, Mimi and Rudolpho. Pessi was much older than she, but ten years difference between husband and wife was not so uncommon among Parsis. He was not exactly handsome, like Kayzad, who had rakish good looks. Pestan was athletic and a fine tenor. Looking into Yasmin's eyes like Don Jose he sang,

Et j'étais une chose à toi!
Yasmin, je t'aime.

But with the withering of her legs, Pessi's passion cooled. Almost overnight, enchantress Carmen turned into hapless

121

Michaela, condemned to spend half of her adult life like a beetle on her back, aching with desire, nuzzling pillows like a bitch in rut. Then for ten years, poor old Bhola came into her bedroom with her afternoon tea and almost mechanically massaged her, keeping his eyes averted all the time. The old fool never stopped crying. But what could she do? Her own hands were limp like tubes on a stethoscope.

After she was struck down with polio, Pestan's attachment to her remained quite strong, but his mother wanted an heir to their large fortune. Besides, what could he have done with a crippled wife in Bombay? Yasmin didn't blame him. If Pestan had been afflicted, why, she would have taken care of him, nursed him and dedicated her life to him. There was no one Yasmin could turn to for sympathy.

Jo Anna was lost in a desperate blizzard unleashed by Maude Aspel, and Yasmin was left all alone. After her husband's suicide, Maude had taken to visiting the Dayan woman who had control over all the ghosts and spectres of Mhow, irrespective of their religion, not just Pir Baba, who was Muslim like herself. If you walked after midnight past the lonely Dargah beyond the signal gantry in the shadow of the Railway Institute, you could see him flitting by in a white robe and green skullcap.

Then there was the young Hindu, Thakurani, who inhabited the Bhut Bungalow where the Masons congregated. The Thakurani had been brutally murdered in the bungalow by the Thakur of Kanshipore's thugs while she was pregnant, and had turned into a shrieking churail. Those two, along with the Lilleys were the major ghosts of Mhow, but there were several other minor ones that lurked in every nook and corner.

The Dayan was said to be Iranian. The Parsis had also migrated to India from Iran, but that was several centuries ago. They were the direct descendants of the original Zoroastrians of ancient Persia; the Dayan had come to Hyderabad before the First World War as maid to a princely bride, and had bewitched the Nabob when he was on a visit to the Nizam's court.

Maude Aspel claimed that Clarissa Lilley had appeared at the Dayan's seance and announced that she was reborn as the younger daughter of Major Chinnery. One day Yasmin went to the Old Cemetery with Jo to place flowers on the Lilleys' tomb, but was so scared when a chameleon jumped out of the shrub and landed straight on her bare arm that she refused to go there again.

ii

THE BASKERVILLE REGIMENT

The day Amanda and Bobby left for England, Grace stayed in her room and cried. Ayah sent a message to the Dog Lady that Grace Baba refused to come down to dinner.

"Now, now Missy we'll have none of this. Let me see you eat at once, chop chop. Or else no one will get any dinner tonight. My orders," said the Dog Lady. "Ayah Roderigues also refuses to touch any food unless Grace Baba has eaten."

Grace looked at old Mr. d'Quodros standing in the doorway with a plate of prawn curry and rice, his wife holding a bowl of what looked like beveca pudding. The tangy whiff of the prawns, fried with fresh coriander and coconut shredded garam masala, the curving slightly browned meat, the puffed red shells all served with tamarind sauce, had already made her mouth water. There was an enormous portion of beveca lying invitingly in the bowl. The anxious eyes of the old couple, the thought of poor old Ayah and others going to bed without food, and the combined smell of hot curry and beveca, finally unshackled her determination to starve herself to death.

Despite her unhappiness, the beveca with sliced almonds in coconut cream and rice went down speedily and she even laughed to hear the Dog Lady's account of her Baskerville Regiment and the attempted burglary at her bungalow.

"The badmash poacher was prowling around the henhouse. What do you suppose little Taffy, my Sealyham did? He was dozing on the verandah when the little tyke heard some rustling behind the henhouse. He tiptoes to the front door and begins to whimper. Tipu is napping inside not far from the door. He is, as you know, the sleepiest Great

Dane in the Empire, but the others take their dressing from him. They surround the henhouse, the poacher can't make a run for it, and he is outflanked. Caught red-handed with two of my best leghorns."

Grace had missed lunch altogether and now, heavy with food and exhausted with crying, she fell asleep.

Next morning Mother Colombier stopped her outside the Chapel at St. Mary's.

"Only the selfish cry when their loved ones go away," she said in a faraway voice. "You mustn't forget that Bobby's future happiness depends on your sacrifice."

A sad smile touched her luminous dark eyes as she spoke.

"I, too, have a brother back in Corsica whom I have not seen these past twenty years. He was just four when I took the vows." Then she looked around and whispered, "I shouldn't be talking to you like this. We all have someone who has gone away. What counts most is that they be happy. Remember what Keats says,

'being too happy in thine happiness' is my lot."

It was around that time when Amanda was away in England that Grace unconsciously slipped into the role of surrogate mother to Baby Jo Anna. For a couple of days the little girl seemed as playful as ever. Amanda used to leave her with Ayah for up to a week and go away to Bombay for shopping. But the combined absence of Amanda, Bobby and the Major, which had merely puzzled the little girl at first, slowly turned into persistent questioning as to when they were coming back. Four days later when the Major returned alone from Bombay, Jo Anna became frantic and then a mild reproof from Ayah unleashed a flood of tears.

She sobbed so forlornly that Grace forgot her own sadness and began to hug and kiss her, reassuring her that Mater and Bobby would be back very soon. Then she sang and played *Alouette* and *Frere Jacques* and suitably altering her voice read Jo Anna's favourite section from *The Wind in the Willows* where the gaoler's daughter is cross with Toad for refusing to escape from the castle disguised as her poor aunt, the washerwoman.

"But have it your own way. You horrid, proud, ungrateful animal, when I am sorry for you, and trying to help you!"

"Yes, yes, that's all right, thank you very much indeed," said the Toad hurriedly. *"But look here! you wouldn't surely have Mr. Toad, of Toad Hall, going about the country, disguised as a washerwoman!"*

A few weeks later a picture postcard arrived from Naples. There was a one-line message saying that they were to disembark at Genoa and catch a train for Paris from Milan. Bobby didn't sound as though he missed her much. Still, Grace was very happy to receive the card and carried it to school to show it to Shirin. She was stunned to hear that Shirin had received one, too. To make matters worse, Shirin's card was full of interesting details. Mater was seasick once, and Scylla and Charybdis were not just a figure of speech. Bobby had also added that Mater was the most popular lady on board the ship, and that she allowed him to stay up till midnight to watch people dance and take part in games.

"Dear, sweet Bobby, oh how I miss him," Shirin added sighing dramatically.

Grace was terribly cut up. How could Bobby do that? After all he was her brother and not that hoity toity Parsi brat's. But, within two days, she was at her desk, writing a long loving letter to him full of sisterly advice, reminding him to wear his scarf all the time when going out. In a postscript she added that Ayah and Baby Jo Anna had cried for two days after his departure, but said nothing about starving herself.

iii

THE CUMAEN SYBIL

Every night the bedroom floor thrums to the rumble of trains. Occasionally there is the drawn-out hoot of an old-fashioned choo-choo engine frantically puffing away in the shunting yard. Mhow is also a railway town; toots and clanger of rolling stock mingle with the horns of lorries. When the Cantonment sleeps, the railways come alive.

Chinnery's was a pleasant shock to Camilla. Not exactly a Chatsworth, but certainly like something out of *Gone With The Wind* with its white facade, columns and tall French windows. Even in its present dereliction its scale was impressive. She feels a sudden surge of pride; it's part of her heritage.

For some reason her mother, who had spent more than half her lifetime yearning to see her old home again, had rushed through it like an intruder looking for hidden family doubloons before bolting. But when accosted by those childbearing women, she'd been magically transformed into a stately public figure. Calling her "Memsahib," the women had surged forward and fitted themselves around her like colourful shards of a shattered vase, recomposing in an instant replay.

One by one Grace had carried the babies to the window to look at them in better light. Camilla had just stood there with the doctor, fascinated by her august manner.

"What was all that about?" Camilla asked later.

"Oh, they thought I was some sort of doctor."

"I had no idea you could speak the lingo."

"Well, it all came back. Most of it. Poor women. Some of them are on their fifth baby and weak as kittens."

127

"What did you say to them?"

"First I told them that I was not a doctor."

"Then why did the others keep calling you?"

"Because they didn't believe it and didn't want to be left out. I said they must get operated to avoid unwanted pregnancies."

"Do you think they would do that?"

"Some of them might, the ones from the towns. The rural girls are at the mercy of their men. They want children to help with farm work. The same old story. At least that hasn't changed," Grace said with a rueful smile.

With that grovelling fat woman, Olinda, Grace had been unnecessarily brusque. First Camilla thought her mother's usual phobia about Anglos had triggered her agitation. But there was also some kind of raw fear in her eyes. She had bustled Camilla away from the hospital as though she were afraid of catching a viral infection.

Yasmin and her mother are two of a kind. There's something Roman matronish about both old friends, although Grace gets tongue-tied with the nuns. Yasmin loves all the attention she gets from the fawning sisters. There she sits fielding their questions like the Cumaen Sibyl.

Even the occasional profanity let off by her eccentric, foul-mouthed parrot does not undermine her authority. Camilla can see why Yasmin is so reluctant to give up her villa. If she went to live in Bombay filled with street-smart little Shivas and hustlers of every kind, she would be like fish out of water. The Debu family elephant has long since padded away, and disappeared in the silence of the forest, but Shiphidol is still like a jewel-encrusted howdah from where Yasmin can view her wasted and savoured world. Even today her elegant rituals, afternoon tea with toothy nuns, and badinage with the barmy parrot, help her beat those interminably cluntering clocks. Poor Grace doesn't have any such snug harbour in London, with doting retainers. It makes perfect sense that Grace whose early passage through life had been steered by the abiding protocols of a cantonment should feel rudderless anywhere else. As a casual but well informed Latinist with an avid interest in Roman archaeology, Camilla herself is not altogether impervious to its seductive geometry. Under its powerful towage she has already crossed the Rubicon so to speak.

Once again that scene replays itself in slow motion. Camilla sees Tehmi disappearing into the club to take a telephone call while she continues to dawdle in the pool. The water has turned cold with the sun setting behind the hills. Children who splashed around earlier have gone home.

Her breasts hefted by the borrowed swimsuit, Camilla feels exposed and cannot help blushing under Ross's intense gaze. The water has stopped churning after Noshir's departure with his wife. He is apt to swim in circles, like a shark closing in on its prey.

The receding light of day flickers on Ross's bronze back as he lances the water in a straight tapering dive. Then he glides underwater like a dolphin. Somehow Camilla finds herself at the tip of the springboard, careening dangerously, but Ross holds her protectively. She feels coddled by this big laconic man. She is airborne and sinks with a splash. His power filling her completely, they come up together, legs paddling in unison. She is no longer conscious of the fat around her waist.

Water drips down their sodden bodies and the two of them are like figures gliding across a rain-splattered glass. They gather their clothes, and the next moment they are at the bottom of the staircase heading for his room at the Guest House. Everybody is at dinner.

In the green tiled bathroom the large antique tub is inviting like a lagoon dappled with soft vegetation.

During their flight from Bombay Camilla had feared that the novelty of being in her place of birth would be short-lived and soon she would start yearning for London, miss the party talk, the new Stoppard or Hare, the latest fare at the Royal Opera House. But here in Mhow she no longer feels ripped from her natural habitat. A bronze hand from Schliemann's seventh layer reaches out and pulls her into its buried music.

iv

HUNGRY CHARLEY'S

When Amanda returned from England she was astounded to learn that during her three month absence, Chinnery's had grown a prosthetic limb in the form of Hungry Charley's, the new cafeteria at the crossroads of Simrole Road and Main Street. In the past, the Major had often regretted the lack of a decent eating place for the Tommies. They frequented cheap unhygienic restaurants on Station Road along with men from Indian regiments. Their salaries, after mess charges and fines, had to be supplemented with continuous high interest loans from the banias on Main Street. Recalling his own plight as a young subaltern, the Major had always wanted to provide the men of British regiments in Mhow with a clean place where they could have good wholesome fare, just your regular steak and kidney, but a real man-size meal.

It so happened that the old Bohra family, who owned a spacious hardware store, suddenly migrated to South Africa. The place, along with living quarters upstairs, was going for a song. The Major leased it and got it fitted with a counter, a huge icebox, and some hardy furniture. Initially, food was carried there hot from Chinnery's, and the Major made it a point to supervise the day-to-day business. It opened everyday at three in the afternoon and closed around nine at night. One evening, roughly two months before Amanda's return, when the Major was back at Chinnery's for dinner, leaving Ayah Fernandez's son Eustace in charge, a woman walked in with a soldier.

The Tommies were always very deferential to the Major and some of them often assisted Eustace, carrying their orders to their own tables. But that night things apparently got a bit out of hand, and a fistfight erupted involving men from different regiments. Each man's mates were about to jump into the fray when Mabel Figgis, the young woman, shamed them into a peaceful settlement.

First they heard an ear-piercing whistle, followed by the sound of a chair crashing to the floor. Everyone turned around to see Mabel standing on a table, eyes blazing, nostrils flaring and her round face livid with anger, her voice dripping with contempt.

"Go on, fight, tear off yer cobblers, yer rotters. Yer think the good Major will open the place t'morrow. This ain't some rub-adub-dub. A fine lot y'are. Lettin' down Blighty like this. Makin' a laughing stock of yerselves in front of the wogs. 'Ere, wot d'they call you lad?" she asked Eustace.

"Eustace, Miss."

"Right y'are Eustace, go and fetch the police. The Major's someone to be reckoned with in this town. A word from 'im to the Colonel and it'll be the bloody pack drill fer yer."

She made the men shake hands and then helped Eustace serve food and drinks for the rest of the evening. The alcoholic drink Hungry Charley's offered was Murrey's Beer, but no one was allowed more than three pints. Next afternoon the Major, who had received the news of the squabble from Eustace, went over to Hungry Charley's. Mabel was singing

Jolly good luck to the girl who loves a soldier
Girl, have you been wed
You know we military men
Always do our duty everywhere . . .

Some of the men were singing along with her, the rest joined in the chorus. The Major waited outside till they finished. There were shouts and applause and voices demanding "More!" "More!" As soon as the Major stepped in, their faces went blank. Mabel was standing behind the counter along with Eustace as though she owned the place.

With bottle-green eyes set in a face tanned to almost chocolate brown, and straggly yellow hair with more than a suggestion of peroxide, it was very difficult to tell whether she was pure British or Eurasian until she opened her mouth. It was obvious that, though her skin had been dyed in some far-flung tropical corner of the Empire, she was born within the sound of Bow Bells.

On seeing the Major, she came smartly to attention, threw him a salute and turning to Eustace said,

"You take the orders, lad, and put some jeldi in it."

Before the Major could say anything, she came forward, pulled out a chair for him to sit at an empty table, and stood before him with hands folded over her apron. Then, without much ado she said,

"Major Sir, I needs a job. I ain't starving but reg'ler work'll keep me outer mischief, if yer see wha' I mean. No' asking much. Leftovers and fifty rupees a month will do nicely, thank yer."

Still somewhat bewildered, the Major looked around. The soldiers' eyes seemed to plead. He did some quick thinking. The place could certainly use someone like her if she were not dressed the way she was, all bulges and dips. Give Mhow something to think about. He pictured the horror on the face of the Colonel's Lady and chuckled. Mabel knew half the battle was won, so she pressed on.

"Ye won't regret it Major, no Sir, and the Lord will bless yer." Then suddenly, looking over her shoulder at a group somewhat boisterously playing cards in a far corner, she snapped, "Shut yer glass case ducky, this ain't some bloomin' boozer. Ye better behave or sod off." Then turning to the Major and dropping a curtsy, she hurriedly added, "Beggin' yer pardon, Sir."

The laughter was suddenly cut off. The only sound was the kettle boiling. She certainly exerted some sort of power over the Tommies. It was either that or they so wanted the Major to give her a chance, that they snapped into orderly postures.

"Can you furnish some references? Do you know anybody here in Mhow who can vouch for you?" the Major asked.

"I knows no one but owld' Pete 'Atchley over there looking like butter won't melt 'n 'is mouth. Besides 'im, I knows nobody 'ere. I knows Pete from Rangoon. Me 'usband Lenny worked on a ferryboat, Rangoon to Chittagong. 'E was drowned at sea. No references save a poor countrywoman from owld Blighty, the same as yer. I ain't got the bees to pay me rent at the Retirin' Room. But I can cook. Nothin' fancy. Kate and sidney and pork pie."

The Major saw no reason to dismiss her request out of hand. If Mabel could cook the snacks here, it would not only spare him the headache of transporting the food, but also provide much needed respite to the d'Quodroses. They were both getting on in years. Besides, the woman certainly seemed to be in command here. "Able Mabel," the old cliché flashed across his mind and he immediately turned red with embarrassment. He got up and stared out at the street. Employees from the Bank of India across the road were filing out. He decided to put her on probation for a month to see how she managed. If she could run the place without an incident for a year, he would recover his investment, wouldn't have to interrupt his nap and drag himself here every afternoon. Besides, the presence of even a retired Major in their midst made the Tommies self-conscious.

Save for one or two Christians in the Indian ranks who dropped in occasionally, the place was almost completely White. Hindu and Muslim soldiers recoiled in horror from the staple of steak and pork pie. Because of the tradition of early marriages, a large number of Indian soldiers were able to have home-cooked meals. The Tommies, on the other hand, were not encouraged to marry. Most couldn't afford to, and the fishing fleeters were generally middle-class suburbanites trying to nail a young lieutenant or captain. Interracial marriages were officially frowned upon and a vast number of men were soon stricken with the clap from frequent forays into the Red Light District. While Mabel couldn't satisfy all their needs, her saucy ways and racy argot proved a powerful attraction, and the cafeteria got off to a flying start. By the time Amanda returned from England, two months after its opening, Hungry Charley's had already become a familiar landmark in Mhow.

It was on the train from Khandwa that Amanda heard about the cafeteria. Mr. Spenser of Ansar, Harford & Company, the sole distributors in India of Dr. D. E. Jongh's Light-Brown Cod Liver Oil, had been visiting the Cantonment at Jhansi. He was planning to stop over at Mhow before heading for Bombay. He had been in Mhow the month before, when the town was just waking up to the presence of the "jolly little café" as he put it, with its "smashing waitress." The Major's letters had been totally devoid of any reference to such a momentous addition to Chinnery's. As soon as the Silver Ghost pulled out of the station yard, Amanda asked rather peevishly, why the Major had rushed into this new venture without waiting for her to return.

"But Mandy, my dear," he said, "had I thought you'd object to us making a little lolly on the side to supplement our income, I wouldn't have dreamed of taking on more responsibility. After you left, Munshi told me that all our savings were practically gone. Your trip and Bobby's school and living expenses could not be provided for from our present income. Salim Ali packed off to Durban. Opportunity knocked and so on. Seemed like a good idea. You know I always wanted a place like that. Going great guns, too. Why, it practically runs itself. You must go and see for yourself."

Amanda looked at him sideways and said, " And where did you find this baggage, this Figgis woman?"

"I didn't find her. She found me, I mean us. In any case she's not a baggage. Far from it. A very capable gal. Bit of a rough diamond, I admit. But she has a good head fixed on her shoulders."

"And a bit of a body too, from what I hear."

"Now, now Mandy. That's droll. Shouldn't jump to conclusions. Wait till you see her. Just what the doctor ordered actually – for the place, I mean," the Major added hurriedly.

"We shall see," Amanda said, "we shall see."

Amanda wasted no time. That very day, following a brief nap in the afternoon, she asked for the Ghost and precisely at five o'clock, a peak hour when Hungry Charley's was chock-full with men of every size and shape who had "taken the shilling" so to speak, the Ghost purred to a halt outside. Call it a woman's instinct, Mabel was ready for her. In reality Mahamud who had been privy to the morning's exchange between the Major and Memsahib, after depositing them at the Hotel, had gone straight to Plowden Road to haul Eustace from bed and dispatch him to Hungry Charley's to alert Mabel, who now lived and cooked upstairs. She had to vacate the Retiring Room at the Railway Station because regulations did not permit a stay of more than a few days. As the Major's driver, Mahamud commanded considerable respect around Mhow, and was always received warmly at Hungry Charley's where, in deference to his religion, a specially prepared chicken sandwich was served to him instead of the popular pork pie. Before turning into Main Street from Simrole, he merrily tooted the horn, although there was no obstruction of any kind on the road. Mabel's alert ears caught the sound; her wolf whistle cut through the air and every man jack dropped his voice to a whisper. Eustace, dapper in his Sunday best, opened the door and in sailed Amanda.

The place was quiet like an empty church. Mabel, who appeared to be busy behind the counter, turned around, eyes widening in surprise. Then, as the men slowly got to their feet, she hurriedly stepped forward, wiping her hands on the white serving apron. In a cream-coloured ankle-length dress, her brown hair with the residual tinge of peroxide tucked firmly under a frilly white serving cap - which she had cajoled Mr. Fernandez to cut to her specifications that very morning - she was a picture of deferential housekeeper. Dropping a curtsy, she pulled out a chair for Amanda. As the men stood there smiling foolishly, the two women took each other's measure.

"Would Madam like a nice 'ot cup of tea. I've just put the kettle on," Mabel said.

"No thank you," Amanda said. "Don't mind me. Please go on with your game," she said to the men who were still standing at their tables. Amanda looked at the menu scribbled on the blackboard, corrected a spelling mistake or two, went and peered behind the counter, and then marched to the sideboard where lay an assortment of invitingly arranged pastries. Satisfied that the place was spotlessly clean, she turned around to face Mabel who stood demurely behind her, while Eustace attended the tables.

"Keep it up," Amanda said to her with a smile. Mabel's eyes sparkled. Amanda realised that at last she had met her match. Then turning to the men she added, "Enjoy yourselves." As she made for the door, Mabel was already there to open it with yet another curtsy, this time dropping almost to the ground.

AUCKLAND HOUSE

Mr. Munshi strongly advocated retrenchment of staff. Except for kitchen crew and bearers, there was not much work for the assistant malis and syces. The chokraboys, who ran minor errands, were a great drain on the kitchen since they consumed more food than the guests whom they vastly outnumbered. On an average, there were fewer than fifteen guests at Chinnery's on a given day. Only when a hunting party organised by Shikari, or the Polo Team from Jaipore, or members of the Railway Board from Ajmer were in town was there enough work for everybody.

But Amanda would have none of it, and even the Major was reluctant to let them go.

"We can't cashier them like that, old boy," he told poor bewildered Munshi. "It's not cricket."

The Major was far from fancying himself a local Roger de Coverley, but the lavish life style at Chinnery's had cast on him the hypnotic spell of a baronial portrait gallery.

The right thing to do, then, was to deny his own family some of the good things of life rather then snatch food away from poor hungry mouths. Accordingly, a moratorium was imposed on the purchase of new clothes and furniture for the household, and plans to send Grace to Simla were abandoned. She was numb with humiliation. The whole town had known for a while that she had been accepted at Auckland House. Shirin, who always had an upper hand in everything, had one more reason to feel superior. And Shirin's family were not even British.

Grace had been planning to reach Simla at the beginning

of the Michaelmas Term, and had received a nice letter from Miss Pearce, the Principal, welcoming her to Auckland House. Unlike St. Mary's with its forbidding wall and cloistered atmosphere, the girls' school in Simla was located in the old majestic residence of Lord Auckland who had been the Governor-General of India prior to the Sepoy Mutiny. The Countess, who had been a pupil there during "dear Miss Pratt's time," had talked about her days at school with a mixture of affection and awe. The assembly hall offered a view of deep gorges and valleys and from the dining room you could catch a glimpse of snowy Himalayan peaks. In vivid terms the Countess had also described the spread at the Vice-Regal Garden Party, the white silk dresses the girls wore and she had taught both Shirin and Grace how to curtsy to the Vicereine and Viceroy. The school magazine *Auktimus*, the old woman still received it, sketched a rosy picture of pony rides to Jacko, tea at Peliti's, and plays at The Gaiety. Through frequent mental flights, Grace had assembled for herself an exciting model of what her life in Simla was going to be.

Like honey oozing on its own out of a comb, the prospectus had offered Grace the ultimate treat, a profile of the concert pianist, Miss Gertrude Toussaint, Head of the Music Department at Auckland House. Miss Toussaint had won the gold medal at the Conservatoire of Music in Leipzig and she often performed as a soloist with the Viceroy's orchestra. It was a great privilege to study under Miss Toussaint but the pupils accepted by her had to pay extra tuition, considerably raising the total cost of education at an institution where no more than fifty pupils were in residence at a time.

The night the doors of Auckland House clanked shut in her face, Grace dreamt that she was all alone in the scorched churchyard of the Old Cemetery where her piano lay on its base, cringing like an empty coffin, its severed legs and wrenched-off lid scattered by its side and, as she watched helplessly, one by one, with soundless flaps of wings the black and white keys rose in the air and flew away like myna birds in the blinding afternoon haze.

V

i

THE DOLL'S HOUSE

The new urban middle-class of India shops for ethnic chic at the Princess's Emporium, which offers some exquisite patterns for curtains as well as bedspreads for Ross. Camilla shares Tehmi's passion for textiles, and when in London often wears clothes designed by her friend Penny, who disassembles antique cloths from Mexico and Guatemala to refashion them as elegant and wearable European dresses. At the Emporium, Camilla picks up enough pieces to fill two thick books of fabric swatches for Penny.

Tehmi also likes to explore the heart of old Indore in her quest for block-printed fabrics in turmeric yellow with a fetching weft of oleander red or peacock blue, woven by local artisans whose primitive hand-operated loom seems to foster a uniquely decorative imagination.

On their way into the old city, they pass through the new Indore, rising like a snarling, digitised nightmare, piling stinking garbage at a furious space alongside architectural designs of astonishing vulgarity, erected no doubt by Noshir's pals in the building racket. Crouching under high-rise structures are tin hovels, covered in grime-laden sheets of yellow or blue plastic, children squatting or playing by slimy green water from broken drainpipes.

Camilla holds her tongue for fear of offending Tehmi, who at one point says in a tone, in which sarcasm jostles with local pride, that Indore has the distinction of being one of the most polluted cities in India.

Jo Anna was born just a couple of miles from here in the British Hospital in the Residency Area, in those days on the outskirts of Indore which leaned more towards the symmetry of Mhow than this medieval bazaar.

Shooing off mangy dogs, Camilla ascends the steps to a shop where hang in overpowering profusion, colourful garments of every imaginable size. She still winces at the word Memsahib, with which beggars and shopkeepers greet her on the street. The word conjures up an image of a large, stertorous woman lounging in a bungalow, being fanned by a lackadaisical punkhawala in an oversized turban.

Camilla picks up three 'batwas' for friends in London. The handloom cloth of these folk handbags feels like velvet and is covered with embroidered creepers and tiny blossoms in bright reds, yellows, and greens.

Coming down the steps of the shop they run smack into Olinda.

After spotting the car the nurse had been hovering around it in the hope of wangling a lift back to Mhow.

"I said to myself, if that isn't our Debu Memsahib's Fiat from Mhow, I am Tipu Sultan," Olinda says. "I came by train to buy readymade clothes for my grandson. Next Sunday is his birthday, no? You can't find such variety in our Mhow and they charge you twice as much there."

"Would you like a lift back to Mhow, Mrs. Lobo?" Tehmi asks without much enthusiasm.

"Oh, Madam, I'd be honoured to travel with two such great ladies. But only if it's convenient."

Olinda cheerfully squeezes herself and her parcels in the passenger seat in the front. She may be loquacious but she knows her place. Fortunately, the rumble of traffic outside drowns Olinda's voice.

During her first trip to Mhow in Noshir's Jeep, Camilla had barely noticed the Ruhr Valley atmosphere of the world outside, smoke billowing for miles into the sky from sooty stacks, makeshift roadside garages and tea-stalls for stranded lorries and their murderous drivers. No one speaks till they are on Bakery Road in Mhow dropping off Olinda. Camilla and Tehmi are unable to put up any resistance against Olinda's most insistent plea to step in and have some tea.

That short visit turns out to be most memorable for Camilla. Right in front of her, in a cabinet with its front glass missing, is the most charming English doll's house she has ever seen.

Apparently it was a parting gift to Olinda from Amanda Chinnery. Camilla would have never known of its existence had she not been highjacked by the nurse that afternoon.

"It belonged to Jo Baba. Of all the Chinnerys," says Olinda, "Jo Baba was my favourite and when she died, my grandparents, the d'Quodros's mourned as though they had lost their own daughter. She was so beautiful and yet always smiling and smiling, but God took her away."

The costumes Jo Anna had made for the dolls are slightly crumpled.

"In those days typhoid was quite fatal wasn't it?" Camilla says. "But I understand now it can be easily brought under control, with penicillin."

"Typhoid?" Olinda says, uncomprehendingly.

"Yes, wasn't it typhoid that killed my aunt?"

A surreptitious look creeps into Olinda's eyes.

"Yes, yes, now I remember, yes it was typhoid," she adds quickly. Then she gets up and tries switching the tiny bulb in the doll's kitchen. But it has fused.

"I'll ask my son, Manuel, to get a new bulb," Olinda says.

On an impulse, Camilla offers to buy the doll's house, but Olinda declines the money.

"Just send me some cheddar from home when you go back," she says. " We can't get good cheese here now. My grandmother always used to bring me some Kraft cheese from the Hotel kitchen. She never allowed me to touch Jo Baba's doll's house when I was a child. I have onlee grandsons and they play cricket all the time. You can send some good English chocolate for them. The boys think onlee of going to America, but I am still loyal to England. It's still my home," she adds fervently.

Camilla notices how Tehmi's aquiline nose crinkles, but there's no bite in her tone when she asks,

"Where is home, which part of England do you call home?"

Olinda hesitates. Her earlier glibness is replaced by a cautious tone. Camilla realises that the poor woman probably gets away with outlandish claims when bragging about English forbears to her fellow nurses at the Hospital. Speaking haltingly Olinda says,

"My father once told me when I was a child but I have forgotten the name of the place. My great-grandfather, Mr. Cornelius Gilbert, came out as a boy and worked his way up in Northern Railways. Here's his picture when he was a young gentleman in England."

Olinda goes to the chest of drawers and brings back a faded old photograph with smudge-marks in what used to be called daguerreotype. There is a dim image of a lanky lad self-consciously smiling at the camera. Two front teeth appear to be missing. The inscription at the back says 'Duddington, Northamptonshire, where the girls are plump and the ale is brown.'

"At the time of retirement he was Foreman of Bareilly Loco Shed," Olinda says. "He married a hill woman from Kumaon. Hill women are much fairer than most Indians."

Before Tehmi could unleash a sceptical rejoinder Camilla cuts her off and says in a friendly tone,

"How wonderful. I really envy you your dual heritage. You are a citizen of the world."

"That I am Madam, that I am. And I am not ashamed of it either. Very few of us left in Mhow now. Others have all gone abroad, some to England some to Canada. There are only two or three other Anglo families here. They live in the Railway Colony. There's Colonel Ross of course. He's a very important man and I'd like to meet him sometime. My dad knew his granddad very well."

Tehmi is unable to let that pass.

"But how can that be," she says. "Why, my Noshir was at school in Darjeeling with Colonel Harrison. We know he is from Calcutta."

"His dad went to Calcutta during the War and never came back. I was away in Ajmer where my dad was stationed, but I used to come here during Christmas and remember seeing him. I am sure Colonel Ross takes after him; he was also very handsome. But he was originally from here. My Aunt Gwen who lives in Ratlam told me just last week. Our whole community is very proud of Colonel Harrison. But his granddad Mr. Busby was quite poor and worked in the Loco Shed here when my dad was station master at Mhow."

The doll's house is conveyed to Shiphidol in an open cart, because it doesn't fit into Tehmi's car. They drive very slowly. Though properly secured with a rope the doll's house wobbles dangerously. Yasmin recognises it immediately and instructs the Mali and his son to place it on a marble-top table in the hall.

"I always wondered what happened to it," Grace's voice seems to come from afar.

"She said your mother, Mrs. Chinnery, presented it to her, before you left for England," Tehmi says wetting a mop to get the dust off the tiny glass windows. Then turning to Yasmin she adds, "By the way, she also told us that Ross's father lived here before he moved to Calcutta. I wonder if you knew him Auntie? Probably not. They were obviously quite poor."

"Who?" Yasmin says, her eyes darting wildly with excitement. "What was his name."

"She didn't tell us," Camilla says, scrubbing a windowpane of what looks like the kitchen section of the dolls' house, "I'll ask when I see her again."

"Oh, she did say Ross's grandfather worked in the Loco Shed here?" Tehmi asks.

"The Loco Shed?" the panic in Grace's voice is unmistakable.

She looks as though she is about to faint. Camilla notices that all colour has drained out of her mother's face. Grace staggers to the nearest sofa and slumps in it. Her chest heaves and a whistling sound punctuates her breathing.

Camilla and Tehmi together half carry her to her room.

"I'd like to rest a while," Grace says, turning her back to them.

Tehmi looks at Camilla who gestures her to leave her alone with her mother.

As soon as the door closes behind Tehmi, Grace flips around, springs up and grabbing Camilla with both hands asks,

"What else, what else did she say? "

"Who?"

"That filthy half-caste hussy, who else do you think?" Grace is almost shrieking.

"Mum, keep your voice down for God's sake. What's got into you? What does it matter what she said or didn't say. And stop abusing people you know nothing about."

A wild gurgle in Grace's throat explodes into a hysterical giggle.

"You think I know nothing about that horrible chi chi baggage who calls herself Olinda. Why, I've known her," here she pauses to let off another giggle; "I've known her practically from the time she was conceived."

"So what," Camilla says. " She told you that herself at the hospital."

"Oh, that," Grace says getting up and feebly waving off Camilla's objection as her hiccuping tapers into sobs. "I don't mean that darling but never mind. Listen dear," she says taking Camilla by her hand. "We must get out of here. Let's go back to England, right away - tomorrow if possible. I am sorry I dragged you away from your work. Not fair, not fair at all. You have your career to consider."

"You listen to me Mum, calm down a bit. Tell me what's all this about. Has the doll's house upset you? We'll just return it to Olinda. End of problem. How can we go back before the new gravestone is in place? What will the Debus think after all they have done for us? You lie down now. Take a nap. I'll come and wake you up at seven. The guests will start arriving at 7-30."

"Guests, what guests?" Grace cries, covering her face with trembling hands.

"The dinner, Mum, have you forgotten? The General and his family are coming."

"And who else?"

"Ross and his daughter. I am so looking forward to meeting her at last."

"I cannot see anyone tonight," Grace's voice has dropped to a barely audible whisper. "Not tonight. We must take stock of this situation. Tomorrow perhaps or the day after but certainly not tonight."

"What situation? What are you on about? Don't tell me now. We'll discuss it later when you are yourself again. Take this pill and lie down for a few minutes," Camilla says, giving her a glass of water.

Back in the hall the doll's house seems to have regained its original lustre under Tehmi's ministrations. Yasmin wheels around the table, pointing out grimy spots on the miniature house that have escaped Tehmi's scrutiny.

The interior is illuminated and Camilla can see tiny gold-framed photographs on the walls of its parlour and fringed furniture on patterned carpets. The dolls sitting primly on a miniature settee wear high-waisted empire gowns developing into bell-shaped crinolines, capes, and poke-bonnets. Two gentlemen sit smoking by the fireplace. They sit awkwardly like people suffering from a stiff neck.

The kitchen, with little pots and pans and cutlery, tea service and silver comfit dishes, is cute, but Camilla is impressed by the minute attention to detail Jo Anna lavished on the beadwork and tassels. The bedroom has a petticoated dressing table and well-draped bed. Camilla is both captivated and moved by the near perfection with which Jo Anna had scaled down the adult world to fit her doll's house.

Replicas of old monuments always look tacky. But within this Lilliputian house there is a sense of life going on in a different time, of a world being remade behind a child's quivering lids as she sleeps, clinging to her sick doll. Camilla cannot take her eyes off that bright scene. She runs her fingers over the dresses the girl Jo Anna had made, touching each miniscule button sewn on the jackets of the stiff-necked gentlemen.

Those tiny figures have memories to which Camilla has no access, but they link her to her lost mother the way the photograph at home in Clapham never could. How beautiful it must have looked then. Camilla imagines Jo Anna's face glowing with pride after the dolls had been dressed. She must have shared her secrets with them. This tiny space is Jo Anna's unrealised future where the old daughter and young mother meet now as equals.

In normal circumstances the doll's house should have come to Camilla very early in life. It was the daughter's legacy. She feels grateful to that strange woman, Olinda, who living in that cluttered house, burning aromatic joss-sticks under a kitsch picture of Christ with blood-dripping heart, had somehow managed to preserve her mother's handiwork.

THE TRANQUILITY OF SYCAMORES

Belt tightening at Mr. Munshi's urging caused only minor discomfort to the guests. With the crunching of the gharry wheel on the gravel in the driveway your eyes snapped open, and there it was, a blue-white silhouette under a moonless sky. Registration could wait until after you'd had your forty winks, and your aching bones were kneaded into shape by the "malishwala" as the Hotel masseur was called. He began the massage by pouring a huge amount of cool coconut oil on the head, rubbing sandalwood paste on the body, then kneading it from head to toe in a prolonged pampering till you felt cosseted. A hot bath after that relaxed you for a post-breakfast siesta from which you were awakened by the gentle tinkling of a bell. It was the hotel khansamah, Abbasbeg, announcing lunch.

The khansamah himself poured for you iced East India Pale Ale and served tapioca pudding. The more venturesome played tennis or cricket for three hours till another bell summoned them to afternoon tea consisting of tirhoot or fruit cake, mince rolls or sandwiches, consumed under the canopy of two ancient banyans.

The d'Quodros's, who were in charge of the kitchen, would bring out a freshly made kul kul or mass plow pastry so the guests would know to whom they were really beholden for the fare. The regulars, who were aware of the rivalry between the khansamah and the cooks, discreetly complimented the latter without undermining Abbasbeg's formal role as chief dispenser of hospitality at Chinnery's.

Sometimes Grace would be awakened by the sound of gharry wheels crunching the gravel and see strong powdery shafts of moonlight making a misty downward passage into the room. She would close the mosquito net, carefully tucking its corners under the mattress, and stand by the window looking at the moon hanging like a lantern over the grey-stone hulk of the Church in the Old Cemetery rising in the distance, its tall roof picked out by the light. It seemed to coggle and bob like a ghost ship. In the cool night air the garden below Grace's balcony was full of tiny reassuring noises: crickets trilling in the foliage, tintinnabulation of a splintering glass fading distantly, the butt-end of a chokraboy's biddie glowing behind a fuchsia shrub. Sometimes after a late night party at Chinnery's there would be a scuffling sound as two silhouettes emerged from the porch. It was always Auntie Maude fumbling to get into their gharry, followed by a husbandly mock reproof,

"Come my girl, don't be naughty, come with Daddy."

Grace would tiptoe out of her room to the balcony over the porch to hear giggling Auntie Maude being pulled into the buggy by Dr. Aspel.

Later in her room, Grace would hear the tap, tap of Constable Haibat Khan's staff hitting the ground like the stick of the blind man Pew approaching the Admiral Benbow. In the shunting yard an engine would go puff, puffing before coming to a screeching halt.

Except for Shirin, who looked unconvinced and shrugged her elegant shoulders when told why Grace could not go to Simla, the face of Mhow betrayed no mockery. The syce saddling her pony looked at her in mute sympathy, Mrs. d'Quodros waddled into the dining hall to serve her the biggest prawn specially saved for her, old Khansahib sighed ruefully and said "Inshallah" several times while pumping air into her bicycle and women sweepers cracked knuckles on their temples to ward off the evil spirit afflicting Missy Baba.

Hulme persuaded the Collector's wife, who was from Switzerland, to teach Grace how to read music. The Burra Mem was a mezzo-soprano and every Sunday Grace cycled down to the Collector's bungalow to accompany her on the grand piano. Mrs. Jenkins sang some of the most haunting melodies from Schubert and Brahms. The Burra Mem was quite patient when Miss Chinnery muffed a key. Grace couldn't pronounce the titles of songs the Burra Mem sang with great passion, eyes closed. But after a while, she was able to spot the close affinity between German and English. Playing the piano at home sometimes Grace would close her eyes and sing:

Was lispeln die Winde, die Vogelein?

Sie lispel die welt in Schlummer ein

from one of Brahms' *Zwei Gesange* in fair imitation of the Burra Mem, just to hear Jo Anna burst into childish giggles. Despite her exalted social status, Mrs. Jenkins was really quite sprightly. She gave a fine rendering in her full-throated mezzo, but was often cross with herself when she failed to hit the high note.

At night alone in her room, Grace would stand in front of the mirror, dramatically clutch her shoulders and, like the Burra Mem, whisper with a deep sigh,

"Musik, Musik ist mein Leben."

iii

THE FISHING FLEET

Jo Anna, Carl and Yasmin were inseparable. As Bobby's friend, Carl had always been warmly received by the Chinnerys. Only Grace continued to chafe at the affection lavished on the little Anglo boy. "The way Mater fusses over that imp," Grace wrote to Bobby, "you'd think he was the Prince of Wales." At sixteen Grace had no need for another brother. Her devotion to Bobby had grown even stronger during the past five years since he had been away. Now it was tinged with pride at the news of his success, especially in sports. During the previous Easter Term, Bobby had been invited to play for the First XI and at the start of Michaelmas Term in autumn, he'd won his cap.

Grace could also get very agitated on the Polo Ground shouting "Ride, ride," when Lieutenant Ponsonby missed a shot and his pony started to wheel and run as if chasing the ball that should have been hit. She had developed a secret passion for that young officer of the 76th Lancers (AKA "The Witchdoctors" because during the siege of Quebec they had treated their wounds with wild herbs provided by their Red Indian guides), recently transferred to Mhow. Dancing with him at the Club she discovered that Adrian Ponsonby had been at Marlborough. So vividly did he describe the Assembly Hall, Chapel, Court, the Bradleian Library, the Gymnasium, Salisbury Plain, Tudor villages nestling by the Wiltshire Downs, the Kennet valley, that she could picture Bobby and his classmates at leisure, roaming over the Spring, tobogganing down the slopes of Forest Hill in winter and devouring masses of scones at the Tea Club on Sundays. In Bobby's letters home, the names of two of his masters always popped up. It was something Mr. Robson or Mr. Harley said that seemed to matter the most. Adrian confirmed that they were two of the most popular teachers at Marlborough. Bobby was expected back for the holidays next Christmas, which made her happiness complete.

Adrian seemed to give a wide berth to the Fishing Fleeters who arrived in November. Most of them had names like Emmeline, Henrietta, Cecilia or Fiona, and they seemed to trill rather than speak.

Grace was thrilled when she entered the Mess with Adrian and uniformed officers got up to greet her in the anteroom before proceeding to the Dining Hall and, during the entire evening, not a single swear word was uttered. At first she was very nervous, but the structured jollity and well-mannered bonhomie of the Mess were designed to make the civilian feel indispensable to the evening's success. Each officer treated her as though she were his personal guest. Their wives, who were usually too busy playing rummy in the Card Room at the Club or gossiping in the Lounge to notice Grace, vied with each other to explain the customs and etiquette that made the Officers' Mess such a special place. When conversation turned to their sons and daughters in England, Grace could boast about Bobby's progress at Marlborough. When dinner ended, the Commanding Officer raised a toast to the Sovereign, and the band struck up "God save the King."

Shirin awed the fishing-fleeters. On her way back from Simla, she usually broke her journey to spend a few days with her cousins in Delhi and had her hair permed. On reaching Mhow, she lightly brushed her upward turning mouth with lipstick, giving it a sardonic cast. The fleeters watched her as if hypnotised. When their unfamiliarity with the bearers' patois made them drop a brick, Shirin, who would be listening with a slightly bored air got up with a fluid boneless movement saying, *"si jeunesse savait, si vieillesse pouvait."*

The language of the cantonment rank and file had

emerged in an attempt to find the right word for many intricate social levels that the imperial caste system had generated. The officer class, as well as the local gentry, could slip back and forth from county to pidgin with breathtaking ease, leaving the fleeters totally befuddled. It would take the fleeters years of effort to get their servants to work at full capacity.

Grace no longer felt any resentment for missing Simla and she watched Shirin play the fine lady with a mixture of pride and wistfulness. From her classmates at Auckland House, Shirin picked up all the latest international gossip concerning opera stars, theatre, as well as other social tattle. She knew which horse had finished first at Ascot and who was the new champion at Wimbledon.

A KING IN BABYLON

Withered hands covered in long sleeves, hair dyed coal black, face pink with rouge, Yasmin, looking like one of her celluloid bibelots, is wheeled into the dining room by Bhola. Her hooded eyes surveying the scene come to rest on Ross. If only she could see him alone for a few minutes! Maybe after dinner. She'd retire early and send Bhola to fetch Ross to her room under some pretext.

The General is nursing his chotta peg, but Ross and Noshir seem bent on finishing the bottle of Scotch. Esmé has grown another inch or two, the puppy fat has receded, bringing into relief her mother's high cheekbones. Outside, in the clear light of the soft winter moon, the trees and the lawn beneath them are covered with silver speckles. The regency chairs around the elegant table and the crystal chandelier give off a festive air.

The General in his evening suit and Sandra in an off-white chiffon sari exude a princely air. And Ross in a blue blazer, hair brushed backwards, looks as though he has stepped off the pages of *PhotoPlay Magazine*. Camilla, her auburn hair falling in soft waves around her shoulders, is a trifle self-conscious in a lavender sari Tehmi has helped her wrap around. But she looks stunning. Even Grace's beige satin gown and fleecy hair secured in a bun give her an air of distinction.

Tehmi has placed Camilla next to Ross. Yasmin knows what her nephew's wife is up to. Much to their chagrin, the Grehwal girls are seated across the table from him, and Yasmin smiles as she watches them squirm with envy. She has just caught the feral expression on Tejinder's face. The dinner has proceeded amidst Noshir's usual clowning, punctuated by giggly rejoinders from Jasbir and Esmé. Yasmin notices how Ross's eyes stray repeatedly to Camilla's fleshy bare arms. Her sleeveless blouse with its boat-shaped neckline stretches tautly across her bosom.

Ross's earlier stiffness is gone; his brooding Flying Dutchman gaze is touched with a lively smile. Yasmin notices how his eyes wander from Camilla's long smooth hands the dress is designed to showcase, to her shapely breasts. When talking, Camilla looks him full in the face. Who knows, she might prove to be just what the doctor ordered, a redeeming Senta.

Yasmin notices that Grace is peeved by the attention her daughter is bestowing on Ross. If she cannot stand the idea of her daughter getting chummy with an "Anglo-Banglo" all Yasmin can say is, 'Serve her right, serve her right with knobs on.'

Ross is at peace with himself. His little girl is there and she is growing into a beauty like her mother.

He is aware of the little bodily movements with which Tejinder is trying to draw his attention. After paying her a compliment on her blue silk sari, which makes her look very pretty and grown up, he pointedly engages Camilla in conversation. Over the past few weeks he has managed to foil Taji's attempts to speak to him alone. Even before reaching Mhow he had decided to make it clear to young Taji that as far as he was concerned, that night in Delhi was an unfortunate accident.

But as usual Camilla's proximity makes his blood froth to his fingertips and he is suddenly assailed by a perverse impulse to reach out to her. Something more than raw sexual energy is driving him, and even in his slightly tipsy state he knows that what he feels is not naked desire to possess her. It is more a howl from within, a constriction in the stomach. Her laughter washes over him like a cloudburst. She inhabits him like a twin.

Looking at them from across the table the bubbly Jasbir suddenly says, "You know, seeing you two together in this light is spooky. You look so alike."

"Yes, you are right," Tejinder says with a sly smile. "How very peculiar!"

Everyone stares at them. Camilla leans closer to Ross like a bride posing for a wedding photograph.

"I don't see much resemblance there," Grace cuts in abruptly.

There is such chill in her voice that the girls stop laughing.

"But then I am getting short-sighted," she adds, looking a little crestfallen.

Camilla laughs and playfully resting her head on Ross's shoulder says,

"Maybe in our previous incarnations I was the Rani and you were the Sultan, what's his name."

"Oh, you mean Sultan Bajbahadur?" Esmé cries out in delight, then begins to recite dreamily,

And ere the knightly years are gone,
With the Old World to the grave
When I was a King in Babylon
And you were a Christian slave.

"I'll drink to that," Noshir says, getting up to serve Golconda wine to his guests.

Scooping up a spoonful of ice cream Esmé looks at her father and says, "Daddy, remember the promise you made last year."

"What promise?"

"Why, he's forgotten already. You promised to take me on a shoot."

"I made no such promise."

"That's not fair. Ask Auntie. She was there," the girl says, appealing to Tehmi.

"Yes, you did Ross, there's no denying it," Tehmi says, enjoying the opportunity to tease him.

"Oo, what fun. Daddy, can we go with them?" Tejinder

asks her father without taking her eyes off Ross's face.

"Only if you promise to follow Ross's instructions. Watch from the machan and don't do anything stupid," the General says, looking at Ross.

"We'll see," Ross says staring at his plate. "There's only the blue bull these days. And it gets very messy, cutting it up. The servants won't touch it; the animal is sacred to them. You have to haul the carcass to the butcher's in Mhow and that's not much fun. What we need is a good-sized tiger for a proper shoot, and as you know, Sir," he says to the General, "there are all sorts of restrictions now. Only when a tiger turns man-eater are we allowed to kill. Not otherwise."

"I am afraid Ross is absolutely right," the General says to his daughter.

"Really? Why's that?" Grace asks suddenly. "I remember in the old days the forest around Manpore was packed with tigers. A friend of our family who sold Shikar kit on Main Street used to help the Maharaja organise hunting parties for the Viceroy."

"Precisely," Ross says. "Burra Sahibs like the Viceroy and his entourage wiped out practically the whole tiger population in this area. When the Burra Sahib wanted to be photographed with a dead tiger at his feet, the Maharaja had no choice but to . . ."

Before Ross can finish the sentence Grace snaps,

"I am sick and tired of hearing what harm the Burra Sahibs did to India. For forty years in England I have heard nothing from the so-called Liberals but how wicked the Burrasahibs were and how they trampled upon the natives. No one remembers all the good we did."

"The less said about it the better," Ross says getting up. His pale blue eyes are now ablaze. "I hope you'll excuse me, Sir," he says to the General. "Noshir's car is giving him some trouble. I must take a look at it."

It's all so sudden. Camilla wishes she hadn't tried so hard to get her mother to come to dinner that night.

Poor Yasmin is stupefied by Grace's outburst and the skin lolling under her chin billows and dwindles. Esmé stares at her father, her lips trembling. The Grehwal girls giggle nervously. Yasmin notices how the veins standing out on Ross's forehead are shaped like a catapult. As usual Tehmi takes charge of the situation and announces that they should retire to the sitting room for coffee.

Ross's daughter is like a tiny but intriguing image in an otherwise kitschy artwork. When he is around, she laughs freely and heartily; there is something eerie about their togetherness. With what maternal ado did she coax him to a second helping of ice cream? That curious combination of innocence and precocity in the girl is very captivating.

When Ross comes back from the garage with Noshir, Esmé giggles, pulls out her handkerchief, pushes him into a chair, and starts wiping off the spots of grime from his cheeks and hands. Then drawing back to inspect the result, she shakes her head in mock despair.

"Look at you, you naughty thing," she chides. "There's soot all over your blazer. Oh, what am I going to do with you?"

Ross pretends to be contrite like a child caught at some wrongdoing and submits himself to his daughter's scolding. It is a fetching sight. Camilla feels strangely drawn to this curious child and gives her a warm hug when she says goodbye. She also promises to attend the concert at St. Mary's where Grace is to be the chief guest the following week.

V

THE SHERLOCK HOLMES

Her mother's petulance at dinner that evening was so utterly uncharacteristic. Ordinarily Camilla would have put it down to Grace's usual beef against the Anglos, but this time she senses something more than racial prejudice behind that outburst, a resurfacing of some ancient grudge against Ross himself. Otherwise, how to explain such an extravagant display of temper in the presence of guests?

Anyway it isn't the first time her mother has been standoffish with a man in her life. Esmé is sheer joy, but other than that, why is Camilla so agitated over her mother's rudeness to Ross? Apart from good looks what else is there to make her go weak at the knees every time she sees him? His favourite films are *Bridge on The River Kwai* and *The Guns of Navarone*, mostly works that glorify warfare and killing. His whole life has been a battlefield strewn with corpses. To put it bluntly, Ross is a professional soldier who initiates others in the art of killing. At the Club he and his friends discuss strategic errors made by their colleagues against the Chinese in the Himalayas or in campaigns botched by General Haig in the Great War. They speak as though they were witness to Patton's unorthodox methods, which had cut a swathe through Hitler's Siegfried Line.

In England, except for brief flare-ups as during the Falklands war, patriotism has fallen into disuse like a cult that has lost its acolytes. But here in Mhow it is alluringly silver-tongued, especially when the usually reticent Ross breaks his silence and speaks movingly about the gallantry of his troops.

Camilla is getting involved with Ross in a way that is

entirely new to her. With Jeremy it was shared idealism, and Eddie, her second, had wooed her with expensive gifts.

Grace could manage to conceal her hauteur when speaking with Eddie but with Jeremy it would splutter like a flame going out. The poor boy was a sitting duck with his "make love, not war" brand of tender vulnerability and ineptitude. Camilla had come down from Oxford to take part in a rally at Trafalgar Square addressed by Bertrand Russell, and in the argy-bargy with the police following a stone-throwing incident, Jeremy and she had fled across Northumberland Avenue like a pair of long distance runners competing for a trophy. He had a cut in the face and, as the police whistles drew closer, they had ducked together into the *Sherlock Holmes*. There, after a few pints in the bar under the blazing eyes of the Hound of the Baskervilles, they had fallen in love.

Camilla had agreed to marry him on condition that he would sit the Civil Service Examination. Stoodgy had given her away at the wedding, but pleading a fierce attack of asthma, Grace had stayed home. Later Camilla had worked as a typist and scrounged, while Jeremy's idealism had died a slow death. Grace's attitude to Jeremy had become progressively more condescending, she made fun of the way he spoke, dressed, and mopped up the gravy from his plate with a piece of bread.

But even with Eddie, who had a degree in Business Management, Grace was only prissily polite. Camilla gradually came to understand that her mother's every gesture of studied politeness concealed inherited arrogance. She often wondered if Grace would have accepted Stoodgy for a husband had he not been the son of a Polish aristocrat.

When shopping for Grace, Eddie would insist on returning coins to the last penny, and would disappear for half an hour to get the right change. He refused to leave even the smallest amount unaccounted for. Grace made no attempt to hide her disdain for such pettifogging.

To the parents of Camilla's men, Grace was a snooty old

colonial bag, best left to stew in her own juice. What made them squirm was the way she tilted her head when listening to them, her perfunctory handshake, her slow drawl, which they took for insolence masquerading as politeness. Grace's inner self was barricaded behind a self-consuming narrative which remained largely opaque to Camilla's men, whose India connection was limited to singsong voices announcing trains in Peter Sellers parodies at Paddington. To them Grace was like a quaintly ornate craft that had been washed ashore.

In order to know where she had been fashioned, from which dry-docks of history launched, they not only needed tact but a willingness to let her past wash over them. But an eerie distance separated their middlebrow, scrimping, suburban world of darned socks and hand-me-downs, from Grace's make-believe England in India. The spectre of Chinnery's always hung in the air like an indictment of Camilla's marriages.

Only Alexis seemed to pass muster with her mother. Alexis had been at Eton and Oxford and he chatted merrily with Grace about polo and Gilbert & Sullivan in a way poor Jeremy or Eddie never could. He had a strange effect on Camilla's mother; his manner suggested the authority of someone born to rule and his self-deprecating wit gave him a sort of weary prince air. It was a caste thing after all, and Grace and Alexis got on like a house on fire.

vi

THE OLD BULL AND BUSH

Hungry Charley's had evolved into a genial little place where, in addition to the Tommies, some hard working boxwallahs flogging their wares on High Street, the likes of Maude Aspel, Anglo nurses from the Civil Hospital, and officers and their wives in town for a day began to drop in for a quick snack and afternoon tea. Also, what began as an occasional turn on his accordion by Eustace during a lull in business became the standard form of entertainment with Mabel's mettlesome rendering of old Music Hall staples,

Come, come, come and make eyes at me
Down at the old Bull & Bush,

she sang and the Tommies cheered, and when she belted out *"Take Me back To Dear Old Blighty,"* even the most self-conscious from the mofussil tapped their feet and joined in the chorus.

The place became a stamping ground for the offbeat, bohemian types looking for fun. Under Maude Aspel's tutelage, Mabel shed her fishwife persona, and Shikari, who caught sight of her several times from his store on Main Street, was completely smitten. A confirmed bachelor, he was used to taking his pleasure where he could find it, and was said to have fathered at least three of the several sandy-haired, light-eyed toddlers with complexions ranging from dark brown to fair, in the crowd of ragged urchins in the native bustee where the poor sweeper women lived. One day he took the Major aside and said,

"Roger, old sport, do you think Mabel could possibly do some cooking for me, my chotta hajeri and such? I dare say she could use some extra cash? I shall make it worth her while."

"I am sure of that," the Major replied with a smile, "but I don't think she'll have the time. Her hands are full in the morning getting the place ready for the afternoon."

Shikari was disappointed, but one day he talked Fred Thompson into accompanying him to Hungry Charley's.

"You should see her, Freddie, me lad. God, I don't half fancy her."

Fred Thompson was a top dog in the railway administration, and didn't relish the thought of being seen in an eatery like Hungry Charley's. It was one thing to get a young heifer like Josephine to drop her knickers, but women like Mabel were a different kettle of fish. However, his curiosity was piqued, so one afternoon before the Tommies arrived, Shikari and Thompson dashed into Hungry Charley's during a sudden downpour. Mabel and Eustace were setting the tables.

"Don't mind us," Shikari said to Mabel. "This here is Mr. Thompson. We were on our way to Dr. Aspel's surgery when it began to come down. Eustace, me boy," Shikari said to the young lad who stood open-mouthed to see Mr. Thompson in the cafeteria, "Go and fetch us a tonga, there's a good lad."

Always ready to please any friends of the Major's, Mabel whipped up a cup of tea, and while the tonga waited outside, Fred had an eyeful of her. His rabbity red eyes followed her every movement. Her long brown hair freshly washed and combed sideways, hung in loose waves beneath her cap, her smooth biscuit-brown arms stuck gracefully out of her puffed sleeves, and her bosom firmly held by the apron, gave an additional lift to her full breasts which brushed Thompson's shoulders when she bent down to place a cup and saucer before him. It was all he could do to keep his hands from flying off to grab her behind.

Fred decided to make an offer Mabel couldn't refuse. He would pay her three times her present wages to serve as his housekeeper in Ajmer. Mrs. Thompson had gone back to England to be near their two daughters who were at school.

If Thompson could prevail on Mabel to give up Hungry Charley's, he wouldn't have to go chasing after young blabbermouth fillies like Josephine. The RMR community was spread across a large area, but gossip travelled from station to station faster than any express train. The Josephine affair had raised quite a smoke in RMR shunting yards and was at least partly responsible for his wife's decision to go back to England. He would have to clear the matter with the Major, of course.

The Major merely shrugged and said Mabel was a free woman and it was entirely up to her, but was secretly very pleased indeed when she turned the offer down without a second's hesitation. Amanda's three month stay in England had aggravated her asthma, and her coughing fits had grown far too frequent for the Major to have a good night's rest, so by mutual consent they had begun to sleep in separate rooms. While his pseudo-baronial life governed his social conduct, deep inside the Major there still lurked a vigorous, country-bred lad from Colne, Lancashire who dreamt every night of Mabel's uplifted breasts. Her deep-throated laughter had begun to work its magic, stirring his loins like cobras at the sound of a Madari's pipe. He had taken to dropping in at Hungry Charley's on Tuesday nights when, following a late session, his fellow masons went home directly from the Lodge. The first time he mustered enough courage to slip out at night on Grace's bicycle, Mabel was still washing up. The Major waited under a clump of trees by the Maidan till he saw Eustace get on his bike to go home. Mabel was about to pull down the curtain that ran the whole length of the glass window when she saw the Major hovering outside. He was nervous and kept repeating himself, but her winsome smile didn't betray any surprise. She had been used to that look in the eyes of men from the time she had been a young lass, pushing a barrow loaded with fruit and vegetables across Putney Bridge for her father, all the way to Sedlescombe Road in Fulham, shouting "pears, tuppence a pound" all morning and afternoon till she was hoarse. Willy Fanshaw, who trained budgies to peck at a row of cards with birthday forecasts printed on them, had popped her cherry when she was sixteen. Without the Major's timely help, she would have probably ended up in the Red Light District of Bombay where many destitute white women disappeared. Besides, the Major never talked down to her, so she took his hand and led him upstairs. Khansahib at the gate was the only one privy to his master's Khalif-of-Bagdad-like peregrinations in the watches of the night. But that old Pathan's loyalty was forged in the hardy Khyber hills, where to lay down one's life for a mentor came as naturally as breathing.

RED BANDANNA

Everyone could see that Carl adored Jo Anna and she made no secret of her preference for him. But it was taken to be simple affection between two children who had grown up together. Many people were drawn to that strange, motherless boy whose physical beauty shone through all the grime and broken fingernails, and who had nowhere to go during the hot season.

Catholic families had homes in Panjim or Vasco or some such place, with Mediterranean-looking houses adorned with wrought iron balconies. Every summer, folks returned from holidays loaded with cashews, jackfruit and feni. The Anglos had really nowhere to go, had no regions attached to them. The Parsis talked of Udwada, location of the main Zoroastrian shrine, and there were ancestral homes in Surat and well-heeled relatives in Bombay, Poona, and Mahabaleshwar. The Anglos were from Mhow, full stop. Some claimed to be from Ratlam or Gangapore, cities with shunting yards for neighbourhoods. The hollowness of their claim on England only provided fodder for cruel party jokes in British homes, and forced some Anglos to declare allegiance to soot-covered railway towns instead of mythical homesteads in far off shires.

Carl was a born raconteur. Standing in front of the globe in the library, he would draw an almost accurate map of the railway network and regale his listeners with a dramatic rendering of the passage of mail trains through different parts of India. Accompanied by much whistling and blowing of imaginary steam, he rendered trains pulling out of Bombay's Victoria Terminus or Calcutta's Howrah Station, simulated their rumbling across expanses of well-known bridges, the way they snaked through tunnels. Everyone in Mhow assumed that when he grew up, Carl would be the engine driver of the Frontier Mail that ran all the way from Bombay to Peshawar lying on the very cusp of the famed Khyber Pass.

It was impossible not to be entranced by his impression of the Punjab Mail speeding across the plains, or the Deccan Queen flashing through the Western Ghats, the Grand Trunk Express hurtling through the dusky boulder-strewn hills of Telengana on its way to Madras, and above all the fabulous Frontier Mail booming through night and day, till the shining dome of the Golden Temple at Amritsar was awash in rosy hues of the setting sun.

On, on went the trains all rattle and roar, eating up miles, purring over nullahs, dementedly shrieking through tumble-down villages, winding past the magnificent Fort at Gwalior, Humayun's Tomb at Delhi, the ochre fortification of New Delhi's Purana Quila. On, on they went rustling across the paddy fields of Bengal, skirting the hills of distant Assam, to descend finally into the lush Burmese foliage around Rangoon. On, they went trumpeting like ferocious prehistoric beasts, leaving tracks smothered in sparks from churning wheels. Carl lived and breathed trains. They coursed through his veins so that listening to him, one felt the ground tremble beneath one's feet, grit filled one's nostrils, wind lashed one's face, and one's head spun in the whirling motion of the hooting monster careening around a precipitous bend, till one saw the soot-smeared face of the engine driver with his salt and pepper beard, leaning out of his cab, eyes glowing like embers under a soiled red bandana.

viii

RULE BRITANNIA

"I am sorry about last night," Grace says after they have finished breakfast in silence.

"It would be better if you apologised to Ross. You were very rude to him. Anyway I have never known you to be so patriotic. But it's not really about patriotism is it? It's not Rule Britannia, something else is bothering you. And I know what it is."

"What?"

"You don't like Ross."

" Don't be silly, dear. I hardly know the man."

"That may be, but there's that look in your eyes."

"What look?"

"You don't say anything, but your eyes are like pebbles. I have seen that look before. Especially when poor Jeremy was around."

"Poor Jeremy, indeed."

"You know what I am talking about. Every time I meet someone I like you get oh-so-lady-like and superior. Jeremy was poor and Eddie was money-grubbing. But what I don't understand is your attitude to Ross. He is just a friend of the Debus, that's all."

"I said I am sorry. If I get a bit rattled, it's because I don't want you to get hurt."

"Please Mum, spare me your concern. Haven't you done enough already?"

"Oh, you mean not telling you about Jo Anna. Well, blame it on me. As if it was all my fault . . . as if Jo..."

"Yes, go on. Out with it. What did my mother do? Did she throw herself at that American Airman? I was born out of wedlock! Is that it? That I'm a bastard? Well, let me tell you. I don't care, you understand. I don't give a damn. Just leave that poor dead girl alone and stop trying to run my life."

"No, no, you don't understand," Grace's shoulders begin to heave and her voice drops to a whisper. "Please, not now, not now. Let your mother alone," she says pressing her fingers against her eyes.

A violent spasm rocks her frame and she stumbles out of the dining room coughing.

They have had heated arguments before, but a new element has entered their relationship. Camilla realises that it's going to be difficult for them to have normal conversation without the spectre of Jo Anna wedging in. Still, Grace's near hysterical reaction that morning makes Camilla extremely uneasy.

The doll's house has a calming effect on her. Chinnery's is no more, Shiphidol is a mausoleum, but the doll's house breathes. Through it Camilla has come to feel a nuzzling closeness to Jo Anna. She pictures her cycling down the road to visit Yasmin, chasing butterflies in the garden and laughing with the girls at the Convent like young Esmé.

Ross's daughter has awakened the dormant mother in Camilla. How explain this uncanny urge to play housewife so late in life? She who, in her youth, had braved cold and drizzle to get Upper Slip seats to watch Margot Fonteyn and Nureyev at Covent Garden, never missed a Bergman or Fellini, regularly haunted the National, the Barbican and the Almeida, needed *The Guardian*, all crisp and crackly, first thing in the morning along with her coffee, is now yearning for motherhood. Jo Anna and Esmé come together before her in natural inclusiveness. It's as if somewhere an unwary house is flooded by a broken levee, and a sodden masterpiece crimps at the edges to reveal an exact likeness concealed under the original.

VI

i

MOTHER HUBBARD

It's obvious that in Camilla's view, Grace is perhaps no better than a grotesque little Mother Hubbard comically clinging to a dead past.

"She went to the Tailor's to buy her Dog a coat
When she came back he was riding a goat."

Such jingles were an essential part of the Countess's arsenal, deployed when the Dog Lady seemed to have an upper hand during their periodic skirmishes.

However, there's no denying that right from the day she first set eyes on him there has been something about that man Ross that has made Grace uneasy. The very sight of Camilla going cheek to cheek with him at dinner last night made her feel that once again her life was balanced on the point of nightmare. It caused her stomach to churn and she felt soiled. That's it, soiled and unwashed. It was like visiting the Loco Shed and watching Jo Anna step down from the engine, buttons of her crumpled frock undone, the fireman's brazen expression, and Carl's smug eyes smiling droopily.

Mhow had been such a small community; she would have remembered a Harrison. Aside from Mr. McGregor the Foreman, the only other Anglo in the Loco Shed had been Mr. Busby, Carl's father. An icy hand passes over her face. The thought of any kinship between Carl and this Harrison is too hideous to contemplate. No, she should simply confront Harrison and tell him to stop stalking her daughter. She would appeal to his sense of honour as a soldier.

It hadn't escaped her that Noshir's blood-red mongoose mouth had twitched as he shot a wink at his friend while that child was going on about Babylon and Christian slaves.

Memory comes flooding back of the time when Tommies would exchange that look at the sight of Maude Aspel in an open gharry on Mall Road in the evening. They had a way of sharing their hunch about what they called a 'chalu', a woman of easy virtue.

It wasn't her imagination; Camilla was trapped between two secretly allied men. For Harrison it would be just another conquest. He obviously has a thing about us, but Camilla would be scarred for life.

The only other time she had felt so utterly helpless was when her grief over Bobby's death was still quite raw and ugly rumours about Pater's liaison with Mabel had begun to circulate once again. Every face in town carried a hint of mockery. Old friends like Hulme and the Countess seemed bewildered by the swiftness with which their serene world had been shattered by the War. The Dog Lady who was in hospital with a broken hip worried that Dr. Vansittart would put her charges to sleep, as indeed he did when she passed away a few months later.

Soon after that Grace had witnessed a ghastly row during which Mater had accused Pater of carrying on with Mabel. Out of his terrible anguish had come Pater's wrenching howl that Bobby would not have died so young had Mater not been so damned keen on sending him to England. In his bitterness he had taken to spending long evenings at Hungry Charley's, leaving Mater to cope with Chinnery's.

Grace had been stunned by the resurgence of sexual hunger in Pater so soon after Bobby's death. He was almost sixty. Grace had grieved for days, but Jack had been very tender and her own appetite flush with his experienced manhood had finally asserted itself. Jack wanted a son and they had tried again and again, consulted swamis, and eaten foul-smelling potions. Within days of the 127th Gurkhas reaching the Burmese Front, Jack was captured by the Japs.

The news of Jap planes over Calcutta had brought the war suddenly to the doorstep. The nightly blackout following the eerie siren announcing curfew made everyone jittery.

For days, the bazaar had been rife with rumour. At this critical time Mr. Gandhi had thought fit to give the British an ultimatum to clear out. Quit India Movement the papers called it. For the first time since the Great Mutiny of the last century, an ocean of unfriendly natives had besieged Mhow. And in every nook and cranny associated with Bobby, one bumped into Ayah on her knees, now almost completely blind, clutching her tiny silver cross. Grace simply had to get away from it all. Then one day in Bombay the news she had been dreading had arrived in the form of a telegram. Three short words. "Pater Gravely Ill."

Pater had indeed had a heart attack, but the reason for the summons was even more devastating. Mater had found out that Jo Anna was pregnant. Battling her asthma night after sleepless night, Mater had been on the verge of physical and mental collapse, but with an iron will she had taken the matter in hand and decided to pack Jo off to Aunt Ethel's Methodist Mission in Poona.

Uncle Matthew was a Methodist minister who thought aborting the foetus a far greater sin than unmarried motherhood. Grace had to pretend to be pregnant and relinquish her position in WAC(I).

OLD BLOOD AND GUTS

"Some goddamned fool once said that flanks must be secured, and ever since then, sons of bitches all over the world have gone crazy guarding their flanks. We don't want any of that in the 3rd Army. Flanks are something for the enemy to worry about, not us."

General Patton's words dance before his eyes as Ross tries to concentrate on Kenneth Macksey's book on Kesserling. Would that master strategist have approved his favourite cadet Johar's unconventional ways of mounting an attack that afternoon? Ross is not sure.

The strain of outflanking the Chinnery woman while bedding her daughter has already taken its toll. Yet this strange sortilege, which sets daughter apart from mother, has its allure. His spine tingles at the memory of Camilla's fingers tracing soft spidery circles on his thighs.

He closes the book and tries to set aside troubling thoughts by reviewing the day's events. Planning new strategies to defend this land he loves is what engages his mind to the fullest. And oh the thrill of waiting for the enemy to make one false move. There's no question that out here in the open an element of kinship is at work, kinship born of being together at the isolated frontier where there's only the sky, the hills and the other man staring into the darkness in much the same way as you do, that throbbing together, alert to each other like animals quivering in the dark.

He knows by heart how the Allies had established a bridgehead in Normandy and rampaged eastwards through France to liberate Paris. But his current model is the Sicilian campaign in which Indian regiments were deployed following their success in the North African theatre. Engagements like El Alamein, Kursk or D-Day could be staged on one of the central Indian plains, but now what is needed in the hills, where airforce surveillance cannot spot guerrilla hideouts, is infantry. Infantry broken into platoons of thirty-six, with a commanding officer and two NCOs and a machine gunner or two, works well to smoke out guerrillas from their hideouts.

That day with an admiring nod at Patton, Ross's chosen warrior, Johar, was able to overcome one obstacle after another by disregarding conventional rules of engagement.

The Veteran believed that well-rested troops made better soldiers. Therefore, instead of getting his men to dig trenches early in the morning, he had them return to the previous night's bivouac for breakfast. On the other hand, young Johar's men started digging trenches at first light, and he sent a van to bring breakfast up to them. By the time the Veteran's men marched up once again and picked up their digging tools, Johar was ready to attack. He carefully examined the ground and avoided the sections where the Vindhya granite was too solid to allow deep digging.

The Veteran wanted to determine the enemy's possible direction of attack. His trenches were sparsely manned. Johar's men pounced and routed the thinly manned trenches and cut off the upward passage of troops waiting in the jungle.

But why isn't Ross out there celebrating Johar's triumph with his men? Why does he still feel like a corralled elephant reduced to an undignified hulk?

Following that heated exchange with Camilla's mother, Ross had been alone with Noshir in the garage. As soon as Ross pulled the bonnet down after locating a leak in the radiator, Noshir had pounced,

"What was all that whispering with Taji in the dining room about? Tehmi was worried."

"Did she notice that? Oh, my God, that girl will be the

death of me. I did something stupid in Delhi last Christmas and now she is making me pay for it."

"Why don't you marry Camilla?" Noshir had said, coming straight to the point. "The way you two have been carrying on. The entire Club is buzzing like a poached beehive. I know how that Camilla dame looks at you, man. I am sure even the General noticed it. Why do you suppose her mother went ballistic during dinner? It's so obvious."

"What will Aunt Yasmin think if I nabbed one of her guests?"

"That old thug would be tickled to death, I can tell you that. Just say the word and Tehmi and I'd manage the rest."

"I am not so sure, Nosh, really I am not."

Ross switches off the lamp.

He knows too well how the old tea planters react once they come to know he is an Anglo-Indian. Then their laughter is only on lips; the eyes are wary bystanders.

He had always visualised the Chinnery women as horse-faced old termagants in tweeds who ordered people about saying "Chop-chop." Instead, there was this decrepit, withered old stump of a woman on the verge of senility who was so pathetically dependent on her daughter.

The campaign against insurgents in Assam is brutal and ugly, but never confusing. Ross waits till he has a pretty shrewd idea where his quarry is hiding. With utmost precision he supervises one spearhead after another to trip rebel ambush. He has come to believe that the success of a guerilla outfit rests on its ingenuity in covering tracks. He also knows from experience that AT guns never come singly, that the one that reveals its presence is a decoy.

His eyelids begin to droop to the reassuring words of Kitchener; "We have to make war as we must and not as we would like to."

iii

IT WAS ROSES, ROSES EVERYWHERE

When Bobby came home for Christmas, dove-breasted chrysanthemums turned slightly yellow round the edges, roses were in full bloom, corncobs grew blonde moustaches, clotted pulp oozed out of custard apples, split-open pomegranates with pearly seeds appeared at breakfast, and in the forest, jejube thickets teemed with red berries. The year was 1936 and the Governor of Central Provinces came down from Nagpore to open the Flower Show.

Away from the Cantonment, the bougainvillea crept all over the fence to form a purple garland around the Railway Colony. The Cantonment was assured of its loyalty in the unlikely event of that man Gandhi descending on Mhow to stir up trouble. In their pressed white shirts and trousers, the RMR Staff carried with them the self-assured air of those who could cajole a recalcitrant locomotive into action with a warning tap and a little turn of the screw. During Christmas, the mainly Anglican Cantonment and the mostly Catholic Railway Colony formed a partnership to the gentle tolling of church bells. The low-slung sun lolled on the grass, and butterflies flitted over the swimming pool at the Club. From carriage windows engulfed in creamy chuffs of engine steam, Mhow looked like a drowned city, and figures on the road had an air of floating disconnection.

There's the Dog Lady at the head of her Pooch convoy, slowly winding up the eastern end of Post Office Road, but rattling up the western flank of Arsenal Road is a coolie-drawn rickshaw with the Matron Miss Barnaby on her way to the station to catch a train for Indore. Walking along Gymkhana Road are Mr. and Mrs. Sanderson with their five plump, marriageable daughters in long ankle-length skirts and parasols, headed for the Polo Match where they can see and be seen by eligible subalterns and captains. There goes Revd. Todd, the Vicar, in his black felt hat and long jacket, spluttering down High Street on his motorbike. Mrs. Martin, the Forest Officer's lady on a visit to town, cheerfully toots the horn of her Morris Oxford to acquaintances shopping on Main Street. RSM McNoggin's wife, Shirley, is pushing her daughter's pram to the dresser's on Simrole. On Mall Road, Mrs. Aspel in frills and velvet, is telling the gharrywala in demotic Hindi, to stop in front of the Mess and take the hood down so that young officers stepping out may admire her new embroidered jacket. A two-seater buggy goes clip clopping across Corbett Road carrying DSP and Mrs. Robinson to tea with friends. On Michael Road the syces are walking ponies with the babalog astride, and the Adjutant's wife is striding down Bakery Road followed by her ayah holding desperately on to Missy Baba who is trying to break loose, whilst from the Collector's bungalow, its red-Mangalore tiles speckled with shiny buttons of light, drifts the heart-rending wail of the Burra Mem mangling an aria from *Madame Butterfly*. The Veterinary paddles his rickety bike, holding a sick cat, and here comes the Colonel's Lady on horseback, on her way to the Mela in the garden of Christ Church to organize the jumble sale.

iv

THE CHRISTMAS OF THIRTY-SIX

During those long dreary November afternoons in London, as she sat in her rocker warming her hands by the fire, Grace was to look back on 'the Christmas of thirty-six' as the most blissful period in her life. She was in love and dying to share her secret with Shirin, if only she could find her alone. But best of all, Bobby was home. Jo Anna followed him everywhere, and Ayah's round chubby face never lost the glow from being gathered up in full view of everybody and being kissed smackingly on both cheeks by Bobby on arriving at Chinnery's. She rarely let him out of sight.

Vague talk of retrenchment, tear-stained faces and whispers, the harassed Mr. Munshi twiddling his thumbs, cast no shadow on the family and friends gathered in the dining hall, vying with each other to find the coin in the Christmas Pudding stuffed with nuts and raisins, candied peel and suet.

That year was special; people came from Ratlam and Khandwa, some even travelled from as far away as Jhansi and Bhusawal. All the rooms were taken, the guests' servants camped in the garden in tents and, save for the Colonel's Lady and a few snooty regimental mems, all of Mhow turned up for the New Year's Eve Ball. The griffins made a beeline for the elegant Sylvia Bickley.

Anglo blondes like Sylvia, and brunettes like Irene Popjoy, with their ever-brightening glances, were not without poise and self-containment. As long as music lasted, the lounge was a medley of colours with rustling silk of Parsi saris, Goan floral designs and the tender lustrous fibre of ladies' evening dresses, set off by the white of men's sharkskin jackets. Little ovoids of light bounced off polished shoes. Unable to keep up with the youthful dancers, buxom matrons plonked down, puffing like steam engines, faces flushed with exertion and heat. But the smooth flesh of Anglo girls never lost its intriguing eloquence, and their eyes looked excited and eager. Dancing for them was a normal part of growing up, since servants did most of the chores including cooking. Chinnery's Hotel was after all a meeting place for the relatively well to do, a salmagundi of races, not classes. Mutual suspicion gave place to bonhomie and some non-toxic flirting took place in the press of bodies, especially under the liberating influence of drinks, games, and nonsense songs. At the stroke of midnight lights were dimmed, partners kissed and everyone joined hands to sing *Auld lang syne*.

Then Irene Popjoy rose to lead the Railway Institute Band in rendering their favourite songs. She closed her eyes, opened her mouth wide, and out flowed the most caressingly tender sound,

I'd love to live in Loveland
With a girl like you
Where everyday's a holiday
And skies are baby blue
Where skies are blue forever
And the hearts are always true
I'd love to live in Loveland
With a girl like you.

It was at the 1936 Gala, when she was eighteen that Grace fell unconditionally in love with Adrian Ponsonby.

One evening she slipped into the garden with Bobby. They headed for the Leprechaun Well to stroll in the grass. When they were children, Bobby used to claim that leprechauns came up at night, sitting on the tiny tubs dangling from the Ferris-wheel-like contraption that went up and down the well, scooping up water. As the tubs came up, they tilted into a tank to empty water before resuming their clanking journey downwards.

After six years in England, even mid-winter seemed fairly mild to Bobby. The fauntleroy, who expected everyone to pick up things after him and wait on him hand and foot, was gone. Somehow he'd sensed that Chinnery's was in financial straits. He seemed determined to start working instead of imposing a further burden on Pater, although Mater was very keen that he should go to Cambridge. But Bobby had other ideas.

"I don't want poor Mater to start fretting. That would only make Pater miserable. Oh, Grace, what a sweetheart of a place Mhow is. Do you remember reading *The Secret Garden* to me? You get off the train and step into this Misselthwaite Manor. In England we hear so much about the troubles in India, the strikes, the bullets, the assassinations in Calcutta, and everyone thinks yet another War is simply waiting in the wings, and here people only talk about Sir Mancherjee's roses and whether they will outshine everyone else's. Such a lotus-eating corner of the world this is."

His pale grey eyes seemed like deep pools in the light of the lantern. He had grown taller, filled out, and carried himself erectly. He polished his own shoes instead of letting one of the chokraboys do it for him, and was full of stories about heroic First World War pilots like the Red Baron.

The athletic training at Marlborough and the Spartan way of life had turned this coddled colonial boy into a thoughtful, self-reliant young man. Grace assured him that while there were financial problems, the income Hungry Charley's brought in had prevented financial disaster. Though they were not as rich as they appeared to be to the outside world, things were all right. She didn't want Bobby to go back to England with unhappy thoughts. Time was fast approaching when he would be leaving and she wanted to savour every moment.

They found Jo Anna waiting anxiously for them in the hall. She caught Bobby's arm and dragged him to the library where, hitching up his several-sizes-too-large shorts, young

Carl armed with a ruler, stood in front of an easel. He was displaying a series of landscapes with various high-speed trains hurtling across sheer passes, clinging to the edges of gorges, snaking across valley floors. Paying close attention to the paintings was a tall and whiskered elderly gentleman with a handlebar moustache, and the ruddy face of an outdoorsman. Mr. Macartney Robbins as the gentleman was called was the editor in chief of *The Railway Magazine* published from London. He was planning to write a series of articles on Indian trains. During a tour of the Central Workshop of the Bombay, Baroda & Central India Railways in Ajmer that had been turning out some excellent engines since the year 1879, he was persuaded by Fred Thompson to visit the Mhow Loco Shed. Having heard from Amanda what beautiful pictures her children's friend Carl had been drawing of some of the famous trains, Mr. Macartney Robbins had expressed a wish to see them. He said he might select a few for publication in his magazine if he liked them.

In some of the watercolours Carl had captured the sweep and expanse of the central Indian plains with their distant trees. But what lent power to his work was what he saw and felt watching the rushing miles from the driver's cab, the thrill of land leaping smotheringly up, the onrush of tunnel mouths on his eyes.

His father, Mr. Busby, had secured him a job at the Loco Shed but every Saturday Carl travelled to Indore where Mr. Abbasi the Court painter, gave him a place to work in his studio. Mr. Abbasi who, in his youth, had accompanied the art-loving Maharaja of Indore to Switzerland and France, was heavily influenced by the Impressionists, and in his studio were several reproductions of their works which powerfully captured realities seized upon at a moment's glance. There one day, Carl had come across Turner's *Rain, Steam and Speed* and had felt the *Great Western* come bearing down and pass through him in sudden perspective.

The flowering of his talent took everyone by surprise.

Propping up his watercolours as visual aid, his voice generating the sounds of wheels hitting tracks, Carl soon whisked them off on a whirlwind tour of the country. From the Himalayas in the North, to Cape Comorin in the South, the Arabian Sea in the West to Rangoon in the East, the land became a shifting web of dependencies on the restless movement of its express trains. In their sheer exuberance of brushwork, the watercolours were a far cry from the rudimentary pencil sketches he had learned to draw at St. Mary's under the supervision of the art teacher, Mr. Misra. Mr. Macartney Robbins was so pleased with the drawings that he paid three hundred rupees for two of them, and gave his card to Carl telling him to look him up at his office at 33 Tothill Street if he should ever visit London. That night everyone went to bed marvelling at that ragtag and bobtail lad's transformation into an artist of no mean talent.

It was Shirin, with an eye for the faintest hanky panky sweltering beneath the most discreet affairs of the heart in Simla, who immediately realised that between Carl and Jo Anna was developing a bond with hints of impending disaster. The violet-eyed, pampered Jo Anna and the Anglo boy with his pale Greek-coin face were coordinated like figures in a dream.

At fourteen there was around Carl a sort of Sinbad the Sailor aura. He would hold back in a crowd or slip unselfconsciously into the lounge filled with well-groomed people in evening dress, watching the proceedings with a distant, assessing gaze. The officers with their mutton-chop good looks and precise, drilled gestures moved like manikins, but Carl passed among them with lithe, unperturbed, cat-like self-assurance, and made for the far corner where Grace and Jo Anna sat with their friends.

Carl and Marje Sanderson demonstrated how to do the tango. Then he led Jo Anna to the floor and their silhouettes flitted across the French windows like a pair of leaves helixing softly down in a wet breeze. Like Grace, Shirin had read *Julius Caesar* for Senior Cambridge, and on one occasion, as she said goodnight to Grace, she leaned forward and whispered in her ears, "Beware the Ides of March."

Grace blushed, thinking Shirin was twitting her about Adrian who was, at that moment, saying goodbye to her mother.

"Whatever do you mean?" Grace said, smiling with pleasure.

"Not you, silly," Shirin said. "It's Carl and Jo. Don't you see?"

"What?" Grace was stunned. "How, how can that be? Carl is not like that."

"Like what?"

"I mean, he wouldn't dare. And Jo is just a baby and treats him like a brother."

"Famous last words. Ask yourself," Shirin said before sliding her arm into her father's as he came up leading Yasmin, "why Jo would not let him dance with anyone besides Marje Sanderson."

Grace was confused. She thought Shirin's mind was addled by all that gossip in Simla. Though tall for her age, Jo was only ten, going on eleven. Why, she still needed Ayah to tuck her into bed. Grace looked at Carl who was talking animatedly to Bobby about the Flying Scot, the Princess Royal, the Cock o' the North, and the King George V, some of the fabled engines that sped across England at seventy miles per hour. He even knew that the Bournemouth Belle with its plush Pullman carriages left Waterloo everyday at 10:30 in the morning, arriving at Southampton precisely at 11:59, and reached Bournemouth Central at 12:39 pm.

Bobby was more interested in airplanes and was a bit bored by all this train talk. His grave, public school manner contrasted sharply with the passion which made Carl's face twitch with excitement. His thin frame shook and strained. Despite the strides he had made as a budding artist, he became so obviously a child again that Grace felt quite relieved, and drove Shirin's words out of her mind.

The week before his departure, Grace and Shirin took Bobby and Adrian to Moonwater Lake for a picnic-cum-shoot. Shirin was in form and the four of them sang songs all the way. Shirin's fondness for Bobby was as strong as ever, and her discerning eye had noticed the evolution of this once callow boy into a self-possessed young man, and she flirted with him outrageously. But instead of feeling jealous as she used to in the old days, Grace was proud that her smarty-pants friend found her brother attractive.

While Bobby and Adrian were trudging the forest in search of deer, Shirin and Grace went for a swim in the twin pools shielded by hoary banyans. Grace was basking in the luxurious warmth of Sunwater Lake when she heard voices. As they clambered out and dressed hurriedly, Shirin jokingly reminded her of the tribals' warning that a quick dip in Moonwater was mandatory because River Alaknanda punished those who ignored her smaller lake-child.

THE WARRIOR PRINCESS

Camilla has taken charge of the restoration of Jo Anna's grave.

Grace feels like a thing banished by some despotic decree. She begins to yearn for London, for the lazy drift of water in the Thames, the blue-green foliage and soft light on the Common, the remote underground rumble followed by the cool draft preceding an incoming train, the cheerful red of a double-decker disappearing round a bend, the unhurried remote rain, the smell of tar mixed with exhaust fumes, the geranium pots on her window sills. If only Camilla had not been so keen on marble, they would be back in London now.

"These days people do not much care for gravestones," Mr. Michael Pinto, Licensed Embalmer of Mhow, had said. "They can't afford marble or headstones. The old masons are dead and gone; people build graves with cement. Most just carve inscriptions on the flat surface while it is still wet. It's all cement now, nothing but cement."

The stone Grace had ordered earlier is gathering dust in Yasmin's backyard. The marble slab from Agra would take some time to arrive. It will have to be cut, polished, transported, and inscribed before it is installed.

Clearly, the smell of death in hospital had addled her brain and, like a fool, she had succumbed to the notion that bringing Camilla to visit Jo's grave would somehow make amends. She who had always been clear-headed had allowed herself to get trapped in this absurd nightmare. How would Camilla react if she knew that the American Airman was a myth?

But . . . but,

Grace rises with a start.

She is missing something here, something frightening, and cruel.

Her mind goes numb.

Merciful Heavens, how could she have been so dense? Why, that makes Camilla an Anglo, too?

She had thought of Camilla only as her sister's baby, and later in England the little girl's link to Jo had got gradually erased from memory. Grace had lulled herself into believing that she would never be forsaken. Hadn't the poor child made so many sacrifices for her sake even after knowing the truth?

Then why this sudden fixation with the gravestone?

A large hot tear comes rolling down Grace's cheek.

Camilla just sits there for hours gazing at the doll's house, carefully brushing the figures, and dry-washing the dresses. As a girl she had been something of a tomboy, was named after Hulme's favourite character the Volscian Princess from *The Aeneid*. In London Camilla had acted as though nothing had changed between them, but all of a sudden, here in Shiphidol, the girl in her has suddenly surfaced alongside the doll's house.

THE QUALITY OF MERCY

As Grace walks up the long driveway at St. Mary's, the years drop away. As chief guest, Grace is expected to distribute prizes. The Mother Principal had come personally to invite her. The nuns have kept the place going, despite all the financial problems the Government's language policies have created for English Medium schools. With the exception of Mother Superior, all the nuns are Indian, wear saris, and speak Hindi. One of them comes forward to escort Camilla and Grace. She is a tall woman with luminous black eyes and an exceptionally striking face. She reminds Grace of Sister Philippa. Perhaps there has to be one beautiful nun in every Convent.

Grace had been unable to get a teaching job in England. Lack of a Diploma in Education had forced her to serve in a school where the oldest students were only seven and the youngest four. She had to shout at the top of her voice to maintain discipline in class. The little five-year-olds were badly spoiled by their mothers, the classroom lapsed into bedlam every day, and arrows and ink blots flew about. She had never forgotten the joy of teaching poetry to bright teenage girls at St. Mary's, but in England her work mainly amounted to babysitting and helping children fill their sheets of paper that had rough outlines of animals with different colours. Worst of all, she hated the baby talk.

"If, within the next minute or so, all the naughty chaps wandering around do not return to the desk, a little birdie tells me they will not be included in the class tour to Pollock's Toy Museum."

Teaching the slightly older six-year-olds was limited to

simple arithmetic, geography, and narrating stories from the Scriptures. Most of her colleagues were considerably older than she. Some of them had lost husbands in the Great War and were like so many Queen Victorias in perpetual mourning with flat hairdos, gold-rimmed glasses, and expanding waistlines. Those spinstered by World War II wore very heavy make-up and eyelashes. Between these two extremes, Grace seemed to be the sole representative of young womanhood and much admired by Mr. Dibble, the only man on the teaching staff and husband of the Headmistress Mrs. Judith Dibble. He had been a failed actor and talked constantly of his theatrical days, of the torrid affair with his leading lady in *Blithe Spirit* which had earned him the wrath of her producer husband, and deprived him of a place in a possible triumvirate with Olivier and Gielgud. The others called him Champagne Charlie because his breath smelt of alcohol. Three or four times he tried to get Grace in a corner. Then she met Stoodgy. The day before she got married, Grace resigned from school, ignoring Mrs. Dibble's warning.

"You won't find it easy to get another decent job like this. I do hope you are not going on the dole like all these so-called Angry Young Men. Don't know what they are angry about. They sit on their bottoms, and grumble all the time."

The driveway forks in front of the Chapel. As she is led to the Principal's Office her heart begins to race. The stage and the assembly hall look just the same. Additions have been made to the periphery, but inside everything is just as it was.

She spots Ross a little distance away talking to Camilla.

"I wonder if I could potter around a bit while guests are still arriving," Grace says to Mother Superior, "I'd like to look at the classroom upstairs where I taught poetry for a while."

Mother Superior asks the nun with the beautiful face to show her around.

To Camilla's surprise Grace comes walking rapidly

towards them and asks Ross if she might have a quick word with him. He walks down with her a few steps, very erect but courteous.

"What did my mother say to you?" Camilla asks Ross as soon as they sit down. The open-air theatre is filled to capacity now and all around is an excited buzz of parents, children and teachers.

"Nothing much," Ross says cautiously. "She apologized to me for the other night."

"Was that all?"

"Yes, of course, what else could there be."

Just outside the Principal's Office Grace almost collides with Olinda.

"Oh, Madam," croons the nurse, "how wonderful it must be to see your old school! It has changed so much, no? My grandson is in the chorus. He has a good voice, but nothing compared to Colonel Harrison's girl. I saw you talking to the Colonel. People say he is conceited. His father wasn't at all like that. And to think that once they were poor like us."

"What was he, I mean Harrison's father?" Heart pounding, Grace forces herself to ask.

"Nothing much as I recall, just an apprentice he was and his father was a boiler mechanic when my father was Stationmaster at Mhow. You remember my father 'Mr. Gilbert', Madam?"

"Boiler mechanic!" Grace freezes and tries to strangle Olinda's words before they can take on meaning. She feels no sorrow or pain, no sensation of any kind, just numbness. The nurse is thrilled with what she takes to be an invitation to gossip. She looks at Grace, archly enjoying the power her knowledge gives her over someone so far above her station.

"Well Madam, as I remember, Colonel Harrison's father Carl Busby was always at the Hotel when I was a little girl, playing with Master Bobby."

Grace's head hangs limp between her shoulders. Before she can blot out Olinda's words, Mother Superior comes out of her office smiling through her thick glasses and Grace is led down the steps. Her mind gone completely blank, her legs carry her across to the place reserved for the chief guest in the front row. At a nod from Mother Superior the red curtain parts and the show begins.

Camilla has coached Esmé and she delivers Portia's "Quality of Mercy" speech in a clear, firm voice. Grace's mouth remains askew, her lips are no longer in alignment and the blood drumming in her ears makes Esmé's words boom like muffled gongs.

It blesseth him that gives, and him that takes,
'Tis mightiest in the mightiest, it becomes
The throned monarch better than his crown.

A few skits, Hindi songs from films, a Bharat Natyam dance, a Bhangra number, follow the Trial Scene from *The Merchant Of Venice.*

Wisely each performer is awarded a prize and then Grace ascends the stage where Mother Superior introduces her as an ex-pupil and teacher. The children's parents, most of whom are army officers, lean forward to listen to her.

"My entire youth lies buried within these walls," Grace tells them in a faltering voice. But with a storm raging in her mind her voice drops to a whisper. She cuts her speech short. Everyone is deeply moved. Afterwards Grace congratulates Sandra Grehwal who teaches English at the Convent and has directed the scene from *The Merchant,* and compliments the beautiful nun who has trained them to sing Mr. Gallagher and Mr. Sheen.

Later that evening Grace says to Yasmin,

"You can have a reunion, or whatever is appropriate with that man, after we are gone." Then she adds in an imploring tone, "I hope you will appreciate how painful it is to me personally, especially when I have come all this way to restore Jo Anna's grave. The marble from Agra is already here. I want to be alone with my memories. We'll be going back very soon."

Yasmin notices with a shock how Grace's face has caved in like a document hastily thrown in a grate. The melancholy in her voice spreads like the afternoon desolation of sunburned leaves in their lonely drift in the garden. It is as though Grace has died in her sleep, leaving behind an empty dress hanging from a peg.

THE SECRET SOCIETIES OF ST. FRANK

Mr. Bamforth the young pianist opened the programme at The Opera House in Bombay with Beethoven's *Aurora Sonata*. Aunt Ethel, who had come down to see Bobby off, thought the concert would cheer up Grace who had stood in the sun at Ballard Pier for a long time till the ship had become a small dot on the horizon. But Grace was driven to despair by the young man's mastery of the keyboard, especially the way he exploited the contrast between highs and lows. The treble notes escaping from the rapid tremolo of the C Major chord took her breath away. After intermission, Bamforth played *The Appassionata*. At the end of that achingly beautiful F Minor, Bamforth's left hand plunged the work into a cavernous valley, even as the right hand was finishing the furiously repeated note of the highest ever C. Grace sadly realised how far away lay the young man's accomplishment from her meagre talent.

While Grace was away, Chinnery's had apparently been knocked sideways by a thunderclap. She had never seen Pater in such a state of raw anger and sensed that something terrible had transpired the night before, and somehow Jo was responsible for it. It made Pater wander around the Hotel mumbling to himself.

The Railways in India, as elsewhere, took care of their people, and from Lahore to Madras, Guntakal to Asansol young strapping Angloboys from low-income families left school early to do a man's job. Accordingly, Carl was apprenticed at the Loco Shed, and was hoping to move on to the locomotive department as fireman to Mr. Lumley, the Senior Driver on RMR. Carl's pocket allowance had suddenly made an upward swing and he had opened his own savings account in the bank across the road from Hungry Charley's. One day he took Jo and Yasmin to the cafeteria for ice cream. Jo adored Mabel because she was the only one who did not treat her like a baby. Moreover Mabel cut Jo's hair to make her look like Simone in *Girl's Dormitory*. With characteristic exuberance, Mabel told Jo that any clever Hollywood director would put her in his pictures if he ever saw her.

"After all, if Merle Oberon could make it, so can you ducks," she said. "And you are prettier and proper British."

However, Mabel felt that the girls were too young to be exposed to the raunchy argot of the Tommies. She was looking for a way to stop Jo from visiting the cafeteria without making her feel unwanted, when the girls were caught trying to sneak into the Ghost House. That put an end to their visits to Hungry Charley's.

Rumours at the Convent had the Thakurani's spirit dancing on the terrace of the Bhut Bungalow. Girls believed that all the well-known shades, including the Lilleys, arrived there one by one on moonless nights for a coven with the Thakurani.

That fateful evening, in the tradition of most upcountry Masonic lodges, all the loyal flock of Mhow congregated at the Bhut Bungalow to reaffirm their imperial fellowship. Just before members arrived in their buggies, carriages, and Morris Minors and passed through the old wrought-iron gate wrenched open by one-eyed Jamal the Chowkidar, Carl cut the barbed wire with a pair of lineman's pliers he'd borrowed from the machine shop at the Loco Shed, and the three of them slipped in through the fence at the back of the Masonic Lodge. He fed the dogs pieces of leftover mutton Jo had picked up from the plates stacked up after lunch at Chinnery's.

Once inside, the three climbed up a banyan, and slithered across a branch to cling precariously to the moulding around the skylight, resting their feet on top of the cornice beneath. It was a greyish evening and the setting sun was behind clouds.

What they saw from their wobbly perch fascinated them. Directly beneath them inside the hall was a slightly raised stone platform with a rough-hewn chunk of stone on a pedestal. There was a fat, leather-bound book on a wooden stand, open at a page, lying on a red velvet pillow, fringed with golden tassels.

From the columns, going towards the altar was a semi-circular passage marked by black marble tiles that contrasted with the shining yellow floor covered with different signs of the Zodiac. At the entrance on the far side, were two bronze columns ornamented with wreaths, and at the top of each column was a globe. Just below the high ceiling was a large eyebrow window, which winked as the sun setting behind it, played hide and seek with the clouds.

Then the side door opened and in came the entire Who's Who of Mhow led by Major Chinnery and Sir Mancherjee. Shining gold medallions dangled on chests from thick silver chains around their necks. Jo and Yasmin couldn't help laughing because both men wore what looked like embroidered aprons covered with strange squares and circles. Uncle Woom, Post Master David, Uncle Shikari, and fathers of other girls at the Convent followed them. His Highness Shah Nawaz, the Nawab of Bhastipore, held the door open for Mr. Jenkins the Burra Sahib, who came in walking solemnly. The Burra had a top hat on and a long green velvet robe.

One by one candles were lighted, and in their glow the hall looked like the inner chamber of "The Secret Societies of St. Franks" in the latest issue of *The Nelson Lee*. The girls couldn't hear anything over the humming of the congregation. In a few seconds DSP Robinson came in leading a blindfolded Jack Sullivan, the newly arrived Lieutenant of the 127th Gurkhas. The buttons of his shirt were undone, his left breast was bare, and there was a noose around his neck. He had only one shoe on and one trouser leg was rolled up.

DSP Robinson raised the naked dagger in his hand and poked Jack's nipple with it. The children saw him wince with pain. Suddenly men in blue goatskin aprons and glistening chains across their chests, encircled him, waving their wands and chanting like Red Indians. The girls looked at each other. There was no sign of any 'bhuts', although the hall seemed like a place where any spectre might feel completely at home. But what was going to be done to Lieutenant Sullivan who was now kneeling down? Were they about to witness human sacrifice as in *"The Fourth Finger of 'Le Chan Suey'"* from *Chums*? The girls began to shake with fear.

The Burra Sahib put down the sword, then, holding a gavel in his hand, he marched down to where the Lieutenant was kneeling in front of the book on the velvet pillow. The Burra stood before Sullivan, facing the altar, and the DSP, holding a staff, was directly behind him. Then the Burra intoned some more, and raised the gavel as if to strike the Lieutenant on the back of his head. It was so quiet you could hear a pin drop. Then the three onlookers, their faces pressed against the window, distinctly heard the Burra say angrily to the Lieutenant,

"Your throat would be cut, your tongue would be torn from your mouth, and your bowels burned to ashes."

At that very moment the sun slipped out of a cloud cover, pierced the eyebrow window with a powerful tracking beam, and illuminated the skylight behind which huddled the three young intruders.

As he raised his head, the Burra's eyes came to rest on the three terrified faces gawking at him through the skylight. He stopped abruptly and whispered something to the DSP, who whirled around to look at them. Now all eyes were trained on them. At that moment the old cornice with its rotted and mildewed bricks buckled, and the three of them plunged down screaming in terror. The dogs began to bark and Carl, who could have run away, got up and helped the girls free themselves from the weeds.

No bones were broken, but Yasmin had a cut across her right calf and she was moaning in pain. The DSP was livid, grabbing Carl by his shoulders; he slapped him hard on the cheek. Carl merely said, "Yasmin needs help, I think she is hurt." The Major and Sir Mancherjee bundled them up in the latter's car and, taking Dr. Aspel with them, rushed to his surgery. The initiation ceremony for Lieutenant Sullivan had to be postponed.

From that time on, Carl was barred from Chinnery's. Although it was Jo who had talked him into it, he was held responsible for everything. His father, Mr. Busby, was summoned by the DSP to his office and warned of dire consequences if he did not control his vagabond son. The Chinnery's saw in that childish prank a good opportunity to separate Jo from Carl.

A TROOP OF DRAGOONS

Like a radio operator tracking a comrade lost in a blizzard, Camilla sits by the doll's house, green eyes focused on its immaculate interior. Yasmin watches the scene silently from behind the silk curtain in the doorway. Little floes of memory starting from different points of her life with Jo Anna quicken into streams that are braided in that tableau. Yasmin had helped sew buttons on the doll's dresses.

In fact Jo Anna never did anything without Yasmin, not even when Carl so obviously wanted to be alone with her. She was included in everything those two did together. After Carl was barred from visiting Chinnery's it was Yasmin who helped them meet in secret. Carl would return from work in the evening, showered and dressed in a loose white shirt and black trousers, looking like Errol Flynn in *Captain Blood,* and scale the wall of the courtyard at the rear of Shiphidol to meet the girls in the potting shed.

The small sturdy locomotive in which he made the short twenty-mile trip to Kalakund and back was named "The Tiger Princess." One day he took them to where the Tiger Princess was being serviced in the Loco Shed. Its tender and boiler barrel had been detached. The girls got on to the footplate of the cab listening, open-mouthed, as Carl demonstrated how to get it going.

A riveting machine stood on one side of the giant phallus-like boiler barrel, lying horizontally on a brick platform with its seams covered with rivets. While Yasmin was staring at the handles, gauges, and tubes that ran down the floor and up into the roof of the cab, Carl and Jo Anna suddenly vanished. Yasmin looked for them everywhere, but they were nowhere in sight. She was scared and started crying. Then she heard voices and muffled laughter. Tiptoeing to the front end of the barrel, she found Jo Anna and Carl lying side by side like sardines. Yasmin tried to get in, but she would have had to walk on top of them. So she just stood there and listened as the two of them hugged and talked. It seemed Mr. Abassi was hoping to catch His Highness Indore in the right mood to get a decent stipend sanctioned for Carl to study in Paris.

"Take me with you to Paris," Jo Anna said.

"First you must finish Senior Cambridge," Carl said to her, "then, as soon as I have saved some money, I'll send for you."

At that moment Yasmin blurted out

"You two must take me with you to Paris."

Startled by her voice, Carl and Jo Anna scrambled out of their hiding, laughing happily. Jo Anna's new frock had a tear where it had been caught in a piece of protruding rivet, but she paid no attention to it. They were all full of such dreams in those days.

When clinging to Carl, Jo Anna would stretch one hand and pull Yasmin into their embrace. The two friends were like young puppies pulling at the same udder. Yasmin loved burrowing in the folds of their dovetailed bodies, to feel the warm kneadable smoothness of Jo Anna's heaving bosom and the hard imprint of Carl's buttons pressing against her cheek. The slightest hint of their not wanting to share something with her caused her to panic. It felt as though all three of them lived in the same body.

When Carl was away, their bodies confluenced involuntarily at the centre of his absence. Then their eyes would snap open, and they would part, giggling like mad. At first they were a bit uncomfortable, but then it became a habit. Both felt as though they were snuggling up against Carl, and they hugged and kissed each other's cheeks. Not until the day Yasmin tried to kiss Jo on the mouth was she pushed away.

"What are you doing?" Jo screamed. Her wide violet eyes

looked wary. Yasmin began to sob, her whole body rocking with anger and betrayal. Lines had been drawn. Yasmin was so afraid of losing Jo Anna that she never attempted to kiss her on the mouth again. Soon after that Jo Anna began to drift away.

By then Mrs. Aspel had graduated from the position of an acolyte of the Dayan's to that of a working sorceress in her own right. But it was difficult to tell when she was joking and when she was not. One day she told them that spirits of English people killed in their prime sought refuge in the bodies of the resident British. Carl was eligible because he had British blood, and since England was too far to travel, even for ghosts, sometimes they had to make do with Anglos. It all sounded very silly to Yasmin, when Maude Aspel told them that Clarissa Lilley had appeared at the Dayan's seance and told them that she was reborn as the younger daughter of the Chinnerys.

Prompted by Maude, Jo would point out the ruins of an old barracks where she had died in her previous incarnation as Clarissa Lilley. But why did she cling so desperately to Maude's bizarre theory and pretend to remember incidents from her former life? Perhaps that was the only way she could fight the alarm she must have felt at Carl being a poor Anglo, lacking proper education. She had to have some way of justifying her love for him. Jo was too smart to believe in spirits, but they became her allies, the way people trapped in categories and distinctions could never be. To the average Briton, the Anglos were like awkward evidence overlooked by criminals during a hasty getaway.

With the exception of the Thakurani turned churail, Clarissa Lilley was the most frequently sighted ghost in Mhow. Since 1862 when she had died and was buried by the men of the 6th Inniskilling Dragoons, Clarissa had been sighted in different parts of the Cantonment. But her agitated spirit had most frequently been seen wandering in the Old Cemetery by those who dared walk alone by it after midnight. The most common account had her kneeling in front of her children's graves, and sobbing disconsolately. But sometimes she wandered all alone in the grounds of the Cemetery, picking wild flowers in moonlight and singing a lighthearted ditty. One day Jo began to hum a song Yasmin had never heard before. She was to hear it so often that she remembers most of it till today.

There once was a troop of Dragoons
Come marching into Fife-eeyo!
Our Captain falls in love
With a bonny wee girl
Who goes by the name of Miss Peggy eeyo!

Yasmin was sure Maude Aspel and not the spirit of Clarissa Lilley had taught that song to Jo, but she couldn't stop worrying about her friend's state of mind. She felt instinctively that some fearful harm would come to Jo Anna and tried to alert Grace through Shirin, but without being explicit. Grace had absolutely no inkling of the darker side of her sister's mind. Only Yasmin knew the real Jo. For instance, she had told her that Mr. Savoy of Carlton & Palmer, who distributed Perfumes and Macassar Oil, had once caught hold of her from behind and tried to kiss her. He had paid her fifty rupees not to tell anyone.

Yasmin was still able to pedal her bicycle with some effort. One evening, while returning home from the bandstand, Jo insisted on accompanying her to Shiphidol. She was eager to listen to the new recording of *Aida* Pestan had ordered from Rose & Company in Bombay. Cycling past the Old British Cemetery, Jo suddenly stopped at the crossroads of the Post Office and Bakery Road and said, "Let's not go home yet. Let's visit my grave in there."

Yasmin was absolutely stunned. There was no one on the road and there was a sudden chill in the air, really quite unusual for October. The sky turned grey as the low sun dipped behind a cloud. The street lamps had not been switched on and a sharp high-pitched laughter cut through the air. Yasmin turned around to see, but there was no one there. Then suddenly amidst tintinnabulation of bells, a tonga galloped by with a very pale woman in a red Marwar sari holding an infant crying in pain.

"There goes the churail, the spirit of Thakurani,"Jo whispered.

Yasmin started shivering.

"Please Jo," Yasmin pleaded. "Come on, let's go home. It's late."

Jo Anna shrugged and wordlessly followed her, but at the end of the road, she said good night with that funny smile, and cycled back towards the Old Cemetery.

Then one day, during the War, Jo went to Kalakund with Carl, riding in the cab of the "Tiger Princess." She told Yasmin that Carl was going to paint her as though rising from Moonwater Lake, like Botticelli's *Venus*. When Grace came looking for her at Shiphidol, Yasmin had to tell her where Jo was.

It was not until after the War when the Chinnerys had gone to England that Yasmin came to know that Carl was beaten mercilessly by the Tommies and left for dead. Captain Gilmore, who was smitten with Jo Anna and was seething with resentment that she should prefer an Anglo upstart to a proper English officer and gentleman, was egged on by Amanda Chinnery to teach Carl a lesson. His handpicked Tommies had waylaid him in the dark with no witnesses to testify, and beaten him within an inch of his life. His legs were broken and his body was dumped at the entrance to the Railway Colony from where he was discovered lying in a coma by his neighbour. He was rushed to the big Railway Hospital in Ratlam and, as soon as he was able to talk, his father dispatched him to far off Calcutta. Mr. Busby was afraid for his son's life.

VII

i

WATERLOO BRIDGE

After a quick hug to Esmé and a promise that he would take her on a tiger shoot, Ross leaves for the Camp. At times Ross can be annoyingly secretive. Is Camilla just another body to him? Tehmi is always hinting at his many conquests. Some of Camilla's friends in London would simply assume that she was trying to stay younger by latching on to a dishy hunk. The more cynical among them might think that she was only hankering after younger flesh that would stay inside her longer than poor spent Eddie.

Her wanting to be with the man is one thing, but how to explain this witless urge to pamper the daughter, the longing to talk to her and share her life? To be a . . . mother! It's the whole package Camilla wants. Not just Ross, but his entire world.

It's not a seizure she is experiencing, but a long gathering storm. Has she allowed her passion to bloom simply to fill her empty spaces? The question of community of interests seems purely academic. So what if he prefers a brass band to Brahms and Le Carré to Proust.

Camilla was shocked at first, by the almost total lack of awareness in Ross about the misery and horror suffered by the victims of the holocaust. She was astonished to learn that a sizeable and prosperous Jewish community had lived and thrived in Western India for nearly two thousand years. Mr. David, the Postmaster, had apparently refused to migrate to Israel with his son's family and after his death was buried in the Jewish Cemetery in Bombay. Everyone spoke fondly of the old Postmaster, yet when Camilla said he was lucky to have escaped the fate of his fellow Jews in Europe, Ross had appeared to be greatly puzzled. Here in Mhow, Auschwitz and Treblinka seemed too distant to have a personal significance to anyone. People were preoccupied with a different bloodbath, that which had followed the partition of India.

Come to think of it, living on the sunny side of affluence her friends in England seem even more unconnected to history. She had tried desperately to hold on to Eddie, even after discovering that he was siphoning off large amounts from their joint account. Gradually she had come to feel estranged from her social circle; sustaining friendships had become a tiresome exercise.

Through the motherless Esmé, Camilla has come to recognise Jo Anna's heartrending claim on her life. It is also quite touching to watch Tehmi, Noshir and Yasmin shower so much affection on Esmé. Those soothing allures of a close-knit community in Mhow tug at Camilla's heartstrings, and remind her of the time when the gentle spirit of Stoodgy permeated their little flat in Clapham Common.

She is so fired by the thought of giving herself to Ross, that her own professional world in London seems unreal and hollow. There can be no life without Esmé and Ross. Individually they are vulnerable; she can resist them as separate entities, but together man and daughter are like a whirlpool sucking her in, together they are her salvation.

She had been swept off her feet by Jeremy's splendid courage and electric Shelley-like presence. With Eddie she had felt assured that someone with his kind eyes would never let her down. But now she doesn't need to justify her feelings or single out a special trait, like Ross's ironic smile for instance, the fetching lift of his eyebrow, or his love for Esmé. It is the entire sum of their many parts, the whole gamut of their different selves, his devotion to his child, and her love for her father, that are pulling Camilla in relentlessly. She has simply fallen in with them and found her feet in their dance.

ii

THE TRIAL

It was during one particularly tranquil day that Mhow was hit by a political tornado. There was an unspoken rule that the British had a right of way on a narrow footpath. The untouchables were expected to step aside for upper class Indians, and the Indians ducked to let the British pass. Even among the untouchables there were distinctions. The lowest of the lowly were the mehters, carriers of night soil; those who swept the streets were one degree higher.

Late one Saturday night, the rickety bike on which old Bhagwan was being conveyed by his grandson to the Post Office, crashed into a pair of Tommies who were on their way back from the Red Light District. Though of the sweeper caste, Bhagwan was appointed night watchman at the Post Office by Mr. David, who like Hulme, considered untouchability a blot on the face of humanity.

Mr. David was of the Bene tribe of Israeli from Bombay. Lately the news of persecution of Jews in Eastern Europe and under the Nazis in Germany had sharpened his sense of solidarity with those denied social justice, merely for the accident of being born under a different label. Mr. David was stocky with large watery eyes under bushy brows, a broad sallow face, and skin smooth as pongee. He was completely bald, but had a resonant, carrying voice. A childless widower, he was not what you might call an orthodox Jew. Mr. David was incapable of hating anybody. He was a one-man synagogue in a town where there were no other members of his tribe.

Come rain or shine, every morning, carefully removing the sacred text from the Tefillin and donning a yarmulk, he recited *B'rasheet.* At dusk it was *Ma'ariv,* and late in the afternoon while still at work, he took a short break behind closed doors for *Minchah.*

The crows were gone, shops were closed on Main Street, and roadside trees were asleep. The Major was in bed with Mabel when he heard the sound of a scuffle outside. The Tommies were kicking a bundle at the street corner and laughing maniacally. Moans emanated from the bundle as one of them landed a blow with a stick. Mabel slipped into her gown and went to the window and began to shout, "Stop it, for god's sake stop it." But the game had peaked. Red faces looked blindly in her direction. One of them shouted,

"Sweetheart, this goal's for you," and landed a hard kick. A small crowd had gathered by then. It was only when the Major, dressing hurriedly, went down that the Tommies swung on to their bikes and pedalled away into the night.

The grandson came out of hiding and started shaking the old man. A low moan indicated there was still some life in him. The Major directed the onlookers to pick up the old man and follow him but the Hindu grocers and moneylenders refused to touch a mehter. So the grandson and the Major together carried the old man to Dr. Aspel's surgery which was round the corner on High Street. Next day, the grandson's account was published in *Nai Duniya,* the local daily from Indore with nationalist leanings. The editorial taunted the British administration for showing utter contempt for the life of the common man but praised the Major for coming to the aid of the unfortunate victim.

DSP Robinson hesitated because the regiment to which the Tommies belonged was none other than the Witch Doctors. The DSP might have been able to hush up the incident to spare the Major any possible embarrassment, but he could not face the wrath of Mr. David.

The self-effacing Postmaster was transformed overnight into a forensic Jeremiah, whose indignation was expressed with the moral force of Rabbi Akiba, whom he quoted from memory, waving his small chubby hands. "Treat your fellowman as you'd like to be treated, the rest is all commentary," he thundered at Robinson and let it be known that British reputation for fair play would be the first casualty if the men went unpunished.

Robinson's dithering, said the Postmaster, would go down as an unmitigated act of cowardice.

That stung. Cravenness was one charge Gordon Robinson could never stomach, especially when hurled at him by a long-time friend. As a young Inspector, with a service revolver and five constables equipped only with truncheons, he had walked into a Jabalpore bazaar against a thousand strong Hindu and Muslim rioters armed to the teeth with fierce looking knives, and prevented mayhem.

Twenty, even ten years before, such an episode could have been hushed up. There would have been some money passed to the family of the man killed, and everything would have been forgotten. There was that case of a subaltern who had kicked his syce in the stomach, causing his death in hospital, but the British surgeon had certified that the man had died of food poisoning and, though the bazaar had been tense for a few days, the matter had received no further attention.

In a hastily scribbled memo the DSP was warned by IGP Nagpore to handle the situation with tact, and not give the agitators a chance to blow up the affair into a national crisis. Nagpore had already become a hot bed of sedition; Gandhi's Ashram at Wardha had transformed college students of the region into a seething mass, clamouring for freedom. And Linlithgow's befriending of Gandhi had considerably increased the Mahatma's influence. Mhow had no experience in dealing with an issue which had relevance beyond its frontiers, and awoke one morning to find that, despite its English road names and army, it could not sidestep local history, and was yoked to the land beyond its perimeters by more than a gleaming railway track.

The very next day the DSP himself drove down in his car

to Colonel Ravenscroft's office. An orderly was dispatched to fetch Lieutenant Ponsonby.

"Oh, do sit down, my dear chap," the Colonel said to DSP Robinson. "What brings you here?"

"I've come to take into custody the two soldiers involved in the beating incident."

"Oh that," the Colonel said casually. "We've looked into it quite thoroughly, old man," the Colonel said. Gesturing towards Adrian he added, "Lieutenant Ponsonby here will tell you there's absolutely nothing to it. The two men are good soldiers. Wouldn't hurt a fly. Just a frightful misunderstanding, that's all."

Adrian remained silent watching the two strong men take each other's measure.

"Criminal charges have been filed against the men," Robinson proceeded politely but firmly. "There are witnesses, Colonel. The whole thing happened right outside Hungry Charley's. People living above their shops across the street saw it clearly. They have identified the culprits."

"Culprits?" roared the Colonel. "Is that what this damned country has come to? Call two of the finest soldiers in His Majesty's Army culprits? The wretched coolie was careless. The men taught him a lesson he'll never forget. What's wrong with that?"

The Colonel's clear blue eyes looked childishly innocent over his platinum-blond moustache.

"In the eyes of the law, Colonel, they are felons."

"Don't you quote law to me, man. You've let the bloody wogs drive you up the wall. For twenty years my men and I chased Pathans right across the Khyber Pass when you were probably sitting comfortably on your behind."

The two men glared at each other. Adrian cleared his throat nervously. Two pairs of gimlet eyes bore through him. He realised he wouldn't get much change out of either formidable adversary and kept mum. He half expected the DSP to get up any moment saying 'Stick it up your Khyber

Colonel," accompanied by a gesture he'd seen him use once during a heated argument with Shikari. He was greatly relieved when the Chief of Police finally decided to force the words back. Instead he said,

"Very well, Colonel, you leave me no choice. Times have changed. I take my orders from the IGP Central Provinces. The Commandant shall hear from him directly in a day or two."

Mr. David's personal involvement catalysed the dormant anti-Semitism within the ranks, and one day a big bucket filled with human excrement was emptied on his doorstep. The Colonel's Lady fumed against Hulme who had not only gone funty, but was now colluding with a Jew, to "extract his pound of flesh" from the poor Tommies.

The thinking at the Club was that once in a while, it was necessary to give the natives a thump and teach them how to sit up straight.

"The English should never give way to an Indian on a narrow footpath," one cheroot-smoking Major declared. "You must keep going ahead till the blighter steps aside. They always do. If one of these cheeky little buggers doesn't, I should kick his arse."

"You're quite right, Sir," a polo-playing Captain said. "There should be never any doubt who's the rider and who the horse."

Adrian knew that the Tommies deserved punishment but he had no stomach to fight the collective will of his fellow soldiers. His visits to Chinnery's grew infrequent, then stopped altogether, plunging Grace into utter despair.

iii

THE LONGEST TONGUE IN THE WORLD

Grace was only nineteen and couldn't handle the terrible mutings of her heart's desire. At every turn in her life she was asked to give up something. When Simla was snatched away from her, she had endured the shame and humiliation for the sake of Bobby whose schooling at Marlborough sliced off a large portion of the family income. Why should she be made to suffer for the sake of some old native who didn't have sense enough to keep out of the Tommies' way? She felt raw and sore like something hung up to dry on a meat hook in the bazaar.

The Chinnerys were already on their second cup by the time Grace returned. She had gone to urge the Postmaster to intervene on behalf of Adrian's men.

"Not possible Grace Baba," Mr. David had said in a kindly voice, pushing a pinch of snuff up his nostril. The desert prophet of a few weeks ago had dwindled to the more familiar avuncular persona. "You are like a daughter to me, but DSP Robinson cannot drop the case, it's too late now."

'But Uncle David," Grace pleaded, "surely he would listen to you. He respects you so much. Everybody does."

The old beetle-browed Postmaster had known Grace since she was a toddler.

"Very nice of you to say so Grace Baba. But I cannot go against my own conscience. It tells me that the culprits must be punished."

Mater was clearing tea things. Both of them looked anxiously at her when she joined them.

"I am afraid something is terribly wrong," Grace said,

looking nowhere in particular. "It's not like Adrian. I hope he is all right."

"Maybe he has come down with malaria. There's a lot of it about. I am sure he'll be here this evening," Pater said.

But looking at him with a sardonic smile, Mater said, "Who knows, he may have got a little sweet patootie tucked away back home in London and doesn't want to marry you."

"Mater, how can you say that?" Grace was close to tears.

"Let's not kid ourselves, honey." Mater's voice always slipped into American register when she was truly distressed. "Two weeks have gone by without a single visit. Do those wretched Tommies mean so much to him that he should stop coming here? No one blames him for what happened. What does that tell you? It tells me that we need to be prepared for the worst. Besides, there's Jack Sullivan, Captain Sullivan now, to consider".

"Mater, I am almost engaged to Adrian."

"Almost! Remember that. It's not official and never will be unless I am mistaken. Look, if I were you, I'd say 'So long Adrian, hello Jack.' The way that Sullivan looks at you when he thinks no one is watching him, why, he would do anything for you. You used to like him. Went riding with him once or twice. Then along came Prince Charming and bang, you dropped poor Jackyboy like a hot potato. Take it from me, honey, he'd make a good husband."

But you could hardly talk to Jack about anything else besides Polo and his Gurkhas. He seemed glued to his saddle and gleamed from head to foot. He could wheel his pony, a lithe Arab this way and that as though it were welded to his thighs. The moment he dug his knee in its flank, it shot out like an arrow straight for the ball. The Gurkhas worshipped him; their small round eyes sparkled when he spoke to them in their language.

During the Polo tournament, while Adrian often bungled a free hit or when taunted by teammates tried to tussle with the opponent, only to fall off his pony and have his breath knocked out of his body, Jack's pony followed the ball with the casual precision of a cat going after a mouse. No one could hit a backhander like Jack, but he thought poetry and music were best left to women.

To add to her misery, Shirin, who attended Elphinstone College in Bombay, came down to attend a cousin's wedding. Instead of sharing her wrenching pain over the loss of Adrian, she warned Grace that Jo Anna continued to meet Carl in secret.

"Personally I have nothing against Anglos," Shirin said. "Look at the Popjoys and our friend Sylvia's family, the Bickleys. They are Anglos and yet you must admit they are extremely cultivated. But the Busbys my dear, they are so common. If this thing's not nipped in the bud you'd all regret it. Mark my words. There was this girl at Auckland House, daughter of one of the ADCs to the Viceroy. Eloped with some Nabob's son by one of his many concubines. They searched the bazaars and gullies of every big city. No trace of them. The pair had escaped into the hills and were found two years later in Khatmandu, after they had crawled out of some remote hamlet in the jungles of Nepal. Their money had run out. There was a frightful row. The poor Nabob was made to pay for his son's indiscretion by being forced to abdicate in favour of some nephew or other."

"That may happen in Simla, not here. Those two have grown up together. Ask Yasmin. She should know. She is with them all the time."

"I did."

"And?"

"I don't know. The little squirt was very evasive."

Grace was irritated and restless and here was Shirin going on about Jo and that little rat Carl. Almost wilfully she ignored the warning.

Suddenly the old Bhagwan died in Hospital and the next day the bazaar erupted. Beyond the river a huge procession began and wound its way through Main Street, down Simrole and up High Street. The Governor of Central Provinces intervened and directed the Commandant to deliver the Tommies into police custody. The offence had taken place in town, and the Police were the only authority to conduct the investigation.

At Sunday morning service the civilian British and the Regimentals nodded to each other stiffly, and the Vicar gave a non-partisan sermon, taking as his text Matthew 5:24:

"Leave there thy gift before the altar, and go thy way; first be reconciled to thy brother, and then come and offer the gift."

Throughout the sermon Mrs. Talbutt kept whispering to Mrs. Ravenscroft whose husband, the Colonel, had refused to hand over his men to the DSP.

The Dog Lady, who was the most vocal of the Chinnery faction, walked right up to the Tommies who were getting ready to go back to the barracks and, waving her forefinger at them cried, "Shame on you." The Pooch Squad growled a warning, ready to spring at the men in case they decided to retaliate

Edward's supreme sacrifice for the woman of his choice played favourably with the girls at the Convent who were heartbroken by the sudden termination of their Grace Madam's romance with the handsome Lieutenant. Jo Anna and Yasmin cast the British Prime Minister Stanley Baldwin in the role of Alfredo's Dad Germont, and with tears streaming down their cheeks, sang

Amami Alfredo
quant'io t'amo.

But they smiled through their tears when, unlike Violetta, Mrs. Simpson finally got her man. On Coronation Day, the entire community assembled at the Club to drink to the health of the new King but with averted eyes.

The Dog Lady now went after Robinson like Jonah provoked by God's leniency to the suddenly reformed citizens of Nineveh, and the DSP was obliged to ask the Major to come forward and identify the Tommies. Dr. Aspel said there was no doubt whatsoever that the victim had died of massive internal haemorrhage resulting from the beating.

The Tommies were convicted. In the untouchable bustees there was much rejoicing.

Amanda continued to hound the Major with accusations of treachery.

One day Grace watched in horror as a mangy cat savaged a nest built by a sparrow in an angle between a joist and a rafter, and proceeded to mangle the one remaining fledgling on the floor, while the sparrow hovered overhead, chirping in despair. Grace couldn't stand it anymore, and one day she broke down before the Dog Lady who urged Amanda to hold her tongue for the sake of the children.

"You must consider Grace's future," she pleaded. "Think what Edith Talbutt would make of it if she gets even a whiff of this. It would be the end of the poor child's happiness. I shouldn't be surprised if it wasn't Edith Talbutt who put a stopper on Ponsonby's visits here. She is quite capable of that, you know. When her tongue's unfurled, it's the longest tongue in the world. Who can forget that it was Talbutt who scuppered poor Amy Broadbent's plans to marry her niece, Pamela, off to that nice young man Greg Tupper from PWD? Edith told Tupper that Pamela's father had killed himself in a fit of madness, that the girl's slight stutter was a symptom of inherited insanity. Everyone knows that, in reality, poor Joseph blew out his brains because he knew his leg would have to come off to stop the gangrene from spreading. Edith can be utterly ruthless."

In the evening the Dog Lady was closeted with the Major for over an hour in the Library.

"It's none of my business, Roger, dear, and I don't want to know whether you bedded that creature or not. May the Lord forgive you if you did. But, if you know what's good for you and your family, you'd get rid of that little hussy."

The Major demurred.

"But Agatha dear, that would only confirm the rumours,

don't you see? I give you my word, I won't ever see her alone. Besides, I cannot manage that place without her. Mandy's condition is not going to improve unless she stops smoking. Her lungs are on the verge of collapse. The hotel is in the red, Mabel brings in the money."

Although gradually civility was restored within the Cantonment community, very few people realised at the time that something precious had been lost irretrievably.

THE TELEGRAM

"What's all this about Aurangabad?" Grace asks.

Camilla helps her sit up in bed and hands her a glass of water along with the pills.

"It's the trip we've been planning to the cave temples to see the frescoes," Camilla says, opening one of the windows.

"Tehmi, Noshir and who else?"

"There will be Ross, of course."

"Of course!"

"He'll drive part of the way when it gets dark," Camilla explains patiently, ignoring the scorn lurking beneath Grace's "of course."

"Noshir doesn't see too well in the dark. Ross will take over from him then."

The ensuing silence is so stark that chimes of varying velocity and amplitude can be heard going off at the same time in different sections of the house. Despite her concern for Grace, Camilla is impelled to ask.

"Mum, for God's sake, will you tell me what you have against Ross?"

"Why, I have nothing against him. I am sure he is all right. I just don't like the way you are throwing yourself at him, and at your age too."

"My age has nothing to do with it, has it?'

"What else then?"

"I don't know. Why don't you tell me? You weren't exactly young when you married Stoodgy."

"Please don't bring Stoodgy into this. If that man were anything like Stoodgy, I should be most happy for you."

"Mum, how do you know what he is like?"

215

"I know the type too well," Grace says, fumbling in her bag. She pulls out a crumpled piece of paper. "Take a look at this. Came yesterday morning. It doesn't say from whom, but there is something here you ought to know."

The letter is made up of typed telegraphic sentences.

ASK COL HARRISON. / REMEMBER CHRISTMAS/ DELHI LAST YEAR/NIGHT OF LOVE/ INNOCENT VIRGIN .

Grace is quite annoyed by Camilla's reaction. Instead of outrage, she detects the beginning of an arch smile such as might be seen on a mother's face on being told of the latest waggishness of her *enfant terrible*.

"Go on, laugh at me. You and your fine ways. I should have known better. You have no respect for truth, no values. Go make a fool of yourself. Jump into bed with that good-for-nothing wretch, that filthy Anglo scum."

That outburst wipes the smile off Camilla's face.

"Steady on, Mum. You'll have a stroke and Dr.Chaudhry said the second one could be fatal, remember? Take a nap. We'll talk about it later."

"Why not now? There's nothing wrong with me. I cannot rest in peace while you are plunging into an abyss."

"Plunging into! What's the matter with you? For god's sake don't be so theatrical Mum. It's not like you. If you'd only calm down and let me explain. That wretched letter is obviously from the General's daughter. The silly girl has had a crush on Ross. She is quite sweet really, but getting desperate now, as you can see. But why should I even bother to explain? Your mind was made up even before you met Ross. You've hated him all along, letter or no letter. Well, let me tell you that I am resolved to marry that 'filthy wretch' as you call him, if he asks me to. Frankly, I'd never thought I'd hear such racist language from a woman I have called mother all my life."

"Oh, I can picture you as a memsahib cooped up in some

dusty barracks."

"Why should I be cooped up? As my husband, Ross could come to England once I've filed papers with the Immigration Office. And so can Esmé. He plans to take an early retirement from the Army."

"Good heavens! You are quite serious about this, aren't you? Think of the consequences."

"What consequences? The world has changed, Mum. Don't you realise? There is nothing wrong with Ross except that he is not white. That doesn't matter to me, because I love him, don't you see?"

"I see all right," Grace says bitterly.

Grace's hands begin to shake, eyes dilate as she collapses in the bed.

"It's Jo Anna all over again. You are just like your mother, all impulse and no patience. Accusing me of being a racist. Look, had I been a racist, I wouldn't have loved you so. Your father was an Anglo too, you know."

Camilla has been staring at the crumpled letter in her hand. She looks up.

"What, what did you say?"

"I said, your real father was an Anglo and yet. . ."

"What! What happened to the American pilot?"

"There was none. We made him up. Mater and I".

"That wasn't the only thing you made up, was it?"

"I don't understand."

"Why don't you tell me?"

"There's nothing more to tell."

"I don't believe it. I have a feeling that there's some code of secrecy at work here. Yasmin seems to know more about the way Jo Anna died. Tehmi thinks she once overheard someone talking to her aunt about it. She thought it was murder. That day at her place Olinda was about to tell me when she suddenly changed her mind. I knew she was lying."

"Olinda! I knew it. From the moment I set eyes on that creature I knew there would be trouble. You should know that Indians love to gossip. It's their worst trait. Look," Grace says, speaking slowly, "when Jo got pregnant Mater sent her to Poona with me. Jack was on the Burmese Front then. Mater wanted to get rid of the baby, but Jo would have none of it. She had you, and I am glad and grateful she did. Otherwise, otherwise I would not have . . ."

Then Grace gets up and speaks in a dead level voice.

"Look dear, I may be prejudiced as you say against the Anglos, although there's a genuine reason for it. I would have told you long ago, even if it meant hurting you badly, but I only found out yesterday. You cannot marry Col. Harrison, he is your brother."

Neither of them moves for a long time. Grace goes limp and sinks down to the floor at Camilla's feet. The worst is over. There are no more skeletons in the cupboard. Camilla need never know about that ghastly business at the Dayan's. That is between herself and Jo. She was the only witness to it and would take it to her grave.

THE WATCHMAKER

Grace's words have a strange effect on Camilla. For a long while her mind stays numb, she is unaware of where she is going. What happens in the next hour and a half after she leaves her mother in a heap on the floor is totally blotted out of her mind, until Tehmi tracks her down at the Railway Station. A policeman in the bazaar tells Rehman the driver that he had just seen a memsahib sitting on a bench on the main platform. Camilla is surrounded by a group of urchins who keep up a steady chant.

only one rupee please
mother dead, father dead
only two rupees please

Rehman chases the urchins away. Camilla seems to be in a deep trance. Tehmi takes her by her shoulders, and helps her get up from the bench. They walk her determinedly to the car, which is parked on the far side of the station yard because a surging wedding procession is blocking all entrances.

Camilla staggers through the crowd with unseeing eyes staring at the grinning wedding guests. Rehman pushes the revellers aside, opening a passage for the two of them.

Vermilion splattered men and women dance and sing to the deafening sound of drums and clashing cymbals.

Stupendous tectonic shifts are rearranging the entire geography of Camilla's being, mountains folding into ocean beds, and new islands scrabbling up like puppies, dripping with bath water. Her mind drifts back to last summer; the news that Grace wasn't her real mother had registered like a delayed shock, its implications unravelling step by step. But this was different.

A wet furry mouth is licking her nape, and she is unable to brush it off.

Doe-eyed women in yellow and magenta saris stop waddling after their husbands and form a circle around her, giggling behind hems of saris. Camilla is paralysed, like that fugitive on the television, before leaping across rooftops to safety.

Her first impulse is to recoil from their extended arms, as the women try to touch her.

A skeletal cow blocks their final passage to the car parked in front of a teashop. The animal looks dolefully at Camilla before moving aside, dragging one mudcaked, injured foot.

Once in the car she glances at her hands. Against her blue dress they are pink, with blond down.

"It can't be true. Mum is making this up in her anger."

But certain regions of her past stand illuminated with unexpected similitude as the car sputters down the road. In his dingy shop, lit by a single dusty bulb, a watchmaker, with a thimble-shaped eyeglass is caught in the attitude of a squirrel squinnying at a nut wedged between its paws.

vi

THE ENGLISH MATRON

The new batch of cadets will arrive in two weeks. Sitting in the front row with the General and Mrs. Grehwal, Ross watches the Passing Out Parade for which the Army Chief of Staff has specially flown in from Delhi. The officers from the batch trained by Ross form only one unit of the elaborate March Past, which includes cadets attending other courses at the College of Combat. Johar has volunteered for training in high altitude combat and is to leave for Ladakh early next morning. 'I shouldn't be surprised,' Ross says to himself, 'if he is not already Major or Colonel Johar when our paths cross again.'

Noshir, Tehmi and Camilla are sitting behind him. There's a sudden prickling along his neck. Without turning around, he feels Camilla's eyes watching him. She knows Ross is annoyed with her. Earlier she had avoided eye contact, and smiled vaguely declining his invitation to the farewell dinner at the Mess for the cadets. He's got to find out from Camilla if they have any kind of future together. He knows Esmé simply adores her. The thought of Esmé and Camilla together lifts his spirit; his lungs feel fresh and clean. Late April and already the air is scented with mango blossom.

The March Past, with those smartly turned-out young officers, is always a heartwarming sight. The women in the stall look very chic in their diaphanous saris, and Camilla, in her white and red polka-dotted summer dress, is the centre of attention. Heaven knows how Tehmi manages these things, but instead of dropping out of college as she had threatened to do, Taji had gone back to Delhi to finish her studies.

With Taji out of his way, he was free to spend all his time

with the "English Matron", as the young girl naughtily referred to Camilla. Tehmi had told him to ignore Taji's threat of suicide, but in her averted gaze was a hatching of something fell that would one day swoop down with dark beating wings.

The sky overhead is intensely blue, but on the horizon, spare clouds with jagged outlines move in ghoulish parody of the parade in progress. Here in Central India, with that military might on display, one felt utterly secure.

Ross looks at the cadets he has trained, boys in their mid-twenties, tall and muscular. They are so different from the slovenly, sweaty crowd shuffling through bazaars, crammed in green and yellow buses, or staring listlessly from wood-framed shops with their painted yellow signs, offering long distance services, STD., STC., and so on. He wonders if these young men realise that within a couple of weeks they might be shivering to their deaths on avalanche-prone slopes, dying of frostbite while facing snipers on Siachin Glacier, or camouflaged and crouching in the jungles of the Northeast under a louring sky. He has helped shape their fate. Their training is not foolproof, and heaven knows how many will return intact to their loved ones. But they are the heart that keeps pumping blood into the remotest artery of the country. There, under the blue sky, is laid bare the nation's interior map, illuminating its fragile hopes and forebodings.

The mountainous terrain of the Northeast, with constant threat of ambush, is different from the Khyber Pass of bygone days. The fine bungalows built by British planters have gone to seed. There are graveyards, churches, and large Italianate villas everywhere in Assam. Some of their houses are so remote they can be reached only by a ropebridge.

The region is filled with wildlife most of the year and the monsoon transforms it almost overnight into a vault filled with blooms of mist.

At the first wet drift in the air, peacocks fluff their plumage, cease their mournful honking, and the hills go silent. On tea plantations, in teak forests, the drone of bluebottles, the gibbering and squawking of beast and fowl are turned off as though at the throw of a switch. Deep inside the jungle it is pitch-black night where, in dreaming self-possession, stand the elephant-folk, and every plant and bush comes alive as though awakened with a kiss.

Ross misses those sudden tints of purple in masses of greenery, the tickle of downy shower, and at night, the mysterious play of lantern light swinging through the foliage. No words can capture the eerie beauty of Assam when, camouflaged from head to foot in vegetation, their olive green fatigues blending with the dun hue of the hills, water dripping constantly down their mud-covered faces, his men stand suddenly silhouetted in lightning flash against the silvery trunks of areca palms and tapering cedar.

In the cities of the plains, the monsoon clogs the streets. In Assam it cascades into the Brahmaputra Valley and slops down to the Bay of Bengal with melted snow, the rhododendrons waving along its banks.

In his early youth, only the tiger used to lure him down to Mhow, now it is concern for Esmé. There are no more tigers left in Assam. The British tea planters and their Indian supervisors have shot them to extinction. Only boar, rhino and deer remain, and they are no challenge. The tiger is Ross's métier. He likes to pit his mind against that of a crafty man-eater. The hunt releases cunning in his tired muscles.

VIII

i

MOONWATER LAKE

The lack of dread while Camilla teeters on the brink of incest is driving Grace to distraction.

The revelation seems to have dredged up something malign and rampant from Camilla's innermost self. For nearly a week Grace has been in a stupor, she has had to jerk herself awake every now and then with a splash of cold water on her face.

True, Camilla hasn't tried to mystify the issue or play down its catastrophic nature. But even while receiving the news she had not blinked, there was no violent reaction, expression of horror or disgust on her face. She had met Grace's terrified eyes with a cold stare.

Grace herself has not quite found a way to step back into the flow of ordinary life, but Camilla goes about looking like a ghoulish child utterly wrapped in some obscure reverie.

Grace is limp with guilt and remorse. She has botched the whole thing. Why couldn't she have waited till they were back in London to break the news as she had planned to do?

One Sunday morning in Clapham, after breakfast, she could have steered the conversation to their recently concluded trip to India and picking up the thread might have said,

"Oh, by the way dear, you got me all wrong back there in Mhow. No racist am I. Perhaps I overreacted when that woman Olinda told us that Ross Harrison was the son of Carl Busby. We all knew Carl. He was an utter blackguard."

She could have then gone to her grave without telling Camilla about her Indian blood. That must have been a shock in itself. On top of it, the news that Harrison was her half brother must have been a cruel, cruel blow. No wonder the poor child is dazed and cannot speak.

Grace feels all hollowed out; she's dead, yet the clock ticks on.

She was left with no choice. Camilla had intended to marry that man.

"God almighty, this thing is just too big for me. Inside I am all finished, there's smell of ash all over me."

She had never been equal to the parts assigned to her by fate.

The pillow feels cold and damp with tears.

If she hadn't, out of sheer selfishness, dragged the poor child all the way to Mhow, none of this would have happened. Without thinking, she had delivered her girl into the hands of her worst enemies.

She cannot face anyone, least of all Yasmin with that smug look on her face. She must be dying to get her claws into Harrison, preening and fussing over him, staking her claim as a long time friend of his father's. God how the wretched cripple must be smacking her lips over this dark comedy enacted right under her roof.

Grace is nibbling at the cold cuts sent in by the cook when Camilla walks in. Her face is slightly flushed and there are dark circles under her eyes as though she might have been crying, but other than that there's no evidence of her crumbling under the weight of monstrous knowledge.

Grace is desperate to find out where she has been the whole day.

"Oh, here and there. Sandra and Tehmi took me to this place called Kala something. There's a reservoir there and a swimming pool of sorts attached to it. There was fresh water in it today in honour of Madam Grehwal. According to Tehmi there were two smaller pools that were sealed off to create a reservoir. I suspect the water is changed only once in six months, judging from the dark wavy fungi on the walls of the pool.

"Moonwater Lake," Grace says.

"What's that?"

"The lakes. One was called Sunwater, the other Moonwater. They were small but had fresh water constantly flowing through them. Moonwater Lake was everybody's favourite because the shady trees that circled its banks cooled the inflow and one could see all the way down to its smooth rocky floor where tiny fish flashed by. The tribals said the Moon came down and lay on its back when everyone was gone. A dip in it cured everything from measles and chicken pox to fevers of every sort."

"All you can see is a greenish floor with brown muck deposited in its corners," Camilla says. "You are bound to pick up something more deadly than chickenpox now."

This casual backchat is too much for Grace. She gets up and goes to Camilla.

"What else, Darling?" she says.

Camilla opens her eyes and looks at her quizzically.

"What else what Mum?"

" I mean are you all right? You are not terribly upset over what I told you?"

"Not terribly."

"Camilla, stop pretending. I have been going out of my mind, lying here imagining all sorts of horrors, and here you are torturing me."

"Me torture you? Mum I wouldn't even know where to start."

"You are all right then?" Grace says, somewhat relieved.

"Of course I am. I must confess, that bit about being part Indian was quite a whack."

"What about Harrison, are you going to tell him what I told you?"

"Of course not."

"You are right. Once we are back in England it wouldn't matter anyway."

"Mum, you are the limit," Camilla says throwing off the sheet. "How can I tell him just like that. I need time, be patient."

"But, but."

"No buts Mum. You'd better keep your mouth shut. Nothing can take him away from me. He is mine, brother and everything else, all rolled into one."

Grace staggers back to her bed.

"That's insane, you are out of your mind. Don't you see how evil it is to defile your body?"

"Mum," Camilla says gently, "how can one defile one's body if one comes to know something is wrong, after the fact?"

"After the.... What are you saying?" Grace screams.

"Nothing Mum, just an expression. Don't shout. You'll wake everyone up."

There's a discreet cough followed by a knock on the door, then Bhola's voice inquiring if Memsahib needs anything?

Grace opens the door, and bundles him off with a curt command in Hindi.

Camilla comes to her from behind and wordlessly leads her back to her bed.

"I'll tell him tomorrow after the hunting trip."

She hands Grace a sedative tablet.

"Please try to get some sleep. I am quite exhausted after that swim in your Moonlake."

"Moonwater Lake," Grace murmurs.

She quickly swallows the tablet like an obedient child but doesn't let go of Camilla who sits there rocking her till her body feels heavy with sleep.

Camilla has not allowed herself to be alone with Ross the past two days. For a few hours she had felt stained, her body had cringed as though something viscid was crawling up her back. But now she knows what needs to be done. It's certainly painful to watch her mother torment herself while her lungs make a stupendous effort to suck in breath.

Camilla's own shock is beginning to wear off; she doesn't feel any repugnance. Why should she deny herself the pleasure she has found in his body, and the spiritual compatibility that goes with it?

Gently she lowers her mother's head on the pillow and pulls a sheet over her.

How can she suddenly go from complete immersion in Ross's being to a total rejection of it? An unbearable tenderness wells up in her heart for this man, this brother. She has never felt that way towards another human being. She cannot let it go even if it means snuffing out her own life.

She opens the window to let in a light breeze. The jasmine-lined passageway to Noshir's wing is a shower of tiny blue bulbs.

She must try and put a recognisable face on the fact that Ross is the same flesh and blood as she. The word 'brother' has to be broken up and swallowed like a tablet till its meaning gets into her bloodstream. Once inside it would be under her control instead of crushing her with its weight.

Trying to bend her yearning for Ross into a manageable shape she rummages for instances of incest she knows, Ancient Egyptians, the Greeks, and Byron with his half-sister, Augusta Leigh.

Ultimately nothing makes sense except the realisation that, whether in the swimming pool or in bed, the atmosphere around Ross is shot through with delicate misty weals. She feels no tug of remorse, nothing, except sweetness of life.

THE REPORT DOESN'T LIE

Late April is the time of tinders in Mhow, jagged outlines of distant hills are grey and rocky and in the Cantonment, pencil-sketch trees stand helplessly in the wind's path while it scoops up crunchy fallen leaves from the roadside and deposits them on people's verandahs. A solitary cuckoo stabs the humid afternoon air with sharp jabbing notes.

Grace finds Camilla huddled with Yasmin at the breakfast table. Camilla is wearing a pair of breeches and a khaki shirt Tehmi has managed to salvage from Shirin's old trunks. The darzi has loosened it around the chest.

She is ready to go on that hunting trip Grace has heard so much about. A man-eater has been carrying away cattle and stray villagers into the forest. The intense pleading in Esmé's big almond eyes has decided the issue for Camilla. Tehmi tries to reassure Grace that Camilla would be well looked after.

"Noshir is a crack shot," Tehmi says, looking proudly at her husband, "and as for Ross, why he never misses his mark."

"I'll bet he doesn't," Grace thinks.

Bhola comes in from the garden humming some sort of tribal ditty.

"Fresh mogra for Missy Sahiba," Bhola says, handing a bouquet of chrysanthemums to Camilla. The dove-breasted flowers are snow white.

"I am afraid Bhola simply adores you," Yasmin says to Camilla, who gives the older woman a peck on the cheek, and follows Tehmi out to the Landrover.

For Grace, that night is one of tossing and turning.

Gradually a tremendous weariness sweeps over her and she feels weak as though the bones in her body were being crushed. Next morning Yasmin sends for Dr. Das and he immediately orders a blood test. A pathologist from his hospital comes to take a sample. In the evening Dr. Das marches in waving the blood report.

"You've had it," he says cheerfully to Grace.

"What do you mean?"

"You've got typhoid." His ability to diagnose correctly wreathes his chubby face in a smug smile.

"Oh no. How could that be? We always boil our water," Yasmin says.

"The report doesn't lie, Madam," quips the doctor. "She must have imbibed tap water somewhere else."

"No. Only boiled water. And juice,'" Grace says.

"What sort of juice?"

"Why, just plain sugar cane juice. I have always loved it."

"Where?"

"At the shop across the road from the Railway Station. You remember," Grace says, turning to Yasmin. "But that was more than a fortnight ago. I went for a stroll. The man had this electric machine and said it was quite safe. I used to have it all the time in the old days."

"Madam, in old days you had immunity. Now you have no immunity. Hence typhoid. The cane juice is the culprit," he says to Yasmin.

"Oh dear, what's to be done now?" Yasmin asks.

"Careful nursing. Nothing else. Take her temperature every hour and I"ll come and check tomorrow."

Yasmin decides to transfer Grace to Shirin's old bedroom that has cross-ventilation, and asks the doctor to send a nurse from the hospital to look after his patient. She, herself, sits by Grace, dozing in her wheelchair till Olinda charges in looking very professional in her nurse's uniform.

"Thank you for giving me chance to serve our Grace, Madam," she says to Yasmin.

Grace turns her face to the wall.

The doctor is of the opinion that it is possible to bring the fever down with penicillin, but decides against it since Grace has already had a stroke, and it might further damage her heart. So the nurse asks Bhola to fill up the ice bag.

Benumbed by ice Grace dozes off until the bag slips from her fingers. She had thought of her trip to Mhow as a homecoming, but is terribly embarrassed to be such a nuisance to Yasmin. What a mess she has got everybody into.

The voluble doctor predicts the fever will come down within a week. Although Yasmin is aware that Grace is uncomfortable having Olinda as nurse, she doesn't have much choice since, according to Dr. Das, she is the only one on his staff fluent in English and can be depended upon to provide Grace with proper nursing. Olinda sleeps on a little cot in the passageway, records the fluctuating temperature and regularly rubs ice on her patient's forehead.

Grace has never had a high fever. In England, except once during a passing bout of flu, such pain had never racked her entire body. In her childhood, Mater used to give them quinine at the slightest hint of temperature. Her breath feels hot and her eyes ache. She drifts in and out of sleep.

iii

THE TIGER AND THE GOAT

Esmé notices that her father's jaw is set. Have the two of them had a fight?

Earlier she had seen him talking to Camilla when they had stopped for sandwiches and tea. He was distraught because his favourite officer Lieutenant Johar had been killed in a helicopter downed by insurgents in Kashmir.

Here in the stubbly fallow land of Malwa shepherds graze goats, squatting wayfarers cook meals, village elders at council recline on charpoys, trying to resolve the contradiction between rival versions of the same story. But there can be no two opinions this time: a man-eater is about and there's safety in numbers.

The man-eater is probably a tigress that has been gored in one eye by a blue bull. A week before, she had killed a man who had stumbled upon her as she lay behind a scrub, broken his neck, and moved on. Another day she had sneaked close to a village in search of food, and found a woman who was cutting wood for fire. The tigress had dragged the woman into the jungle and eaten her arms after killing her. Since then, there have been nearly seven kills, which include unwary humans. All very true, say the hookah-sucking elders, but who is foolhardy enough to go stalking a man-eater crazed with hunger? You need patience, unlimited patience, for days may go by without any sign of the tiger.

"When is a forest not a forest but a jungle?" Camilla asks, breaking the oppressive silence. The question baffles Tehmi.

"A jungle," says Noshir, "is where animals do not recognise our special status as human beings and kill only when they are hungry."

He remembers a story of a tigress that had chanced upon a toddler soon after feeding on a water buffalo. She had merely sniffed the child and walked away.

Across the ridge to the east, is the silhouette of a train, its carriages are skewed cardboard cutouts with dark interiors. Reduced in scale by distance, it is like a wooden toy of poor workmanship. At a railway crossing they pass a busload of passengers who stare at them silently. Thorny babul bushes, like grey-haired hags, grasp at the hood of the Landrover as it pitches over fallen branches and knolls.

Leaving the women at the Dak Bungalow, Noshir and Ross go to inspect the place where the partly dismembered kill is lying. After following the pugmarks that go in loops without leading anywhere, the men return to the Dak Bungalow in time for supper. The little hamlet that clings to the spur of the hill lies hushed in the wake of the latest fatality. Thin, spiralling smoke from cooking fires licks the air, claylamps flare nervously amid the usual murmur of voices, the wailing from the hut of the man-eater's victim stops suddenly and the baying of jackals fades to low, tentative growls.

Late at night Camilla's cot is rocked violently as the tucked-in ends of the mosquito net are pulled off. Breath reeking of whisky, Ross rips apart her nightgown and pounds into her like a demented machine. For the first waking moments, Camilla thinks the man-eater is attacking her. A savage hand clamps her mouth, choking her cry of terror. Afterwards, he lies on top of her sobbing like a child; her face is drenched in his tears. She cannot understand the ferocity of his attack.

During the lunch break that afternoon he had asked her angrily why she had been avoiding him at the Club and she had merely shrugged her shoulders, saying everything would be all right once they'd had a chance to sort out a few things. She had refused to go to his room that night saying he must get good sleep after all that trudging in the forest, tracking the spoors.

The crying sobers him, and he slinks away in the dark without a word.

Next morning at breakfast, Ross is missing. The Khansamah says word had reached them at dawn that another buffalo had been attacked in the night, within two miles of the Dak Bungalow and Ross had gone to check the kill. When they drive up to the place of the latest kill, machans are going up on two neighbourly banyans. Noshir explains that shooting from a machan at a moving animal can be tricky, as well as time-consuming. Besides, one is able to aim at the crucial sections of the animal's body with greater precision from ground level.

Esmé and Tehmi huddle on the smaller machan, and Camilla, assisted by Noshir, scrambles up the rope ladder to the larger one fastened to the banyan across the pathway. The villagers vanish.

Ross decides to hide behind a lantana bush on a small hummocked ground, below which, about a hundred yards from the machans, is the kill.

"You will cover me, won't you ?" he says to Noshir as he picks his way through a clump of lantana bushes.

The wait begins.

"We are dealing with at least two man-eaters," Noshir tells Camilla. Ross has told him that another tiger had mauled a woodgatherer ten miles away to the west.

The jungle lifts its latch and opens its gloom. The battered, twisted vegetation has a hushed look as if it were aware of the impending slaughter. In the space between tree trunks is the fluid traffic of furry backs and twisted horns. Occasionally a splattered snout rises from the half-eaten carcass, teeming with flies. The air is thick with the smell of something putrefying in the gloom. Camilla had always imagined a jungle to be a netted world, like Mowgli's enchanted retreat of dappled foliage looming over green entanglements and couplings, not this grey, petrified place with stunted, gnarled shapes and jagged bark, the smell of mouldering and rut.

Morning drags into midday. The air is still and Camilla's back is drenched with sweat. Esmé fidgets and trains her binoculars on her father every five minutes. Camilla wonders if Ross is deliberately putting himself in harm's way to atone for last night. Would a disciplined hunter indulge in such bravado? Through a pair of binoculars, Camilla can see the shrine of the local goddess a mile and half away behind the foliage. It seems to tilt in the thick shafts of turmeric light. The overgrowth around its collapsed dome implies long-gone worshippers, but Noshir whispers that it is forbidden to kill game within a one-mile radius of the shrine. Even in that destitute state, the tiger-riding goddess protects her animal.

Under armpits of branches hang gutted, multi-storeyed facades of honeycombs. Over the kill in the ditch begin to hover carrion birds with wattled necks and grey muddy wings. One by one they swoop down and rise with bloodied beaks, protesting the unruliness of scavenging jackals.

"There might be nothing but bones left, if the animal does show up," Noshir mutters.

A little after twelve, Noshir suddenly turns around and points his binoculars at a spot behind the lantana bush. "There she is," he whispers. The huge beast comes surging up silently like an electric locomotive on grass-covered tracks. It stops abruptly, then resumes in slow-motion arcs, without touching the ground.

Wet sticky locks of hair blur Camilla's vision. She reaches frantically for the pair of binoculars and accidentally knocks a thermos flask with her elbow. It rolls over and drops down with a thud. Ross can be seen gesturing angrily, signalling them to be quiet. The man-eater, which has just emerged from a scrub, is motionless, one paw raised like a taxidermist's exhibit, dreaming on three legs.

Has the absentee divinity warned it?

In the eerie dream space of the tigress, the birds are frozen on bone-white branches, Camilla feels strapped by thick shafts of sunlight, and there's Ross running towards the diminutive goddess who has just emerged from the direction of the shrine in the form of a little girl leading a goat. Very slowly the enormous head of the beast turns and, with a sudden lurch, its three legs start loping in the direction of the bleating.

A shot rings out as Ross, trying to divert the animal, fires while running to intercept it. His leg gets caught in a snaky root and he stumbles as he fires, merely grazing the animal's flank. With an earsplitting thunder, the tigress whips around and charges at him, rising about five feet in the air with a white flash of underside, as if to smother him in a lover's embrace. The wiry Noshir, whom none of the women has seen slither down the tree, rears out of a bush and shoots the tigress in the neck, deflecting her fall about half a foot from Ross. Before she can rise again, Ross shoots her straight in the head. There's an agonised roar as limp and heavy she goes down, section by section to make an abject heap at his feet.

The goat has broken loose from the little girl and is bleating at some distance from the hunters and their prey.

Tehmi and Esmé have already thrown down the rope ladders and are descending from the machans. As Camilla descends step by wobbly step, the villagers come out of hiding. In her hurry to reach Ross, Esmé seems to have swung close to the tree and cut herself in the arm on the rough bark. She cries, beating him on the chest and brushing off the dust and leaves from his safari jacket all at the same time.

"I should have known better than fire at a speeding beast," Ross says, "but if I hadn't, she would have certainly got the child."

He has twisted his ankle and now stands up, leaning against his gun. Camilla goes to him and kisses him silently on the cheek. The villagers mill around the carcass, lash it to an improvised stretcher to be carried to the headman's house for skinning.

Esmé asks the little girl what she was doing all alone in the jungle.

"I was taking the goat to my sister's. She has a new baby. The baby needs milk. And now the goat is gone. My father will beat me."

"Don't worry," Esmé assures the girl, "my father won't let your father beat you. Isn't that true, Dad?"

"But why didn't your father bring the goat himself," Noshir asks.

"He has gone to the Friday market to sell vegetables."

"And your mother?"

"She is cooking."

"Weren't you afraid of the tiger?"

The little girl merely shrugs her scrawny shoulders.

Ross asks one of the villagers to retrieve the goat. Esmé insists that they give the child a lift to her sister's.

"But that would make us very late. The sun will go down in a couple of hours and we might miss the other tiger," Noshir pleads.

"That's enough tigers for one day," Tehmi says, walking the girl with the goat to the Landrover. "Besides, that poor man can hardly walk," she adds, looking at the limping Ross.

"That's why I am against bringing petticoats on a shoot," Noshir grumbles. "They are only interested in the excursion."

The kill has whetted his appetite. Bagging two tigers in one day is a tempting idea. Nothing brings out the ultimate killer in man as much as a tiger hunt. The presence of women violates that instinct not because they are incapable of killing, but their ruthlessness is channelled toward protecting their brood.

The little girl has never been in a car, and is very pleased with herself, but the goat refuses to budge. Finally, Noshir picks it up and deposits it at the back of the Landrover. An acrid whiff hits their nostrils as soon as the goat is lowered; they clamp handkerchiefs to their noses. Fortunately it takes them only twenty minutes to reach the farmhouse where the girl's sister lives. After depositing the goat at her sister's, the child is driven back to her home. Noshir reprimands the mother, and warns her that he would have her husband arrested and thrown in gaol if ever again they sent their daughter out alone. The woman begins to cry and touches Noshir's feet.

iv

OUR LADY OF FATIMA

Typhoid is no longer considered fatal but there are always exceptions. However, when she goes to Grace's room, Camilla is surprised to see her sitting propped up against a pillow. The nurse is spooning some milk into her mouth.

"How do you feel?" Camilla asks.

"Don't come too close, darling," Grace protests. "It wouldn't do for both of us to come down with fever."

"No problem," Olinda volunteers. "Typhoid's not contagious."

From the open window come the sounds of young girlish voices singing a hymn.

"You are wondering about singing, no?" Olinda asks Camilla. "I'll tell you, in a few days it's the feast of our Lady of Fatima."

"Our Lady of Fatima," Camilla repeats the words like some magic formula.

"But of course, I remember how Ayah used to pray and fast during the feast," Grace says.

"All of us did, Madam. My grandmother Mrs. d'Quodros prayed also. If any of us children had fever, she would immediately pray to Lady Fatima. We still do that. Tonight I shall pray for Madam's recovery."

"That's very kind of you," Camilla says.

"It's my duty, no?" Olinda says. "We are like members of one family. My granddad, Mr. d'Quodros used to say, 'The Major's family is our family. No difference'."

"Where's the Feast celebrated?" Camilla asks.

"At Church Madam. Sacred Heart. Everybody prays to our Lady of Fatima, not just Catholics. Hindus and Muslims also

239

pray. Now, very few Catholics left in Mhow. Slowly, slowly everyone is leaving for Dubai and Kuwait."

The doctor's theory about the cane juice is not very convincing.

"I had it, too," Camilla says.

"Where did you have the juice?" Olinda asks.

"At the restaurant in Ashoka Hotel in Indore."

"Ah, but that's a five-star hotel," Olinda says. "Makes a difference. Besides, Grace Memsahib is weak, no?" Olinda explains.

It was strange about that flask. Camilla was sure she had placed it in her shoulder bag. How it popped out to roll down at that precise moment was a mystery. The tigress had been killed well within the forbidden one-mile radius. Was Grace's typhoid the Goddess's way of settling a score, an old woman for an old tigress? But surely Mum was struck down with typhoid, before that?

"Good heavens," Camilla thinks, "I am beginning to think like Indians."

FOREVER YOUNG

Shirin and her husband, Kayzad, stare down at Grace. Shirin is in a traditional Parsi sari and looks calmly at her. The room is stacked with a young girl's memorabilia and pictures taken at school in Simla. In the far corner under a white shroud lies her old piano.

Shirin had been a true friend in adversity, especially after Jo Anna's death. When the two of them met for the last time in London, both their lives had been shattered.

In the morning Grace's temperature shoots up to a hundred and five. She is delirious.

"During Christmas, we sang carols," she mumbles. "We used to assemble at St. Mary's Chapel and started at the Robinsons. Mr. Robinson was the DSP, you know, then we worked our way up Post Office Road all the way to Mall Road, stopping at the Dog Lady's. All the big officers lived on Mall Road."

After the nurse goes home to shower and change, Camilla sits rubbing her mother's forehead with ice till her hands are numb. The temperature steadies around 101. Grace lies inert, breathing heavily, but with body temperature dropping, she begins to writhe.

"Camilla needs a new dress for Christmas, poor child."

In her mind she has travelled back to England and is talking to Stoodgy.

Suddenly her eyes snap open and she stares at Camilla with knitted brows.

"Ayah, you shouldn't have come. You are not well."

Then she closes her eyes and says in a clear voice. "Where is Camilla?"

"Here, Mum."

"No more ice please. It gives me a headache."

She is deathly pale. Camilla is certain that this time she is going to die. She sits down by her and begins to wipe her forehead. Gently, she brushes away a tear from Grace's cheek. The nurse slips in and takes away the icebag. Grace continues to mutter in sleep.

Her temperature drops very slowly, day by day, her body aches, but now she is able to sleep for longer stretches of time. Camilla hovers around her bed all the time, Yasmin wheels in to check if she needs anything, Olinda wakes her up every four hours to give her medicine, Bhola stands panting outside the door, Noshir tiptoes in, loaded with oranges, and Tehmi changes flowers in the vase every morning. Grace lies quietly, luxuriating in the ocean of sympathy.

Sometimes in her sleep she is back in her old bedroom at Chinnery's. Missy Baba's engagement to the dashing, true-blue English officer Captain Sullivan has sent a massive wave of excitement throughout the servants' quarters, and the Cantonment hums with wedding-related chores; the Goan bakers have started working on daring new recipes for the wedding cake.

After Bobby's death Mhow had gathered the Chinnerys to its bosom, like a vast banyan, some fragile little shrine of a hometown deity.

That Mhow had died long ago. All that really remained was that cracked gravestone and Jo Anna's dying words ripping through her nightmares.

Only Grace had heard those words. Mater had simply collapsed when told that Jo's death was just minutes away. Rabies had eaten into her brain. It had all happened so suddenly. Over Mater's objection, Jo had continued to breast-feed the baby in secret and their mutual attachment had grown so strong that the baby constantly cried unless she sang her to sleep. Grace could have protested when Mater snatched the baby away from Jo. She could have refused to take little Camilla with her to Poona to live with Aunt Ethel. Amanda's plan was to send the baby to England with Grace after the War. Grace could have objected to Mater's cruelty; instead she'd started packing the baby's things. Like Mater, she, too, had not wanted the Chinnery name to be tarnished by scandal. Fortunately, the baby's complexion had showed no sign of darkening, and the world believed that Grace was the mother. Sometimes Anglo complexions skipped a generation, before reverting to a sootier hue of their Indian pedigree.

But the day before Grace was to leave for Poona, Jo Anna, and the baby had disappeared. If only Grace had had more sense, been less self-righteous, pinned that moment down to reflect, she could have prevented the disaster. But she had acquiesced, given in to Mater's rage. Aunt Ethel had telegraphed back to say Jo had not sought refuge with her in Poona. DSP Robinson's men had combed the entire township without producing a single clue.

Three weeks later, Jo Anna was found dying of rabies in the Dayan's bungalow outside the town. The Iranian woman's mongrel had died the day after it had bitten her, but its corpse was discovered much later. It had bitten her in the face while she stooped down to pick up her baby when the dog was about to attack it. Jo had saved her child, but lost her own life.

In little over a fortnight, she had turned into one seething mound from which emanated droolings and whistling punctuated by hoarse whispers. The Dayan had locked her up in her room and sent for Maude Aspel. It was to her that Jo had first fled, but fearing police investigation, Maude had arranged a hideout at the Dayan's. The Aspel house was the first to be searched. Robinson had personally examined every corner, brushing aside Maude's objection.

For fear of being followed, Maude had not ventured to contact Jo till the Dayan's message arrived. Being a doctor's widow, Maude had immediately suspected rabies, taken the baby away, and, leaving the child at home with her maid, personally gone to fetch Dr. Vansittart. But it was too late. Dr. Vansittart had put Jo under quarantine and forbidden any physical contact with her. For two days she had lain unconscious on the floor. Through the bars of the door, Grace could see the remains of the Indian style cradle, its wooden legs had been pulled out as if Jo had frantically searched for her baby in the patchwork folds of the hammock, which lay on the floor. On the third day there was a lull in moaning. From behind the wooden frame of the door, Grace had heard furious scrabbling and Jo's blotched face had appeared behind the bars. Kneeling on the floor she had spoken in her slightly husky voice, "Grace, I am very thirsty. Why won't they let me out?"

Mater was under heavy sedation at home, and Pater, who had slumped in a chair in the forecourt of the Dayan's bungalow, had not stopped crying. But for Yasmin's father, who never let him out of sight, Pater would have put a bullet through his brain that very day. By the time Jo was discovered, she was already beyond all hope. According to Dr. Vansittart, her condition had deteriorated so rapidly because she had been bitten in the face and the back. Grace had struggled to break away from the doctor's grip and run to that thing that kneeled there with outstretched hands, moulting alternately from daughter, beast, sister.

"Grace," it had said distinctly, "Grace, let me hold my baby, please, Grace just once, let me hold my little girl."

As Dr. Vansittart dragged Grace out of the room, she had heard the voice behind her turn to a whine, and the barred door had rattled and rattled and rattled.

A spasm rocks Grace's body. She opens her eyes. Camilla is sitting by her, gently rubbing her hand.

"It's all right Mum, everything is okay. The fever is gone finally. It's all been a dream."

Grace stretches her hand and touches Camilla's cheek.

"Of course it's all right. Why shouldn't it be? I have you here, haven't I."

"Let's give you nice, nice sponge bath today, Grace Memsahib," Olinda says, coming in with a basin full of water and towels. "You would feel fresh."

After the bath Grace falls into a prolonged sleep, and when she opens her eyes, it is late in the afternoon. The smell of Green Label Darjeeling tea is wafting in. Camilla is talking to Yasmin in the passageway. If you closed your eyes you might imagine it was Jo and young Yasmin all over again, plotting some mischief. Grace suddenly feels excluded and rings the bell. She presses the button so hard that everyone comes running into the room. Even Yasmin's wheel chair is heard hurtling across the passageway.

"Are you all right, Mum?" Camilla asks.

"Yes, of course. Why?"

"Nothing. You gave us a start. The bell rang and continued to ring."

"Sorry, dear. Didn't mean to startle you. I'd like some tea though."

"I'll ask Bhola to get it right away," Yasmin says and trundles away in search of Bhola. But there it is again, a quick flashing exchange between the invalid and Camilla, a secret dialect of glances. Grace is numb with exhaustion. She'll think about it later. Her lungs which have been working overtime, are silent, and she has the sensation of floating softly down, down into bottomless darkness.

When tea is brought in they find Grace to be fast asleep. Her breathing is light and steady, and she sleeps for a long time. When she wakes again, the sun is shining, there are fresh chrysanthemums in the vase, and the nurse is already shaking the thermometer. The temperature is just a point over 98. Grace realises how sick she has been. The toast tastes like mud and the tea feels oily on the tongue.

After the nurse has gone home to see her family, Camilla comes in and sits on the bed. Propped up against two fat pillows Grace is staring out of the window.

"What is it, Mum?" Camilla asks.

"What's what dear?"

"You were crying in your sleep yesterday."

"I wasn't crying. It's the fever, causes the ducts to run somewhat."

"Fiddlesticks. Tell me the truth. Remember what day it is today. One shouldn't lie on one's birthday. Now tell me," Camilla says.

"What is there to tell? I was suddenly reminded of poor Jo."

"How old would she have been if she had lived?"

"About the same age as Yasmin. She was a year older than Jo Anna. She would have been sixty-two by now. I always think of her as forever young."

"Mum, why did we really come here? All it has brought us is pain and misery, there is nothing for us here."

"Fortunately the new gravestone is already in its place, we should leave as soon as I am able to sit up."

"The gravestone. How long will it survive?"

"I don't know. But I want to carry its image with me. That would be enough. Now that I have seen what time has done to the old one."

"And who will see what time has done to you or to me for that matter?"

Grace presses Camilla's hand.

"You mustn't get all morbid dear, and you mustn't hang around me all the time. The nurse takes good care of me."

"We'll see about that. You haven't touched normal yet. I don't think I'd enjoy going to the Club with you lying in bed here. Anyway, Noshir is away in Bombay."

"What about the Colonel?"

Camilla is silent.

"I have been remiss, very remiss," Grace says, fumbling for her napkin. "It's your happiness that counts. Do what you think is best. Oh, I've been such a fool."

246

"We'll talk about it later."

"What I am trying to say in my own stupid way is . . . ."

"Mum, for God's sake don't upset yourself. You don't understand, I might as well tell you. He was horrified when I told him the truth about us. He is back in Assam with his regiment. Auntie Yasmin will explain all. Incidentally, I had to tell her I was not your daughter. She says she had suspected it all along. I haven't seen Ross since the day we returned from the hunt."

vi

THE UNTOUCHABLES

Like a water bird tormented by an insect lodged under its wing, Camilla's mind keeps jabbing at that harrowing moment of parting with Ross.

In reality, her carefully fashioned script had careened and looped, causing the plotline to buckle and the crucial bit of information about their common parentage had slipped out prematurely.

Once again every cruel detail stands illuminated.

The night the man-eater was killed, Ross and she lingered on the verandah after coffee. Everyone turned in early. The two of them sat in silence, and then Camilla took Ross's hand and led him to her room. He was still in some pain from his twisted ankle.

She sensed that he wanted to talk about the previous night, but she put a finger on his lips and told him to be quiet. Then she drew him to her and undressed him without looking at him. She was the tigress ready to devour him. Life was too precious to be squandered away on guilt. She felt no embarrassment in their buffeting bodies, or burrowing deep into each other, breathing in draughts of forepleasure and sourness.

Outside, the jungle was unnaturally quiet. Afterwards neither of them spoke for almost ten minutes. Finally, Ross got up and, looking out of the window, said,

"I seem to be losing my grip, I have seen hundreds of men fall in action. But when one of them dies for no reason, it . . . it . . . "

He was unable to complete the sentence and stared blindly at the darkness outside while Camilla leaned against him.

"That young fellow, Johar, had no business dying in that crash," Ross said slowly. "We cannot afford to lose someone like him. He had a rare instinct for survival and, left to himself, he would have become a Major within the next five years."

"But Ross, you said it was an accident," Camilla said. "You are not responsible for his death. According to Noshir your man was escorting some politician who wanted to be photographed with the troops in the forward area. If anyone is responsible, it's that wretched politician."

"Well," Ross continued, shaking his head in confusion, "you seemed to turn away just when I was trying to cope with the news from the Front. I got tanked up and wanted to kill somebody. But that wasn't the real me, the real me would never hurt you. Let us just say some old demon got the better of me last night. Forgive me."

"There's nothing to forgive. But last night you cried, I couldn't understand that."

"It's a long story. If you must know, my father was almost killed for his friendship with an English girl."

"Really, why?"

"Because he was an Anglo."

"But, but what's that got to do with us?"

"Well, for one thing, I don't think your mother approves of me."

"There's nothing personal in that," Camilla said, "She thinks because you have Indian blood . . ."

"There, you see. I am an Anglo and will always be one."

"But so am I, Ross, so am I."

"Now you are laughing at me."

"No Ross, how can I laugh. Listen to me carefully. This isn't going to be easy. Remember that whatever happened long ago was no fault of ours. We are victims of a terrible accident. Like young Johar."

"Victims, what are you taking about?"

"If you really care for me as you say you do, you will not

let this upset you. Just remember we are not to blame. What we have is too precious for words, beyond life itself. Nothing should be allowed to destroy that."

"Camilla, please come to the point. Are you trying to tell me that it's over between us? Tell me, I can take it."

"I am sure you can. I'll help you with it. We must help each other. The truth is we have every right to love each other."

Ross's expression softened, but he still couldn't look at her.

"Before we came to India Mum told me that she was not my real mother, that I was her sister Jo Anna's daughter. First I was told that my father was an American pilot, but last week the whole truth came out. My father was Carl Busby."

Ross repeated the name Carl Busby three times as though he were trying to remember where he had heard it before. Then amazement slowly turning to disgust, he stumbled out of the bedroom leaving behind an image of horror-stricken, recoiling eyes.

After that night's lovemaking, for him to walk out like that made Camilla feel like a cheap streetwalker, who had only served to relieve him of a sudden itch. Were the passion in his lovemaking, and the deep beat of his pulse that inflamed her inmost being nothing more than a passing spasm of lust?

She picked up the lantern. A strong whiff of kerosene hit her nostrils.

In the dim light of the verandah he was like a corpse, mouth wrenched open in surprise, while the eyes were dying.

"Ross, what's wrong? Please don't cry. I didn't mean to hurt you."

It was horrible to see the transformation of this big man into a cowering fugitive. He was shaking with terror. Camilla had had a head start; it was now up to her to help him face the truth.

"Lord, forgive me," he cried. "How was I to know? Why didn't you tell me before?"

"I told you I was in the dark till last week. Now you know.

But why are you so agitated? We didn't choose to be brother and sister. On the other hand we should be happy that we are."

"How could you after you knew about our father, how could you bring yourself to do what we did just now?"

"Ross my darling, I wanted to see if knowing what I did would make any difference. To me it didn't. Don't you see, it's the knowing that's sinful, not what we did?"

"How can you separate the two. What kind of a woman are you?"

"I'll tell you what kind. Just think, ten days back I was purebred English, now I am half Indian. A few months back you were just a man I fell in love with and now you are my brother. I had to work that one out all by myself. But now we are in this together. You once said we Anglos were mongrels, remember? And if what Mum says is true, most of us are also Untouchables on our Indian side. And the less said about our British side the better."

"Yes but that's not the same thing," Ross said uncertainly.

"Yes it is. We are truly untouchable; free to be whatever we want. Don't you see my darling that at least part of us belongs with that goat girl, a world where mothers routinely send out their little girls through tiger-infested jungles to sell goats? There's nothing normal about us. We don't have to worry about pedigree. We two are of a kind, brother and sister."

For a mad instant he stared at her. She thought he was going to strangle her.

"My sister," he whispered. "You must be. Till the end Dad used to say there was a baby."

With a cry he swept her up in his arms and hugged her, laughing and crying at the same time.

She hadn't seen him since that night.

When Noshir finally did manage to track him down, Ross was on his way to the Front. He had asked for a transfer.

Ross, the soldier's soldier, was unable to fight the greatest battle of his life.

The only relief was the calm, almost serene manner in which her mother spoke about him. When Grace woke up from that dream, with tears streaming down her cheeks, there was a momentary flare-up of dread in her eyes like that of a deer encircled by a pack of wild dogs. But the next moment, terror was replaced by infinite sadness.

Later in the week when she was able to sit up without any help, Grace staggered to the piano and started plucking the keys. Camilla and Tehmi were strolling in the garden and were startled to hear the faint, scattered tinkle build to a full-blown harmony pouring out of Grace's bedroom. They hurried in to find Yasmin in her wheelchair, blocking their path and shushing them to be quiet. Camilla had forgotten how beautifully her mother could play. It was as if an iron door had clanked open and a foul cackling bird to which Grace's memory had been ransomed had flown away, leaving in its wake a melody like a distant river, flecking gently into a shadowy valley.

MUFFLED DRUMS

EAST GRINSTEAD 1995

i

LAME DOGS OVER A STILE

"Did Your Grace sleep well last night?" Nurse Barclay asks.

"Very well, thank you."

"Time for morning tea, then, I am thinking?"

"How clever of you, did you work that out all by yourself?"

"Oh, yes, I does me best to please I am sure," says Nurse Barclay dropping a curtsy.

It's a little game they play every morning. In that cramped lower middle-class nursing home where fate has brought them together, the music hall routine provides some relief from the drudgery of physical therapy, inanities of whist-drives, and benumbing games of bingo favoured by the hoi poloi. Nurse Barclay is there because she wants to be near her son who is a paraplegic computer expert. He works from a wheelchair at home. Camilla, who had stayed on in India to have Ross's baby, could afford nothing fancier by way of a retirement home for Grace than St. Jude's on the outskirts of East Grinstead.

If the staff were not vigilant, most would head for the dining room in their nightgowns. Grace is perhaps more infirm than most inmates, with skin lolling from skeletal hands, dewlap under the chin, yet she somehow manages to look well groomed with a fresh, after-shower glow. The Matron is talking to a woman called Gillian who has broken teeth, and whom Grace has taught to play the piano. The woman is a notch above the others, with taste in music which extends beyond the numbers plunked out at their old local.

It's been only five years since she arrived at St. Jude's, but she has regained enough of her skill to play old favourites, and accompany the doddering inmates in the lounge after dinner. All they sing is *"My Old Man Says, Follow the Van"* or *"I do like to be Beside the Seaside."* In recognition of her playing, Matron has assigned her a separate table by the French window. It sports a single purple petunia or rose, in a proper vase, whereas, on the other tables, sit squat, potbellied jam bottles with sprigs of aster.

From the moment news of Camilla's death in Indore during childbirth arrived in the form of a long grieving letter from Tehmi, Grace has felt weightless like an image on a television. Often she turns her head sharply, hoping to catch a glimpse of that other Grace who speaks to her from just outside the line of vision.

At first she thought the reproving whisper came from Nurse Barclay. Like a self in a dream, she hears it distinctly. Sometimes the other woman cries softly behind doors, while Grace is engaged in that Noel Cowardish persiflage with Nurse Barclay. Occasionally the whispering voice turns crisp and snaps like a Sergeant Major briefing a platoon.

"On your pins, come on jump to it, time for a shower."

Sometimes it sings,

"It's time to put on make up,
It's time to dress up right,"

like the opening chorus of the Muppet Show. Oh yes, Grace loves the Muppets, especially Miss Piggy dancing with that Russian ballet dancer Nur...nur... something.

"Nureyev, Your Ladyship, his name is Nureyev," Nurse Barclay corrects her.

Nice woman Nurse Barclay, always cheerful and smiling with a kind word for everybody. Like Camilla . . .

She is not sure why Camilla had to die. Hadn't there been enough of that already?

"Was she somebody?" Grace hears the voice of the new maid over the hoovering. Nurse Barclay has rolled Grace out into the passage while her bed is being made. The new girl is a bit slow on the uptake, and is not very good with electrical appliances.

"Yes," says Barclay. "Very famous. Before your time. Silent films as a matter of fact."

"Coo, what's she doin' in this dump, then?"

"Because this 'dump' as you call it, is all she can afford. You know how it is. In those days actresses didn't make the obscene amounts of money they do now."

"I could tell, just by looking at her," says the young maid as she comes out cradling the unplugged hoover in her arms and stands respectfully aside. Barclay comes out to wheel Grace in.

"I heard that," Grace says. "Silent films indeed. Next you'll have me saying 'Let 'em roll, Mr. de Mille,' like that woman in the film we saw last Sunday on the television."

"*Sunset Boulevard*, dear, and that was Gloria Swanson. But she was off her chump, I mean the old actress she plays. Paranoid, couldn't face. . ."

"I know that," Grace cuts her off abruptly.

The nurse is taken aback. Never before has Grace spoken in that tone to anybody, least of all to Barclay. But the nurse has noticed Grace's agitation. That afternoon some guests are coming, Barclay only knows they are from India. She hopes the visit does not upset Grace too much. Now the weather has turned warm, Grace's asthma seems less virulent. But she must warn Nurse Plunkett to keep a sharp eye on her when the visitors arrive. They are expected at four in the afternoon, a good hour after Barclay's shift ends.

"Time for your nap, dear," she says, helping Grace into bed.

"Thank you," Grace says, and doesn't let go of Barclays' hand.

"I am sorry, dear, I am a bit nervous. I am to meet my granddaughter today, for the first time."

"Well isn't that nice. How old is she?"

"Not very old. Just five. You see it was a late marriage, my daughter's."

"I'll tell the Matron to serve you a little something with tea then. I'm sure we still have some of that nice cake from yesterday's birthday party for Mrs. Congleton," Barclay says cheerfully.

"Remember, dear Nurse, to keep that sweet smile
It helps us lame dogs over many a stile."

Grace's eyes moisten as those lines, penned by a wounded soldier, flash through her mind.

"Now, now," says Nurse Barclay. "Chin up. We want to look our best today. It won't do to get eyes all swollen and red when the grandchild arrives."

Grace nods her head and closes her eyes.

If that man Ross had married Camilla, she would have come back to England with him. The doctors here would not have let her die. But he had waited till the last minute. It turned out that he was brought up a devout Catholic. The Anglos in Mhow used to be Church of England, but somehow Ross had turned out to be a Catholic.

By the time Ross relented and agreed to marry Camilla, it was too late. The baby was due any day, and she couldn't take the risk of an in-flight delivery. Besides, there were very good doctors in India now. Why, Grace's own doctor in London, Dr. Chaudhry, was Indian. It had to do with Camilla's age, they said. Forty-four was rather old. Even Camilla's friend, Joyce, said so. It was through Joyce that Camilla had arranged a room for Grace at St. Jude's. Fortunately, Camilla did not die at Chinnery's, that is to say in Dr. Das's Hospital in Mhow. That would have been too monstrous to think of.

Soon after Grace returned to England, there was a fire at Chinnery's. Luckily, they were able to evacuate all the patients. No, Camilla had died in a posh clinic in Indore. After a normal delivery she had simply bled to death. Her body had sunk like a leaky boat in her own gushing blood.

A hysterectomy might have saved her, but the woman doctor who had delivered the baby had to rush home because her five-year-old had swallowed a coin. The nurses couldn't do anything. By the time another doctor arrived, it was too late. Ross filed a case against the Clinic, but each member on the so-called Commission of Inquiry, smothered under tons of banknotes by the Management, acquitted the doctor on grounds that chances of death after normal delivery were one in a hundred thousand.

The child, Jo Anna, is coming today with her sister, Esmé. Noshir and Tehmi are in London on their way to the United States, where they will spend three months visiting Shirin and other relatives. Esmé is to attend the University of California. On their way back to India, the Debus plan to fly across the Pacific and visit Tehmi's old parents in Hong Kong. Yasmin has a flat of her own in the Bombay suburb of Parel, with a day nurse and a night nurse. After Bhola's death, she could no longer live in Mhow alone. She says in her letter that she is well looked after. With Yasmin's departure Grace's last link to Mhow is snapped. She will never see it again, and that's all right with her.

Grace wasn't surprised when news of Camilla's death arrived. The pattern had been all too familiar. It was like visiting an old scene of carnage. In 1947, when Grace was struggling to make a new life in England, trainloads of bleeding women had shrieked across the newly-marked boundaries in the Punjab, their breasts torn like fruit from a bough, infants hanging out of ripped wombs, the red paint of carriages blurred at the windows with their men's blood. On the Frontier Mail, save for the demented driver, there wasn't a complete body on either side of the border.

Camilla had died in peace.

Her passing away had a logic of loss by instalment. Clarissa Lilley's revenge had been relayed to Jo Anna, and Camilla was the next in line.

During her illness in Mhow, something had happened to Grace. Tiny details she had missed earlier had sprung to life, as though an invisible hand had passed over her eyes, opening shutters. Again, she could see Jo Anna vividly, framed in that door at the Dayan's house, every trace of her honey-coloured hair all matted, her husky voice, her violet eyes no longer human, the slavering mouth, the face emulsifying into nothingness. In her delirium at Yasmin's place, she had relived her past minute by minute till her eyes had come to rest on the noontide stillness of Sir Mancherjee's garden. All she'd wanted was for Camilla to be happy, to have the joy of living.

Now she looks at the world out of another body. Her time belongs to death but it can do nothing to hurt. She continues to breathe, eat, and go to the toilet, but another being performs all her bodily functions. Her mind feels empty like a sparrow's nest cast to the ground, which makes the flapping of wings in search of food seem achingly arduous, a solitude like granite, a silence of roads where no footsteps echo.

After lunch, she tries to read but that carping voice is at it again. "One hopes," it says snortingly, "one sincerely hopes the little girl is not dark, a throwback to Carl's mother who was black as a kettle." Grace replies, "I don't give a hoot."

"Whom are you talking to, Your Grace?" Nurse Barclay asks. She has come in to say good-bye at the end of her shift.

"No one, dear. Don't you fret; I shall be all right. I promise."

Precisely at four, Nurse Plunkett wheels her out into the garden where a table is laid for tea. It's a mild day in late August, the sun is mewed by clouds to a bracing mellow, and trees are covered in green coppery leaves, when a taxi rolls up the gravel driveway and stops under the porch where the Matron is waiting to receive the guests. Then Noshir, looking dapper in a blazer, and Esmé, grown astonishingly beautiful, come walking hand in hand towards Grace. "Please don't get up," Noshir says as he bends to kiss her cheek. Esmé stands there demurely, as Tehmi, now plumper, leads by hand a little girl in pigtails, nut-brown freckled face, silky black hair, and round eyes, the colour of a monsoon-blue sky, when it droops low like a blind on an open window. When the girl shyly offers her a posy, Grace gathers her up and holds her tight till she feels the heart beating behind her fragile ribcage. Camilla was right; shame cannot violate a child.

"Daddy sends his regards," Esmé says sitting down. "He is in Africa with the UN Peace Keeping Mission."

"Look, a horse!" says the child with a delighted squeal, and runs across the lawn that slopes down to a country lane. A young man on horseback appears beyond a spinney. Tehmi pours tea and tells Grace that the little girl has learned to ride a pony at Matheran where the Debus spend their summers. Time holds its nostrils and dips, imbricating two moments like pretty red Mangalore tiles. Grace has a sensation of watching Pater instruct Jo Anna how to guide her pony.

"Eyes in front, heels down, toes forward."

As the pony trots in circles, little Jo Anna's face, framed by hat and chin strap, is a picture of intense concentration, her mount's sandy mane bounces gently in the sun. Suddenly, it picks up speed and her violet eyes are filled with glee mixed with fear. "No pulling at the reins," Pater shouts, while the syce runs with the pony, making clucking sounds.

And here comes the Dog Lady, each member of her retinue meticulously dressed in regional colours. Junker the German Shepherd is in a green and white tunic, the brown Sussex Spaniel wears a tweed cardigan, the silky coat of the Gordon Setter is wrapped in red and green tartan, and the Welsh Corgi has a creamish jacket on with a red velvet cap that has openings at the top through which her erect ears stare out at the world.

Buggies flit past bougainvillea bushes, the sun sinking behind the hills illuminates the columns red with clematis. Grace's heart begins to pound, as the Silver Ghost draws up to the porch.

Peacocks dance in the grass by the lilypond. Grace knows she is not in the Prince of Wales Park with Shirin. But never mind that. Those are peacocks. Yasmin and Jo are silhouettes going round and round the bandstand. A massive cloud of parrots detaches itself from a tree, and unfolds like a carpet, making the sky one green. But it is some other garden, in another time and in the lounge Grace's toothless pupil begins to touch the delicate opening bars of *Kinderscenen*. Plinking slightly off-key, they seem to say, soon the swallows and swifts making a racket by the window in the morning will migrate with the cuckoo to Africa. Grace too would love to go there with them, but inside St. Jude's it is getting dark. Across the flat top of a distant hill the sun is setting like a pat of butter on toast, and little Jo Anna is walking away, clutching Tehmi's finger, to the fading strains of *A Curious Story.*

Printed in the United Kingdom
by Lightning Source UK Ltd.
105062UKS00001B/68